Histoire d'une mouette et du chat qui lui apprit à voler

Luis SEPÚLVEDA

Histoire d'une mouette et du chat qui lui apprit à voler

Traduit de l'espagnol (Chili)
par Anne-Marie Métailié

SUITES
Métailié / Seuil
2004

Titre original: *Historia de una gaviota y del gato que le enseñó a volar*
© Luis Sepúlveda, 1996
by arrangement with Dr. Ray-Güde Mertin, Litterarische Agentur,
Bad Homburg
Traduction française © Éditions Métailié et Éditions du Seuil, Paris, 1996
ISBN: 978-2-86424-490-5
ISSN: 1281-5667

À mes enfants Sebastián, Max et León,
le meilleur équipage de mes rêves.
Au port de Hambourg car c'est là
qu'ils sont montés à bord et
au chat Zorbas évidemment.

Première partie

1

Mer du Nord

— Banc de harengs à bâbord! annonça la vigie et le vol de mouettes du Phare du Sable Rouge accueillit la nouvelle avec des cris de soulagement.

Il y avait six heures qu'elles volaient sans interruption et bien que les mouettes pilotes les aient conduites par des courants d'air chaud agréables pour planer au-dessus de l'océan, elles sentaient le besoin de refaire leurs forces, et pour cela quoi de mieux qu'une bonne ventrée de harengs.

Elles survolaient l'embouchure de l'Elbe dans la Mer du Nord. D'en haut elles voyaient les bateaux à la queue leu leu, comme des animaux marins patients et disciplinés, attendant leur tour pour gagner la pleine mer et là, mettre le cap vers tous les ports de la planète.

Kengah, une mouette aux plumes argentées, aimait particulièrement regarder les pavillons des bateaux, car elle savait que chacun représentait une façon de parler, de nommer les choses avec des mots différents.

— Comme c'est difficile pour les hommes. Nous, les mouettes, nous crions de la même manière dans le monde entier, cria un jour Kengah à l'une de ses compagnes de vol.

— C'est comme ça. Et le plus étonnant c'est que parfois ils arrivent à se comprendre, répondit sa compagne.

Au-delà de la ligne de la côte, le paysage était d'un vert intense. C'était un immense pré dans lequel on distinguait les troupeaux de moutons en train de paître à l'abri des digues et les ailes paresseuses des moulins à vent.

Suivant les instructions des pilotes, la bande de mouettes du Phare du Sable Rouge prit un courant d'air froid et se jeta en piqué sur le banc de harengs. Cent vingt corps trouèrent la mer comme des flèches et en ressortant de l'eau chaque mouette tenait un hareng dans son bec.

Délicieux harengs. Délicieux et gros. Juste ce qui leur fallait pour reprendre de l'énergie avant de continuer à voler jusqu'à Den Helder, où les rejoindraient les vols des îles Frisonnes.

Le plan de vol prévoyait de continuer ensuite jusqu'au Pas-de-Calais et à la Manche où elles seraient reçues par les bandes de la Baie de Seine et de Saint-Malo, en compagnie desquelles elles voleraient jusqu'au ciel de Biscaye.

Elles seraient alors un millier qu'on verrait comme un rapide nuage d'argent et que grossiraient les bandes de Belle-Ile, d'Oléron, des caps Machichaco, de l'Apio et de Peñas. Lorsque toutes les mouettes autorisées par la loi de la mer et des vents voleraient au-dessus de la Biscaye, la grande convention des mouettes des mers Baltique, du Nord et de l'Atlantique pourrait commencer.

Ce serait une belle réunion. Kengah y pensait en pêchant son troisième hareng. Comme tous les ans on y raconterait des histoires intéressantes, en particulier celles des mouettes du Cap de Peñas, voyageuses infatigables, qui parfois volaient jusqu'aux îles Canaries ou aux îles du Cap-Vert.

Les femelles, comme elle, feraient de grands festins de sardines et de calamars pendant que les mâles construiraient les nids au bord d'une falaise. Elles y pondraient leurs œufs, les couveraient à l'abri de toutes les menaces, et quand les premières plumes résistantes pousseraient aux poussins viendrait la plus jolie partie du voyage : leur apprendre à voler dans le ciel de Biscaye.

Kengah plongea pour attraper un quatrième hareng et n'entendit pas le cri d'alarme qui ébranla l'air.

— Danger à tribord, décollage urgent!

Lorsque Kengah sortit la tête de l'eau, elle était seule sur l'immensité de l'océan.

2

Un chat grand noir et gros

— J'ai beaucoup de peine de te laisser tout seul, dit l'enfant en caressant le dos du chat grand noir et gros.

Puis il continua à remplir son sac à dos. Il prenait une cassette du groupe PUR, un de ses favoris, la rangeait, hésitait, la sortait et ne savait pas s'il la remettait dans le sac ou s'il la laissait sur la table. Il n'arrivait pas à décider ce qu'il allait emmener en vacances et ce qu'il allait laisser à la maison.

Le chat grand noir et gros le regardait avec attention, assis sur le bord de la fenêtre, son endroit préféré.

— J'ai pris mes lunettes pour nager ? Zorbas, t'as pas vu mes lunettes ? Non, tu ne les connais pas, toi, tu n'aimes pas l'eau. Tu ne sais pas ce que tu perds. La natation est un des sports les plus amusants. Des croquettes ? proposa l'enfant en prenant une boîte de croquettes pour chat.

Il lui en servit une ration plus que généreuse, et le chat grand noir et gros se mit à mastiquer lentement, pour faire durer le plaisir : quelles croquettes délicieuses, craquantes, au bon goût de poisson ! "C'est un garçon formidable", pensa le chat la bouche pleine. "Comment ça, un garçon formidable ? Le meilleur", corrigea-t-il en avalant.

Zorbas, le chat grand noir et gros, avait de bonnes raisons de penser cela de cet enfant qui dépensait son argent de poche en délicieuses croquettes, qui nettoyait la litière de la caisse où il faisait ses besoins et qui l'instruisait en lui parlant de choses importantes.

Ils passaient de longues heures ensemble sur le balcon à regarder l'activité incessante du port de Hambourg, et là, par exemple, le garçon lui disait :

— Tu vois ce bateau, Zorbas ? Tu sais d'où il vient ? Du Liberia, un pays d'Afrique très intéressant parce qu'il a été fondé par des hommes qui avaient été des esclaves. Quand je serai grand, je serai capitaine d'un grand voilier et j'irai au Liberia. Tu viendras avec moi, Zorbas. Tu seras un bon chat de mer. J'en suis sûr.

Comme tous les enfants des ports, il rêvait de voyages dans des pays lointains. Le chat grand noir et gros l'écoutait en ronronnant et se voyait aussi à bord d'un voilier sillonnant les mers.

Oui. Le chat grand noir et gros avait beaucoup de tendresse pour le garçon et il n'oubliait pas qu'il lui devait la vie.

Zorbas avait contracté cette dette exactement le jour où il avait quitté le panier dans lequel il vivait avec ses sept frères.

Le lait de sa mère était tiède et doux mais lui, il voulait goûter ces têtes de poisson que les gens du marché donnaient aux grands chats. Il ne pensait pas en manger une entière, non, il voulait la traîner jusqu'au panier et là, miauler à ses frères :

— Assez de téter notre pauvre mère ! Vous ne voyez pas comme elle a maigri ? Mangez du poisson, c'est la nourriture des chats des ports.

Peu de temps avant de quitter le panier, sa mère lui avait miaulé très sérieusement :

— Tu es agile et malin, c'est très bien, mais tu dois faire attention et ne pas sortir du panier. Demain ou après-demain les humains vont venir décider de ton destin et de celui de tes frères. Ils vont sûrement vous donner des noms sympathiques et vous serez assurés d'être nourris. C'est une grande chance de naître dans un port, car dans les ports on aime et on protège les chats. La seule chose que les humains attendent de nous, c'est que nous éloignions les rats. Oui, mon enfant, être chat de port est une grande chance, mais tu dois faire attention car il y a en toi quelque chose qui peut faire ton malheur. Mon enfant, si tu regardes tes frères, tu verras qu'ils sont gris ou rayés comme les tigres. Toi, tu es né tout noir, sauf la petite tache blanche que tu as sous le menton. Il y a des humains qui croient que les chats noirs portent malheur; c'est pourquoi, mon petit, il ne faut pas sortir du panier.

Mais Zorbas, qui était alors une petite boule de charbon, quitta le panier. Il voulait goûter une de ces têtes de poisson. Et il voulait aussi voir un peu le monde.

Il n'alla pas très loin. La queue dressée et vibrante, en trottant vers un étal de poissonnier, il passa devant un grand oiseau qui somnolait, la tête penchée. C'était un oiseau très laid avec une énorme poche sous le bec. Soudain le petit chat sentit que le sol s'éloignait de ses pattes et, sans comprendre ce qui lui arrivait, il se retrouva en train de faire une cabriole en l'air. Se souvenant de l'une des premières leçons de sa mère, il chercha un endroit pour retomber sur ses quatre pattes, mais en bas l'oiseau l'attendait le bec ouvert. Il tomba dans la poche, il y faisait noir et ça sentait horriblement mauvais.

— Laisse-moi sortir! Laisse-moi sortir! miaula-t-il, désespéré.

— Ah bon. Tu parles. Quelle bête tu es? croassa l'oiseau sans ouvrir le bec.

— Laisse-moi sortir ou je te griffe, miaula-t-il, menaçant.

— Je crois que tu es une grenouille. Tu es une grenouille? croassa l'oiseau, toujours le bec fermé.

— Je m'étouffe, oiseau idiot! miaula le petit Zorbas.

— Oui. Tu es une grenouille. Une grenouille noire. Comme c'est étrange, croassa l'oiseau.

— Je suis un chat et je suis en colère! Laisse-moi sortir ou tu vas le regretter! miaula le petit Zorbas en cherchant où planter ses griffes dans la poche sombre.

— Tu crois que je ne sais pas distinguer un chat d'une grenouille? Les chats sont poilus, rapides et ils sentent la pantoufle. Toi, tu es une grenouille. Une fois j'ai mangé des grenouilles, c'était pas mauvais, mais elles étaient vertes. Dis donc, tu ne serais pas une grenouille vénéneuse par hasard? croassa l'oiseau inquiet.

— Oui! Je suis une grenouille vénéneuse et en plus je porte malheur!

— Quel problème! L'autre jour j'ai avalé un hérisson vénéneux et il ne m'est rien arrivé. Quel problème! Je t'avale ou je te crache? réfléchit l'oiseau, mais il ne croassa rien de plus car il s'agita, battit des ailes et ouvrit finalement le bec.

Couvert de bave, le petit Zorbas sortit la tête et sauta par terre. Il vit alors le garçon qui tenait l'oiseau par le cou et le secouait.

— Tu es aveugle ou quoi? Pélican imbécile! Viens mon chat. Un peu plus tu finissais dans le ventre de cet oiseau, dit l'enfant, et il le prit dans ses bras.

C'est ainsi qu'avait commencé cette amitié qui durait depuis cinq ans.

Le baiser de l'enfant sur sa tête éloigna ses souvenirs. Il le vit enfiler son sac à dos, marcher vers la porte et de là lui dire encore adieu.

– À dans deux mois. Je penserai à toi tous les jours Zorbas, je te le promets.

– Au revoir Zorbas ! Au revoir mon gros ! crièrent les deux petits frères du garçon.

Le chat grand noir et gros entendit qu'on fermait la porte à double tour et il courut jusqu'à la fenêtre sur la rue pour voir sa famille adoptive avant qu'elle ne s'éloigne.

Le chat grand noir et gros poussa un soupir de satisfaction. Pendant deux mois il allait être le seigneur et maître de l'appartement. Un ami de la famille viendrait tous les jours lui ouvrir une boîte de nourriture et changer sa litière. Deux mois pour se prélasser dans les fauteuils, sur les lits, ou sortir sur le balcon, grimper sur les toits, aller jusqu'aux branches du vieux marronnier et descendre le long de son tronc jusqu'à la cour, où il retrouvait les chats du quartier. Il n'allait pas s'ennuyer. Pas du tout.

C'est ce que pensait Zorbas, le chat grand noir et gros, car il ne savait pas ce qui allait lui tomber dessus très bientôt.

3

Hambourg en vue

Kengah déplia ses ailes pour prendre son envol, mais la vague fut plus rapide et la recouvrit toute. Quand elle sortit de l'eau, la lumière du jour avait disparu, et après avoir secoué énergiquement la tête, elle comprit que la malédiction des mers obscurcissait sa vue.

Kengah, la mouette aux plumes argentées, plongea sa tête dans l'eau à plusieurs reprises jusqu'à ce que quelques étincelles de lumière arrivent à ses pupilles couvertes de petrole. La tache visqueuse, la peste noire, collait ses ailes à son corps et elle se mit à remuer les pattes dans l'espoir de nager vite et de sortir du centre de la vague noire.

Tous les muscles tétanisés par l'effort, elle atteignit enfin la limite de la tache de pétrole et le frais contact de l'eau propre. Lorsque, à force de cligner des yeux et de plonger sa tête sous l'eau, elle réussit à nettoyer ses yeux, elle regarda le ciel et ne vit que quelques nuages qui s'interposaient entre la mer et l'immensité de la voûte céleste. Ses compagnes de la bande du Phare du Sable rouge devaient être loin, très loin.

C'était la loi. Elle aussi, elle avait vu des mouettes surprises par les vagues noires mortelles, et malgré son désir de descendre leur apporter une aide aussi inutile qu'impossible, elle s'était éloignée, respectant la loi qui interdit d'assister à la mort de ses compagnes.

Les ailes immobilisées, collées au corps, les mouettes étaient des proies faciles pour les grands poissons, ou bien elles mouraient lentement asphyxiées par le pétrole, qui en glissant entre leurs plumes bouchait tous leurs pores.

C'était le sort qui l'attendait et elle désira disparaître rapidement dans le gosier d'un grand poisson.

La tache noire. La peste noire. Tandis qu'elle attendait l'issue fatale, Kengah maudit les humains.

– Pas tous. Il ne faut pas être injuste! cria-t-elle faiblement.

Souvent elle avait vu d'en haut comment les grands pétroliers profitaient des jours de brouillard côtier pour aller en haute mer nettoyer leurs réservoirs. Ils jetaient à la mer des milliers de litres d'une substance épaisse et pestilentielle qui était entraînée par les vagues.

Elle avait aussi vu que parfois des petites embarcations s'approchaient des pétroliers et les empêchaient de vider leurs réservoirs. Malheureusement, ces petits bateaux aux couleurs de l'arc-en-ciel n'arrivaient pas toujours à temps pour empêcher qu'on empoisonne les mers.

Kengah passa les heures les plus longues de sa vie, posée sur l'eau à se demander, atterrée, si ce n'était pas la plus terrible des morts qui l'attendait ; pire que d'être dévorée par un poisson, pire que l'angoisse de l'asphyxie, mourir de faim.

Désespérée à l'idée d'une mort lente, elle remua et se rendit compte avec étonnement que le pétrole n'avait pas collé ses ailes contre son corps. Ses plumes étaient imprégnées de cette substance épaisse mais au moins elle pouvait étendre les ailes.

– J'ai peut-être encore une chance de sortir de là et, qui sait si en volant haut, très haut, le soleil ne fera pas fondre le pétrole.

Une histoire racontée par une vieille mouette des îles Frisonnes revint à sa mémoire. Cela parlait d'un humain, nommé Icare, qui pour réaliser son rêve de voler s'était fabriqué des ailes avec des plumes d'aigle et avait volé très haut, tout près du soleil, si bien que la chaleur avait fait fondre la cire qui collait les plumes et qu'il était tombé.

Kengah battit des ailes, replia ses pattes, s'éleva de quelques centimètres et retomba dans l'eau.

Avant de recommencer, elle plongea complètement et remua ses ailes sous l'eau. Cette fois elle s'éleva d'un mètre avant de retomber.

Ce maudit pétrole collait les plumes de sa queue, de sorte qu'elle ne pouvait pas guider son ascension. Elle replongea et avec son bec retira la couche de saleté qui couvrait sa queue. Elle supporta la douleur de l'arrachage des plumes jusqu'à ce que sa queue soit un peu moins sale.

Au cinquième essai, Kengah réussit à s'envoler.

Elle battait des ailes désespérément car le poids de la couche de pétrole l'empêchait de planer. Un seul arrêt et elle tomberait. Par chance, elle était jeune et ses muscles répondaient bien.

Elle vola très haut. Sans cesser de battre des ailes, elle regarda en bas et vit à peine la côte comme une ligne blanche. Elle vit aussi quelques bateaux comme de minuscules objets sur une nappe bleue. Elle monta plus haut, mais les effets du soleil qu'elle attendait ne l'atteignaient pas. Peut-être les rayons donnaient-ils une chaleur trop faible, peut-être la couche de pétrole était-elle trop épaisse.

Kengah comprit qu'elle n'aurait pas suffisamment de force pour continuer à battre des ailes et vola vers l'intérieur des terres en suivant la ligne verte et sinueuse de l'Elbe, à la recherche d'un endroit pour se poser.

Son battement d'ailes devint de plus en plus lourd et lent. Elle perdait ses forces. Elle ne volait plus aussi haut.

Dans un effort désespéré pour reprendre de l'altitude, elle ferma les yeux et battit des ailes avec ses dernières énergies. Elle ne sut pas combien de temps elle vola les yeux fermés, mais quand elle les rouvrit elle était au-dessus d'une haute tour ornée d'une girouette d'or.

— Saint-Michel! cria-t-elle en reconnaissant la tour de l'église de Hambourg.

Ses ailes refusèrent de la porter plus loin.

4

La fin d'un vol

Le chat grand noir et gros prenait le soleil sur le balcon en ronronnant et en pensant comme c'était bon d'être là à recevoir les rayons du soleil, le ventre en l'air, les quatre pattes repliées et la queue étirée.

Au moment précis où il se retournait paresseusement pour présenter son dos au soleil, il entendit le bourdonnement d'un objet volant qu'il ne sut pas identifier et qui s'approchait à grande vitesse. Inquiet, il se dressa d'un seul coup sur ses quatre pattes et arriva tout juste à se jeter de côté pour esquiver la mouette qui s'abattit sur le balcon.

C'était un oiseau très sale. Tout son corps était imprégné d'une substance noire et malodorante.

Zorbas s'approcha et la mouette essaya de se redresser en traînant les ailes.

— Ce n'était pas un atterrissage très élégant, miaula-t-il.

— Je regrette. Je ne pouvais pas faire autrement, croassa la mouette.

— Dis donc, tu es dans un drôle d'état. Qu'est-ce que tu as sur le corps? Tu sens vraiment mauvais!

— J'ai été atteinte par une vague noire. La peste noire. La malédiction des mers. Je vais mourir, croassa plaintivement la mouette.

— Mourir? Ne dis pas ça. Tu es fatiguée et sale. C'est tout. Pourquoi ne vas-tu pas jusqu'au Zoo? Ce n'est pas loin et il y a des vétérinaires qui pourront t'aider, miaula Zorbas.

— Je ne peux pas. C'était mon dernier vol, croassa la mouette d'une voix presque inaudible, et elle ferma les yeux.

— Ne meurs pas! Repose-toi un peu et, tu verras, tu iras mieux. Tu as faim? Je vais t'apporter un peu de ma nourriture mais ne meurs pas, miaula Zorbas en s'approchant de la mouette évanouie.

Surmontant son dégoût le chat lui lécha la tête. Cette substance qui la couvrait avait un goût horrible. Quand il lui passa la langue sur le cou il remarqua que la respiration de l'oiseau était de plus en plus faible.

— Écoute, mon amie. Je veux t'aider mais je ne sais pas comment. Essaye de te reposer pendant que je vais demander ce qu'on fait avec une mouette malade, miaula Zorbas avant de grimper sur le toit.

Il s'éloignait vers le marronnier quand il entendit la mouette l'appeler.

— Tu veux que je te laisse un peu à manger? miaula-t-il, soulagé.

— Je vais pondre un œuf. Avec les dernières forces qui me restent je vais pondre un œuf. Chat, mon ami, on voit que tu es bon, que tu as de nobles sentiments. Je vais te demander de me promettre trois choses. Tu vas le faire? demanda-t-elle en secouant maladroitement ses pattes dans un essai manqué pour se redresser.

Zorbas pensa que la pauvre mouette délirait et qu'avec un oiseau dans un état aussi lamentable on ne pouvait qu'être généreux.

— Je te promets tout ce que tu voudras. Mais maintenant repose-toi, miaula-t-il avec compassion.

— Je n'ai pas le temps de me reposer. Promets-moi que tu ne mangeras pas l'œuf, dit-elle en ouvrant les yeux.

— Je promets de ne pas manger l'œuf.

— Promets-moi de t'en occuper jusqu'à la naissance du poussin, croassa-t-elle en soulevant la tête.

— Je promets de m'occuper de l'œuf jusqu'à la naissance du poussin, miaula Zorbas.

— Et promets-moi que tu lui apprendras à voler, croassa-t-elle en regardant fixement le chat dans les yeux.

Alors Zorbas pensa que non seulement cette malheureuse mouette délirait, mais qu'elle était complètement folle.

— Je promets de lui apprendre à voler. Et maintenant repose-toi, je vais chercher de l'aide, miaula Zorbas en sautant sur le toit.

Kengah regarda le ciel, remercia les bons vents qui l'avaient accompagnée et juste au moment où elle poussait son dernier soupir, un petit œuf blanc taché de bleu roula à côté de son corps imbibé de pétrole.

5

À la recherche d'un conseil

Zorbas descendit rapidement le long du tronc du marronnier, traversa la cour de l'immeuble à toute vitesse en évitant de se faire remarquer par les chiens vagabonds, sortit dans la rue, s'assura qu'il n'y avait pas d'auto, traversa et courut jusqu'au Cuneo, un restaurant italien du port.

Deux chats qui reniflaient une caisse à ordures le virent passer.

— Eh, mon pote, tu vois ce que je vois ? Quel joli petit gros ! miaula l'un des chats.

— Ouais, mon vieux. Comme il est noir, c'est pas une boule de graisse, c'est une boule de goudron. Où tu vas petite boule de goudron ? demanda l'autre.

Même préoccupé par la mouette, Zorbas n'était pas disposé à laisser passer les provocations de ces deux voyous. Alors il s'arrêta, hérissa les poils de son dos et sauta sur le couvercle de la poubelle.

Lentement il étira une patte de devant, sortit une griffe longue comme une allumette et l'approcha du museau de l'un des provocateurs.

— Elle te plaît ? J'en ai neuf autres du même modèle. Tu veux les essayer ? miaula-t-il très calmement.

Le chat qui avait la griffe sous le nez avala sa salive avant de répondre sans quitter la griffe des yeux.

— Non chef. Quelle belle journée ! Pas vrai ?

— Et toi, qu'est-ce que tu en dis ? demanda Zorbas à l'autre chat.

— Moi aussi je dis que c'est une bien belle journée, idéale pour se promener, un peu fraîche peut-être.

Cette affaire réglée, Zorbas reprit son chemin jusqu'à la porte du restaurant. À l'intérieur, les garçons préparaient les tables pour les clients de midi. Zorbas miaula trois fois et attendit assis sur le seuil. Peu après, Secrétario, un chat de gouttière très maigre avec seulement deux poils de moustache, un de chaque côté du nez, s'approcha de lui.

— Nous regrettons beaucoup, mais si vous n'avez pas réservé, nous ne pouvons pas vous accueillir. Nous sommes complet, miaula-t-il en guise de salut.

Il allait ajouter quelque chose encore, mais Zorbas le coupa :

— Je dois miauler avec Colonello. C'est urgent!

— Urgent! Toujours des urgences de dernière minute. Je vais voir ce que je peux faire, mais c'est bien parce qu'il s'agit d'une urgence, miaula Secrétario, et il rentra dans le restaurant.

Colonello était un chat d'un âge indéterminé. Certains disaient qu'il avait le même âge que le restaurant qui l'abritait, d'autres soutenaient qu'il était encore beaucoup plus vieux. Mais cela n'avait pas d'importance, car Colonello avait un étrange talent pour conseiller ceux qui avaient des problèmes, et même s'il ne résolvait jamais aucune difficulté, ses conseils réconfortaient. Par son âge et par son talent Colonello était une autorité chez les chats du port.

Secrétario revint en courant.

— Suis-moi. Colonello va te recevoir, exceptionnellement.

Zorbas le suivit. Passant sous les tables et sous les chaises de la salle, ils arrivèrent à la porte de la cave. Ils descendirent en sautant les marches d'un escalier étroit et, en bas, trouvèrent Colonello, la queue dressée, en train d'examiner les bouchons des bouteilles de champagne.

— *Porca miseria!* Les rats ont rongé les bouchons du meilleur champagne de la maison. Zorbas, *caro amico,* salua Colonello qui avait l'habitude de miauler des mots en italien.

— Excuse-moi de te déranger en plein travail, mais j'ai un problème grave et j'ai besoin de tes conseils, miaula Zorbas.

— Je suis là pour ça, *caro amico*. Secrétario! Sers à *mi amico* un peu de ces *lasagnes alforno* qu'on nous a données ce matin, ordonna Colonello.

— Mais vous les avez toutes mangées! Je n'ai même pas pu les sentir, se plaignit Secrétario.

Zorbas remercia en disant qu'il n'avait pas faim et raconta rapidement la tumultueuse arrivée de la mouette, son état lamentable et les promesses qu'il avait été obligé de faire. Le vieux chat écouta en silence, puis il réfléchit en caressant ses longues moustaches et finalement miaula avec énergie.

— *Porca miseria!* Il faut se débrouiller pour que cette pauvre mouette puisse reprendre son vol.

— Oui, mais comment? demanda Zorbas.

— Le mieux c'est de consulter Jesaitout, indiqua Secrétario.

— C'est exactement ce que j'allais suggérer. Pourquoi faut-il toujours qu'il m'enlève les miaulements de la bouche, celui-là? protesta Colonello.

— Oui? C'est une bonne idée. Je vais aller voir Jesaitout, approuva Zorbas.

— On va y aller ensemble. Les problèmes d'un chat du port sont les problèmes de tous les chats du port, déclara solennellement Colonello.

Les trois chats sortirent de la cave et coururent à travers le labyrinthe des cours des maisons alignées en face du port jusqu'au temple de Jesaitout.

6

Dans un endroit étrange

Jesaitout habitait un endroit assez difficile à décrire car, à première vue, cela aurait pu être un bric-à-brac d'objets étranges, un musée des extravagances, un dépôt de machines hors d'usage, la bibliothèque la plus chaotique du monde ou le laboratoire d'un savant inventeur d'engins impossibles à nommer. Mais ce n'était rien de tout cela, ou plutôt, c'était beaucoup plus que cela.

L'endroit s'appelait "Harry, Bazar du Port" et son propriétaire, Harry, était un vieux loup de mer qui au cours de cinquante ans de navigation sur les sept mers s'était employé à réunir toute sorte d'objets dans les centaines de ports qu'il avait connus.

Lorsque la vieillesse s'installa dans ses os, Harry décida de troquer sa vie de navigateur contre celle de marin à terre et d'ouvrir le bazar avec tous les objets qu'il avait réunis. Il loua une maison de trois étages dans la rue du port, mais elle était trop petite pour exposer ses collections insolites, si bien qu'il loua la maison voisine, à deux étages, mais ce n'était toujours pas suffisant. Finalement, après avoir loué une troisième maison, il réussit à ranger tous ses objets — ranger évidemment selon son sens de l'ordre très particulier.

Dans les trois maisons réunies par des couloirs et des escaliers étroits, il y avait près d'un million d'objets parmi lesquels il faut signaler :

7 200 chapeaux à bord souple pour que le vent les emporte

160 gouvernails de bateaux pris de vertige à force de faire le tour du monde

245 feux de navires qui avaient défié les brumes les plus épaisses

12 télégraphes de commandement écrasés par des capitaines irascibles

256 boussoles qui n'avaient jamais perdu le nord

6 éléphants de bois grandeur nature

2 girafes empaillées contemplant la savane

1 ours polaire naturalisé, dans le ventre duquel se trouvait la main, naturalisée aussi, d'un explorateur norvégien

700 ventilateurs dont les pales rappelaient les brises fraîches des crépuscules tropicaux

1 200 hamacs de jute, garantissant les meilleurs rêves

1 300 marionnettes de Sumatra qui n'avaient interprété que des histoires d'amour

123 projecteurs de diapositives montrant des paysages où l'on pouvait toujours être heureux

54 000 romans dans 47 langues

2 maquettes de la tour Eiffel, l'une construite avec un demi-million d'aiguilles à coudre et l'autre trois cent mille cure-dents

3 canons de bateaux corsaires anglais ayant attaqué Cartagena de Indias

17 ancres trouvées au fond de la Mer du Nord

200 tableaux de couchers de soleil

17 machines à écrire ayant appartenu à des écrivains célèbres

128 caleçons longs de flanelle pour hommes de plus de 2 mètres

7 fracs pour nains

500 pipes d'écume de mer

1 astrolabe s'obstinant à indiquer la position de la Croix du Sud

7 coquillages géants dans lesquels résonnait l'écho lointain de naufrages mythiques

12 kilomètres de soie rouge

2 écoutilles de sous-marins

Et beaucoup de choses encore qu'il serait trop long de nommer.

Pour visiter le bazar d'Harry on devait payer une entrée et une fois à l'intérieur il fallait un grand sens de l'orientation pour ne pas se perdre dans le labyrinthe de chambres sans fenêtres, couloirs étroits et escaliers qui faisaient communiquer les trois maisons.

Harry avait deux mascottes : un chimpanzé nommé Matias qui tenait la caisse à l'entrée, assurait la sécurité et jouait aux dames avec le vieux marin – évidemment très mal. Il buvait de la bière et essayait toujours de tricher en rendant la monnaie.

La deuxième mascotte c'était Jesaitout, un chat gris, petit et maigre, qui consacrait l'essentiel de son temps à l'étude des milliers de livres qu'il y avait là.

Colonello, Secrétario et Zorbas entrèrent dans le bazar la queue en l'air. Ils regrettèrent de ne pas voir Harry derrière le comptoir car le vieux marin avait toujours des paroles affectueuses et des saucisses pour eux.

— Un instant sacs à puces! Vous oubliez de payer l'entrée! glapit Matias.

— Et depuis quand est-ce qu'on paye, nous les chats? demanda Secrétario.

— Sur la porte il y a : *Entrée deux marks.* Nulle part il est écrit que les chats entrent gratis. Huit marks ou vous fichez le camp! glapit énergiquement le chimpanzé.

— Monsieur le singe, je crains que les mathématiques ne soient pas votre fort, miaula Secrétario.

— C'est exactement ce que j'allais dire. Une fois de plus vous m'enlevez les miaulements de la bouche, protesta Colonello.

— BLABLABLA! Payez ou fichez le camp! cria Matias.

Zorbas sauta sur le comptoir et regarda fixement le chimpanzé dans les yeux. Il soutint son regard jusqu'à ce que Matias cligne des yeux et commence à pleurer.

— Bon, en réalité, ça fait six marks. Tout le monde peut se tromper, reprit timidement Matias.

Sans cesser de le regarder dans les yeux, Zorbas sortit une griffe de sa patte droite de devant.

— Ça te plaît Matias? J'en ai neuf autres pareilles. Tu peux les imaginer plantées dans ce cul rouge que tu as toujours à l'air? miaula-t-il tranquillement.

— Pour cette fois je ferme les yeux. Vous pouvez passer, glapit le chimpanzé en prenant un air calme.

Les trois chats, la queue orgueilleusement dressée, disparurent dans le labyrinthe de couloirs.

7

Un chat qui sait tout

— Terrible! Terrible! Il est arrivé quelque chose de terrible, miaula Jesaitout en les voyant.

Nerveux, il se promenait devant un énorme livre ouvert sur le sol, et par moments il portait ses pattes de devant à sa tête. Il avait l'air vraiment inconsolable.

— Qu'est-ce qui est arrivé? miaula Secrétario.

— C'est exactement ce que j'allais demander. Il semble que m'enlever les miaulements de la bouche soit une obsession chez vous, protesta Colonello.

— Allons. Ce n'est pas si grave, suggéra Zorbas.

— Quoi! Pas si grave. C'est terrible! Terrible. Ces maudites souris ont mangé une page entière de l'Atlas. La carte de Madagascar a disparu. C'est terrible! insista Jesaitout en tirant sur ses moustaches.

— Secrétario, rappelez-moi qu'il faut organiser une battue contre ces mangeurs de Masagas…

Masagamas… enfin vous voyez ce que je veux dire, miaula Colonello.

— Madagascar, précisa Secrétario.

— Continuez. Continuez à m'enlever les miaulements de la bouche. *Porca miseria!* s'exclama Colonello.

— On va te donner un coup de main, Jesaitout, mais maintenant nous sommes ici parce que nous avons un grand problème et comme tu sais tant de choses, tu peux peut-être nous aider, miaula Zorbas, et il lui raconta la triste histoire de la mouette.

Jesaitout écouta avec attention. Il approuvait en remuant la tête et quand les mouvements nerveux de sa queue exprimaient avec trop d'éloquence les sentiments qu'éveillaient en lui les miaulements de Zorbas, il essayait de la retenir avec ses pattes de derrière.

— … et je l'ai laissée comme ça, très mal, il y a un instant… conclut Zorbas.

— Terrible histoire! Terrible! Voyons, laissez-moi réfléchir. Mouette, pétrole… pétrole… mouette… mouette malade… c'est ça. Il faut consulter l'encyclopédie! s'exclama-t-il plein de jubilation.

— La quoi? miaulèrent les trois chats.

— L'en-cy-clo-pé-die. Le livre du savoir. Il faut chercher dans les tomes 13 et 16, les lettres M et P, indiqua Jesaitout d'un ton décidé.

– Voyons cette enplico... empyco... hum! proposa Colonello.

– En-cy-clo-pé-die, épela lentement Secrétario.

– C'est exactement ce que j'allais dire. Je vois que vous ne pouvez pas résister à la tentation de m'enlever les miaulements de la bouche, protesta Colonello.

Jesaitout grimpa sur un énorme meuble dans lequel étaient alignés de gros livres à l'air imposant et après avoir cherché les lettres M et P, il fit tomber les deux volumes. Il descendit et, d'une griffe très courte, usée à force de feuilleter les livres, il tourna les pages. Les trois chats gardaient un silence respectueux tandis qu'il marmottait des miaulements presque inaudibles.

– Je crois qu'on va y être. Comme c'est intéressant! Merlan, Migration, Milan. Comme c'est intéressant! Écoutez ça: Il semble que le milan est un oiseau terrible! Terrible! Il est considéré comme l'un des rapaces les plus cruels! Terrible! s'exclama Jesaitout avec enthousiasme.

– Le milan ne nous intéresse pas. Nous sommes ici pour une mouette, l'interrompit Secrétario.

– Auriez-vous l'amabilité de cesser de m'enlever les miaulements de la bouche? grogna Colonello.

– Pardon. Mais pour moi l'encyclopédie est irrésistible. Chaque fois que je regarde dans ses pages j'apprends quelque chose de nouveau. Morue. Mouette. On y est! s'écria Jesaitout.

Mais ce que l'encyclopédie disait des mouettes ne leur fut pas très utile. Ils apprirent que la mouette qui les préoccupait appartenait à l'espèce argentée, appelée ainsi à cause de la couleur de ses plumes.

Ce qu'ils trouvèrent sur le pétrole ne les amena pas non plus à savoir comment aider la mouette, même s'il leur fallut supporter une interminable dissertation de Jesaitout, qui parla longuement d'une guerre du pétrole dans les années 70.

— Par les piquants du hérisson! Nous sommes toujours au même point, miaula Zorbas.

— C'est terrible! Terrible! C'est la première fois que l'encyclopédie me déçoit, s'exclama Jesaitout, désolé.

— Et dans cette enplico… encymolé… enfin tu vois ce que je veux dire. Il n'y a pas de conseils pratiques, du genre comment enlever les taches de pétrole? s'enquit Colonello.

— Génial! Terriblement génial! C'est par là qu'on aurait dû commencer. Je prends tout de suite le tome 4, la lettre D, Détachant, annonça Jesaitout en grimpant sur le meuble.

— Vous vous rendez compte, si vous aviez évité cette odieuse habitude de m'enlever les miaulements de la bouche nous saurions déjà quoi faire, indiqua Colonello au silencieux Secrétario.

À la page consacrée au mot "Détachant" ils trouvèrent, outre la façon d'enlever les taches de confiture, d'encre de Chine, de sang et de sirop de framboise, la solution pour éliminer les taches de pétrole.

— "On nettoie la surface affectée avec un linge humecté de benzine." Ça y est! miaula Jesaitout, euphorique.

— Ça y est pas du tout! Et où on va trouver de la benzine? grogna Zorbas avec une mauvaise humeur évidente.

— Mais, si je me souviens bien, dans la cave du restaurant il y a un pot avec des pinceaux qui trempent dans de la benzine. Secrétario sait ce qu'il doit faire, miaula Colonello.

— Pardon monsieur, mais je n'ai pas bien saisi votre idée, s'excusa Secrétario.

— Très simple: vous humectez convenablement votre queue avec la benzine et nous irons nous occuper de cette pauvre mouette, répondit Colonello en regardant ailleurs.

— Ah non! Ça alors non! Pas question! protesta Secrétario.

— Je vous rappelle qu'au menu de ce soir il y a une double portion de foie à la crème, susurra Colonello.

— Tremper ma queue dans la benzine... Vous avez dit du foie à la crème? miaula Secrétario consterné.

Jesaitout décida de les accompagner et les quatre chats coururent jusqu'à la sortie du bazar d'Harry. À leur passage le chimpanzé, qui venait de boire une bière, leur adressa un rot sonore.

8

Zorbas commence à tenir ses promesses

En arrivant sur le balcon les quatre chats comprirent qu'il était trop tard. Colonello, Jesaitout et Zorbas regardèrent avec respect le corps sans vie de la mouette tandis que Secrétario agitait sa queue dans le vent pour en chasser l'odeur de benzine.

— Je crois qu'on doit lui fermer les ailes. C'est ce qui se fait dans ces cas-là, affirma Colonello.

Surmontant leur répugnance devant cet être imprégné de pétrole, ils replièrent ses ailes le long de son corps et en la déplaçant ils découvrirent l'œuf blanc taché de bleu.

— L'œuf! Elle a réussi à pondre l'œuf! s'exclama Zorbas.

— Tu t'es fourré dans une drôle d'histoire, *caro amico*, une drôle d'histoire, remarqua Colonello.

— Qu'est-ce que je vais faire avec l'œuf? s'interrogea Zorbas de plus en plus angoissé.

— Avec un œuf on peut faire plein de choses. Une omelette par exemple, proposa Secrétario.

— Oh oui! Un coup d'œil dans l'encyclopédie nous dira comment préparer la meilleure des omelettes. Ce thème est traité dans le tome 15, lettre O, assura Jesaitout.

— Pas question. Pas un miaulement de plus! Zorbas a promis à cette pauvre mouette qu'il s'occuperait de l'œuf et du poussin! Une promesse sur l'honneur faite par un chat du port engage tous les chats du port. Aussi on ne touche pas à cet œuf! déclara solennellement Colonello.

— Mais je ne sais pas comment on s'occupe d'un œuf! Je n'ai jamais eu d'œuf, moi! miaula Zorbas désespéré.

Alors les chats regardèrent Jesaitout. Peut-être y avait-il quelque chose là-dessus dans sa fameuse ency-clo-pé-die.

— Je dois consulter le tome 15, lettre O. Il y a sûrement tout ce que nous devons savoir sur l'œuf, mais pour l'instant je conseille la chaleur, la chaleur du corps, beaucoup de chaleur du corps, indiqua Jesaitout sur un ton pédant et didactique.

— C'est-à-dire se coucher sur l'œuf, mais sans le casser, conseilla Secrétario.

— C'est exactement ce que j'allais suggérer. C'est effrayant cette capacité que vous avez de m'enlever les miaulements de la bouche. Zorbas, reste près de l'œuf, nous, nous allons accompagner Jesaitout pour voir ce que dit son enpylo...

encymo… enfin tu sais ce que je veux dire. Nous reviendrons ce soir avec les informations et nous donnerons une sépulture à cette pauvre mouette, décida Colonello avant de sauter sur le toit.

Jesaitout et Secrétario le suivirent. Zorbas resta sur le balcon, avec l'œuf et la mouette morte. Il se coucha en faisant très attention et attira l'œuf contre son ventre. Il se sentait ridicule. Il pensait aux railleries que pourraient faire les deux voyous qu'il avait affrontés le matin si jamais ils le voyaient.

Mais une promesse est une promesse et, réchauffé par les rayons du soleil, il s'assoupit avec l'œuf blanc taché de bleu tout contre son ventre noir.

9

Une nuit triste

À la lumière de la lune Secrétario, Jesaitout et Zorbas creusèrent un trou au pied du marronnier. Peu auparavant ils avaient jeté la mouette du haut du balcon dans la cour en faisant attention qu'aucun humain ne les voie. Ils la déposèrent rapidement dans le trou et le recouvrirent de terre. Alors Colonello miaula gravement :

— Camarades chats, cette nuit nous disons adieu à la dépouille d'une malheureuse mouette dont nous ne connaissons même pas le nom. Tout ce que nous savons d'elle, grâce aux connaissances de notre camarade Jesaitout, c'est qu'elle appartenait à l'espèce des mouettes argentées et qu'elle venait peut-être de très loin, du pays où le fleuve rejoint la mer. Nous savons peu de choses d'elle, mais ce qui importe c'est qu'elle est arrivée mourante chez Zorbas, l'un des nôtres, et qu'elle a mis en lui toute sa confiance. Zorbas a promis de s'occuper de l'œuf qu'elle a pondu avant de mourir, du poussin qui naîtra et, ce qui est plus difficile, camarades, il a promis de lui apprendre à voler.

— Voler, tome 23, lettre V, entendit-on Jesaitout murmurer.

— C'est exactement ce que monsieur Colonello allait dire. Ne lui enlève pas les miaulements de la bouche, conseilla Secrétario.

— ... Promesses difficiles à tenir, poursuivit Colonello impassible, mais nous savons qu'un chat du port respecte toujours ses miaulements. Pour l'y aider, j'ordonne que notre camarade Zorbas n'abandonne pas l'œuf jusqu'à la naissance du poussin et que notre camarade Jesaitout regarde dans son enplico... entiplo... enfin dans ses bouquins tout ce qui concerne l'art de voler. Et maintenant disons adieu à cette mouette, victime du malheur provoqué par les humains. Tendons nos cous vers la lune et miaulons le chant d'adieu des chats du port.

Au pied du vieil arbre les quatre chats se mirent à miauler une triste litanie et à leurs miaulements se joignirent très vite ceux des chats des alentours, puis ceux des chats de l'autre rive du fleuve, et aux miaulements s'unirent les hurlements des chiens, le pépiement plaintif des canaris en cage et des moineaux dans leurs nids, le coassement triste des grenouilles, jusqu'aux glapissements désordonnés de Matias le chimpanzé.

Les lumières de toutes les maisons de Hambourg s'allumèrent et les habitants s'interrogèrent sur les raisons de l'étrange tristesse qui s'était subitement emparée des animaux.

Deuxième partie

1

Portrait de chat en mère poule

Le chat grand noir et gros passa des jours couché contre l'œuf, le rapprochant avec toute la douceur de ses pattes de velours chaque fois qu'un mouvement involontaire de son corps l'éloignait de quelques centimètres. Ce furent des jours longs et inconfortables qui lui parurent parfois totalement inutiles, car il s'occupait d'un objet sans vie, une sorte de pierre fragile, même si elle était blanche tachée de bleu.

Un jour, ankylosé par le manque de mouvement, puisque, suivant les ordres de Colonello, il n'abandonnait l'œuf que pour aller manger et se rendre à la caisse où il faisait ses besoins, il eut la tentation de vérifier si un poussin de mouette grandissait vraiment à l'intérieur de l'ogive de calcaire. Il approcha alors une oreille de l'œuf, puis l'autre, mais il n'entendit rien. Il n'eut pas plus de chance lorsqu'il essaya de mirer l'intérieur de l'œuf en le plaçant à contre-jour. La coquille blanche tachée de bleu était épaisse et on ne voyait absolument rien à travers.

Toutes les nuits Colonello, Secrétario et Jesaitout venaient le voir, ils examinaient l'œuf pour vérifier si ce que Colonello appelait "les progrès espérés" se manifestait, mais après avoir constaté que l'œuf était le même qu'au premier jour, ils changeaient de sujet.

Jesaitout ne cessait de regretter que son encyclopédie n'indique pas la durée exacte de l'incubation et que la donnée la plus précise qu'il avait réussi à trouver dans ses gros livres était que cela pouvait durer entre dix-sept et trente jours, selon les caractéristiques de l'espèce à laquelle appartenait la mère.

Couver n'avait pas été facile pour le chat grand noir et gros. Il ne pouvait oublier le matin où l'ami de la famille chargé de s'occuper de lui avait pensé qu'il y avait trop de poussière par terre et avait décidé de passer l'aspirateur.

Tous les matins pendant les visites de l'ami, Zorbas avait caché l'œuf au milieu des pots de fleurs du balcon pour consacrer quelques minutes à ce brave type qui changeait sa litière et ouvrait ses boîtes de nourriture. Il lui miaulait sa gratitude, se frottait contre ses jambes et l'humain s'en allait en répétant qu'il était un chat très sympathique. Mais ce matin-là, après l'avoir vu passer l'aspirateur dans la salle de séjour et dans les chambres, il l'entendit dire :

— Et maintenant, le balcon. C'est entre les pots de fleurs qu'il y a le plus de saleté.

En entendant le bruit d'un compotier volant en mille éclats, l'ami courut dans la cuisine et cria depuis la porte :

— Zorbas, tu es devenu fou ? Regarde ce que tu as fait ! Sors de là, chat idiot ! Il ne manquerait plus que tu t'enfonces un bout de verre dans une patte.

Quelles insultes injustes ! Zorbas sortit de la cuisine en prenant l'air penaud, la queue entre les pattes, et trotta jusqu'au balcon.

Ce ne fut pas facile de faire rouler l'œuf jusque sous un lit, mais il y arriva et il y attendit que l'humain ait fini le ménage et s'en aille.

Le soir du vingtième jour Zorbas somnolait et ne s'aperçut pas que l'œuf bougeait, légèrement, mais il bougeait, comme s'il voulait se mettre à rouler par terre.

Un chatouillement sur le ventre le réveilla. Il ouvrit les yeux et ne put s'empêcher de sauter en voyant que par une fente de l'œuf apparaissait et disparaissait une petite pointe jaune.

Zorbas prit l'œuf entre ses pattes de devant et vit comment le poussin donnait des coups de bec pour faire un trou par lequel sortir sa petite tête blanche et humide.

— Maman! cria le poussin de mouette.

Zorbas ne sut que répondre. Il savait qu'il était noir mais il crut que la chaleur de l'émotion le transformait en un chat violet.

2

Il n'est pas facile d'être maman

— Maman! Maman! cria le poussin qui avait quitté son œuf.

Il était blanc comme du lait et des plumes minces, clairsemées et courtes couvraient à moitié son corps. Il essaya de faire quelques pas et s'écroula contre le ventre de Zorbas.

— Maman! J'ai faim! piailla-t-il en lui picorant la peau.

Qu'est-ce qu'il allait lui donner à manger? Jesaitout n'avait rien miaulé à ce sujet. Il savait que les mouettes se nourrissaient de poisson, mais d'où est-ce que, lui, il allait sortir un morceau de poisson? Zorbas courut à la cuisine et revint en faisant rouler une pomme.

Le poussin se dressa sur ses pattes mal assurées et se précipita sur le fruit. Le petit bec jaune toucha la peau et se tordit comme s'il était en caoutchouc et en se redressant il catapulta le poussin en arrière en le faisant tomber.

— J'ai faim! Maman! J'ai faim! cria-t-il en colère.

Zorbas, regrettant d'avoir vidé son plat avant la naissance du poussin, essaya de lui faire picorer une pomme de terre, ses croquettes — avec les vacances de la famille il n'y avait pas beaucoup de choix. Rien à faire. Le petit bec était tendre et se pliait contre la pomme de terre. Alors, dans son désespoir, il se souvint que le poussin était un oiseau et que les oiseaux mangeaient des insectes.

Il sortit sur le balcon et attendit qu'une mouche se pose à portée de ses griffes. Il ne tarda pas à en attraper une et la donna à l'affamé.

Le poussin la mit dans son bec, la serra et l'avala en fermant les yeux.

— C'est bon! Encore! Maman, encore! cria-t-il avec enthousiasme.

Zorbas sautait d'un bout à l'autre du balcon. Il avait chassé cinq mouches et une araignée lorsque du toit de la maison d'en face lui parvinrent les voix connues des chats voyous qu'il avait rencontrés quelques jours auparavant.

— Dis donc, regarde! Le petit gros fait de la gym. Quel corps, c'est un vrai danseur, miaula l'un.

— Moi je crois qu'il fait de l'aérobic. Quel joli petit gros. Qu'il est gracieux et quel style! Holà boule de graisse, tu vas te présenter à un concours de beauté? miaula l'autre.

Les deux voyous riaient, à l'abri de l'autre côté de la cour.

Zorbas leur aurait volontiers fait goûter le fil de ses griffes, mais ils étaient loin, si bien qu'il revint vers l'affamé avec son butin d'insectes.

Le poussin dévora les cinq mouches mais refusa de goûter à l'araignée. Rassasié, il eut un hoquet et se blottit tout contre le ventre de Zorbas.

— Maman, j'ai sommeil.

— Écoute, je regrette mais je ne suis pas ta maman, miaula Zorbas.

— Bien sûr que si, tu es ma maman. Et tu es une très bonne maman, fit-il en fermant les yeux.

À leur arrivée Colonello, Secrétario et Jesaitout trouvèrent le poussin endormi contre Zorbas.

— Félicitations! C'est un très joli poussin. Il pesait combien à la naissance? demanda Jesaitout.

— Qu'est-ce que c'est, cette question? Je ne suis pas la mère de ce poussin! rétorqua Zorbas.

— C'est la question qu'on pose d'habitude. Ne le prends pas mal. C'est vraiment un joli poussin, miaula Colonello.

— C'est terrible! Terrible! miaula Jesaitout en posant ses pattes sur sa bouche.

— Tu pourrais nous dire ce qui est terrible? demanda Colonello.

— Le poussin n'a rien à manger. C'est terrible!
Terrible! insista Jesaitout.

— Tu as raison. J'ai dû lui donner des mouches
et je crois qu'il va très vite avoir encore faim,
miaula Zorbas.

— Secrétario, qu'est-ce que vous attendez?
interrogea Colonello.

— Excusez-moi, monsieur, mais je ne vous suis
pas, se défendit Secrétario.

— Allez au restaurant et ramenez une sardine,
ordonna Colonello.

— Et pourquoi moi? Hein? Pourquoi c'est
toujours moi qui fais les courses? Moi qui
trempe ma queue dans la benzine? Moi qui vais
chercher une sardine? Pourquoi c'est toujours
moi? protesta Secrétario.

— Parce que ce soir, monsieur, il y a des calamars à la romaine pour le dîner. Ça ne vous
semble pas une raison suffisante? indiqua Colonello.

— Et ma queue qui empeste encore la benzine?... Vous avez dit des calamars à la romaine?...
demanda Secrétario en sautant sur le toit.

— Maman, qui c'est? cria le poussin en montrant les chats.

— Maman! Il t'a dit maman! C'est terriblement attendrissant!... arriva à s'exclamer Jesaitout
avant que le regard de Zorbas ne lui conseille de
fermer sa bouche.

— Bon, *caro amico,* tu as tenu ta première promesse, tu es en train de tenir la deuxième, il ne te reste plus que la troisième, déclara Colonello.

— La plus facile! Lui apprendre à voler, miaula ironiquement Zorbas.

— On y arrivera. Je consulte l'encyclopédie, mais le savoir a besoin de temps, assura Jesaitout.

— Maman, j'ai faim! coupa le poussin.

3

Le danger à l'affût

Les difficultés commencèrent le lendemain de la naissance. Zorbas dut agir énergiquement pour éviter que l'ami de la famille ne le découvre. Dès qu'il l'entendit ouvrir la porte il retourna un pot de fleur vide sur le poussin et s'assit dessus. Par chance l'humain ne sortit pas sur le balcon, et de la cuisine on n'entendait pas les cris de protestation.

Comme d'habitude l'ami nettoya la caisse, changea la litière, ouvrit la boîte de nourriture et avant de partir vint à la porte du balcon.

– J'espère que tu n'es pas malade, Zorbas, c'est la première fois que tu n'accoures pas quand j'ouvre une boîte. Qu'est-ce que tu fais assis sur ce pot ? On dirait que tu caches quelque chose. Bon, à demain, chat fou !

Et s'il avait eu l'idée de regarder sous le pot ? Rien que d'y penser il eut mal au ventre et dut courir jusqu'à sa caisse.

Il était là, la queue bien dressée, soulagé, à penser aux paroles de l'humain.

"Chat fou." Il avait dit "chat fou". Il avait peut-être raison, parce qu'il aurait été plus pratique de lui laisser voir le poussin. L'ami aurait pensé qu'il avait l'intention de le manger et il l'aurait emmené pour s'en occuper jusqu'à ce qu'il grandisse. Mais lui, il l'avait caché sous un pot, est-ce qu'il était fou ?

Non, pas du tout. Simplement il suivait rigoureusement le code d'honneur des chats du port. Il avait promis à la mouette agonisante qu'il apprendrait à voler au poussin, et il le ferait. Il ne savait pas comment, mais il le ferait.

Zorbas recouvrait consciencieusement ses excréments lorsque les cris effrayés du poussin le ramenèrent sur le balcon.

Et ce qu'il vit lui glaça le sang.

Les deux voyous étaient devant le poussin, excités ils remuaient la queue et l'un le maintenait d'une griffe posée sur le croupion. Par chance ils tournaient le dos à Zorbas et ne le virent pas arriver. Zorbas banda tous ses muscles.

— Qui aurait pensé qu'on allait trouver un déjeuner comme ça, mon pote. Il est petit mais il a l'air délicieux, miaula l'un.

— Maman, au secours ! criait le poussin.

— Dans les oiseaux, ce que je préfère ce sont les ailes. Là, elles sont petites mais les cuisses ont l'air bien charnues, remarqua l'autre.

Zorbas sauta. En l'air il sortit les dix griffes de ses pattes de devant et en retombant entre les deux voyous il fit cogner leurs têtes par terre.

Ils essayèrent de se relever, mais ne le purent pas car chacun avait une oreille transpercée par une griffe.

— Maman! Ils voulaient me manger! cria le poussin.

— Nous, manger votre enfant? Non, madame. Pas du tout! miaula l'un la tête contre le sol.

— Nous sommes végétariens, madame, super-végétariens, assura l'autre.

— Je ne suis pas "madame", imbéciles! miaula Zorbas en les tirant par les oreilles pour qu'ils puissent le voir.

En le reconnaissant les deux voyous se hérissèrent.

— Vous avez un très joli petit, mon ami. Ce sera un beau chat! affirma l'un.

— Oui, ça se voit de loin. Quel joli chaton! confirma l'autre.

— C'est pas un chat! C'est un poussin de mouette, imbéciles!

— Je le dis toujours à mon copain, il faut avoir des enfants mouettes! Pas vrai? déclara le premier.

Zorbas décida d'en finir avec cette farce, mais ces deux crétins allaient se souvenir de ses griffes. D'un mouvement décidé il replia ses pattes et ses griffes déchirèrent les oreilles des deux lâches. Miaulant de douleur, ils s'enfuirent en courant.

— J'ai une maman très courageuse, pépia le poussin.

Zorbas comprit que le balcon n'était pas un endroit sûr, il ne pouvait pas mettre le poussin dans l'appartement, il allait tout salir et l'ami de la famille le découvrirait. Il fallait chercher un endroit sûr.

— Viens, on va se promener, miaula Zorbas avant de le prendre délicatement entre ses dents.

4

Pas de repos pour le danger

Réunis dans le bazar d'Harry les chats décidèrent que le poussin ne pouvait pas rester dans l'appartement de Zorbas. Les risques qu'il courait étaient nombreux et le plus grand n'était pas la présence menaçante des deux voyous mais bien l'ami de la famille.

— Les humains sont hélas imprévisibles! Souvent, avec les meilleures intentions du monde ils causent les pires malheurs, déclara Colonello.

— C'est bien vrai. Prenons Harry, par exemple, c'est un brave homme, il a bon cœur, mais, comme il a une grande affection pour le chimpanzé et qu'il sait qu'il aime la bière, chaque fois que le singe a soif il lui en donne une bouteille. Ce pauvre Matias est un alcoolique qui a perdu toute honte, et quand il se soûle il se met à glapir des chansons terribles. Terribles! miaula Jesaitout.

— Sans parler du mal qu'ils font intentionnellement. Pensez à cette pauvre mouette qui est

morte par la faute de cette maudite manie d'empoi-
sonner la mer avec des ordures, ajouta Secrétario.

Après une courte délibération, ils décidèrent
que Zorbas et le poussin vivraient dans le bazar
jusqu'à ce que le poussin ait appris à voler.
Zorbas irait chez lui tous les matins pour que
l'humain ne s'inquiète pas et il reviendrait ensuite
s'occuper du poussin.

— Ce ne serait pas mal que ce petit oiseau ait
un nom, suggéra Secrétario.

— C'est exactement ce que j'allais proposer. Je
crains qu'arrêter de m'enlever les miaulements
de la bouche ne soit au-dessus de vos forces ! se
plaignit Colonello.

— Je suis d'accord. Il doit avoir un nom, mais
d'abord il faut savoir si c'est un mâle ou une
femelle, miaula Zorbas.

Il avait à peine terminé sa phrase que Jesaitout
avait fait tomber de la bibliothèque un tome de
l'encyclopédie : le volume 19 correspondant à la
lettre S, et il le feuilletait en cherchant le mot "sexe".

Malheureusement l'encyclopédie ne disait rien
sur la façon de reconnaître le sexe d'un poussin
de mouette.

— Il faut bien dire que ton encyclopédie ne
nous a pas été très utile, maugréa Zorbas.

— Je n'admets pas qu'on mette en doute
l'efficacité de mon encyclopédie ! Tout le savoir
est dans ces livres, répondit Jesaitout, vexé.

— Mouette. Oiseau de mer. Vent-debout, le seul qui puisse nous aider à savoir si c'est un oiseau ou une oiselle, c'est Vent-debout! miaula Secrétario.

— C'est exactement ce que j'allais miauler. Je vous interdis de continuer à m'enlever les miaulements de la bouche! grogna Colonello.

Pendant que les chats miaulaient, le poussin se promenait au milieu de douzaines d'oiseaux empaillés. Il y avait des merles, des perroquets, des toucans, des paons, des aigles, des faucons, qu'il regardait avec crainte. Soudain un animal aux yeux rouges, et qui n'était pas empaillé, lui barra la route.

— Maman! À l'aide! cria-t-il désespéré.

Zorbas fut le premier à arriver près de lui, et à temps car à cet instant précis un rat tendait ses pattes de devant vers le cou du poussin.

En voyant Zorbas, le rat s'enfuit vers une lézarde ouverte dans le mur.

— Il voulait me manger, cria le poussin en se serrant contre Zorbas.

— On n'avait pas pensé à ce danger. Je crois qu'il va falloir miauler avec les rats, déclara Zorbas.

— D'accord. Mais ne fais pas trop de concessions à ces insolents, conseilla Colonello.

Zorbas s'approcha de la lézarde. Dedans il faisait très noir, mais il réussit à voir les yeux rouges du rat.

– Je veux voir ton chef, miaula-t-il, décidé.

– Je suis le chef des rats, lui répondit-on dans l'obscurité.

– Si c'est toi le chef des rats, alors vous ne valez même pas les cafards. Préviens ton chef, insista Zorbas.

Zorbas entendit le rat s'éloigner. Ses griffes faisaient grincer le tuyau par lequel il se glissait. Quelques minutes après il vit reparaître les yeux rouges dans la pénombre.

– Le chef va te recevoir. Dans la cave des coquillages, derrière le coffre du pirate il y a une entrée, couina le rat.

Zorbas descendit jusqu'à la cave. Il chercha derrière le coffre et vit dans le mur un trou par lequel il pouvait passer. Il écarta les toiles d'araignée et s'introduisit dans le monde des rats. Cela sentait l'humidité et les ordures.

– Suis les tuyaux d'égout, cria un rat qu'il ne put voir.

Il obéit. À mesure qu'il avançait en rampant sur le ventre il sentait que sa peau s'imprégnait de poussière et de saleté. Il avança dans l'obscurité jusqu'à un réservoir d'égout à peine éclairé par un faible rai de lumière du jour. Zorbas supposa qu'il était au-dessous de la rue et que le rai de lumière entrait par la grille de l'égout. L'endroit empestait, mais était suffisamment haut pour qu'il puisse se redresser sur ses quatre pattes.

Au milieu coulait un canal d'eaux immondes. C'est alors qu'il vit le chef des rats, un grand rongeur à la peau sombre, couturé de cicatrices et qui s'amusait à nettoyer les anneaux de sa queue avec une griffe.

— Eh bien, eh bien! Regardez qui vient nous voir! Le gros chat, couina le chef des rats.

— Le gros! Le gros! glapirent en chœur des dizaines de rats dont Zorbas ne voyait que les yeux rouges.

— Je veux que vous laissiez le poussin tranquille, miaula-t-il fermement.

— Alors comme ça les chats ont un poussin. Je savais. On raconte beaucoup de choses dans les égouts. On dit que c'est un poussin délicieux. Hé! Hé! Hé! glapit le rat.

— Vraiment délicieux! Hé! Hé! Hé! reprit le chœur des rats.

— Vous le mangerez quand il sera grand? Sans nous inviter? Égoïstes! couina le rat.

— Égoïstes!

— Égoïstes! répétèrent les autres rats.

— Comme tu le sais j'ai liquidé plus de rats que j'ai de poils. S'il arrive quoi que ce soit au poussin vos heures sont comptées, affirma Zorbas avec sérénité.

— Écoute boule de graisse, tu as pensé comment tu peux sortir d'ici? On peut faire de toi un bon pâté de chat, menaça le rat.

— Pâté de chat! Pâté de chat! reprirent les autres rats.

Alors Zorbas sauta sur le chef des rats. Il lui tomba sur le dos en lui tenant la tête entre ses griffes.

— Tu es sur le point de perdre tes yeux. Tes sbires vont peut-être faire de moi un pâté de chat, mais tu ne pourras pas le voir. Alors, vous laissez le poussin tranquille? miaula Zorbas.

— Comme tu es mal élevé! Ça va. Ni pâté de chat, ni pâté de poussin. On peut tout négocier dans les égouts, couina le chef des rats.

— Négocions. Qu'est-ce que vous demandez en échange du respect de la vie du poussin? demanda Zorbas.

— Le libre passage dans la cour. Colonello a ordonné qu'on nous coupe le chemin du marché. Libre passage dans la cour, couina le chef des rats.

— Libre passage dans la cour, reprit le chœur.

— D'accord. Vous pourrez passer dans la cour, mais la nuit, quand les humains ne vous verront pas. Nous les chats, nous devons faire attention à notre prestige, déclara Zorbas en lui lâchant la tête.

Il sortit de l'égout à reculons, sans perdre de vue le chef des rats et les dizaines d'yeux rouges qui le regardaient pleins de haine.

5

Oiselle ou oisillon

Il leur fallut trois jours pour arriver à voir Vent-debout, un chat de mer, un authentique chat de mer.

Vent-debout était la mascotte du *Hannes II,* un puissant bateau de dragage chargé de nettoyer et d'enlever les écueils du fond de l'Elbe. L'équipage du *Hannes II* appréciait Vent-debout, un chat couleur de miel aux yeux bleus, qu'il considérait comme un compagnon supplémentaire pendant les durs travaux de dragage du fleuve.

Les jours de tempête ils le couvraient avec un ciré jaune à sa taille, semblable à ceux qu'ils utilisaient eux-mêmes, et Vent-debout se promenait sur le pont avec l'air sombre des marins qui affrontent le mauvais temps.

Le *Hannes II* avait nettoyé les ports de Rotterdam, Anvers, Copenhague, et Vent-debout racontait des histoires amusantes sur ces voyages. Oui. C'était un authentique chat de mer.

— Ahoy! miaula Vent-debout en entrant dans le bazar.

Le chimpanzé cligna des yeux, perplexe, en voyant s'avancer le chat qui remuait son corps en chaloupant de gauche à droite à chaque pas et qui ignorait l'importance de sa dignité de caissier de l'établissement.

— Si tu ne sais pas dire bonjour, paie au moins l'entrée, sac à puces, glapit Matias.

— Idiot à tribord! Par les crocs du barracuda! Tu m'as appelé sac à puces? Sache que cette fourrure a été piquée par tous les insectes de tous les ports. Un jour je te miaulerai l'histoire de certaine tique qui s'est hissée sur mon dos et qui pesait tellement que je ne pouvais pas la soulever. Par la barbe de la baleine! Et je te miaulerai les poux de l'île de Cacatua, qui doivent sucer le sang de sept hommes à l'apéritif pour être rassasiés. Par les ailerons du requin! Lève l'ancre, macaque. Ne me coupe pas le vent! ordonna Vent-debout, et il suivit son chemin sans attendre la réponse du chimpanzé.

En arrivant dans la pièce des livres, il salua depuis le seuil les chats qui y étaient réunis.

— *Miaou*! miaula Vent-debout qui aimait miauler le dialecte à la fois rêche et doux de Hambourg.

— Tu arrives enfin, *capitano*. Tu ne sais pas comme nous avons besoin de toi! répondit Colonello.

Ils lui miaulèrent rapidement l'histoire de la mouette et des promesses de Zorbas, promesses qui, ils le répétèrent, les engageaient tous.

Vent-debout écouta en hochant la tête, préoccupé.

— Par l'encre du calamar! En mer il arrive des choses terribles. Parfois je me demande si quelques humains ne sont pas devenus fous, ils essayent de faire de l'océan une énorme poubelle. Je viens de draguer l'embouchure de l'Elbe et vous ne pouvez pas imaginer la quantité d'ordures que charrient les marées! Par la carapace de la tortue! Nous avons sorti des barils d'insecticide, des pneus, des tonnes de ces maudites bouteilles de plastique que les humains laissent sur les plages, indiqua Vent-debout avec colère.

— Terrible! Terrible! Si ça continue comme ça, bientôt le mot "pollution" occupera tout le tome 16, lettre P de l'encyclopédie, s'exclama Jesaitout scandalisé.

— Et qu'est-ce que je peux faire, moi, pour ce pauvre oiseau? demanda Vent-debout.

— Toi seul, qui connais la mer, peux nous dire si ce poussin est un mâle ou une femelle, répondit Colonello.

Ils l'emmenèrent auprès du poussin qui dormait rassasié après avoir réglé son compte à un calamar apporté par Secrétario qui, selon les ordres de Colonello, était chargé de son alimentation.

Vent-debout tendit une patte de devant, lui examina la tête et ensuite souleva les plumes qui commençaient à pousser sur sa queue. Le poussin chercha Zorbas de ses yeux effrayés.

— Par les pattes du crabe! C'est une jolie petite qui un jour pondra autant d'œufs que j'ai de poils sur la queue, s'exclama le chat de mer amusé.

Zorbas lécha la tête de l'oiselle. Il regretta de ne pas avoir demandé son nom à la mère, car si la fille était appelée à poursuivre son vol interrompu par la négligence des humains, il aurait été beau qu'elle porte le même nom.

— Si on considère que l'oiselle a eu la chance, la fortune, de tomber sous notre protection, je propose qu'on l'appelle Afortunada, la fortunée, déclara Colonello.

— Par les ouïes de la merlu! C'est un joli nom. Il me fait penser à une charmante mouette que j'ai vue en mer Baltique. Elle s'appelait comme ça, Afortunada, et elle était toute blanche, miaula Vent-debout.

— Un jour elle fera quelque chose de remarquable, d'extraordinaire, et son nom sera dans le tome 1 de l'encyclopédie, lettre A, assura Jesaitout.

Tous tombèrent d'accord sur le nom proposé par Colonello. Alors les cinq chats se mirent en rond autour de l'oiselle, se dressèrent sur leurs pattes de derrière en tendant les pattes de devant pour former un toit de griffes et miaulèrent le rituel de baptême des chats du port.

— Nous te saluons Afortunada, la fortunée, amie des chats!

— Ahoy! Ahoy! Ahoy! s'écria Vent-debout heureux.

6

Afortunada, vraiment fortunée

Afortunada grandit rapidement entourée de l'affection des chats. Au bout d'un mois dans le bazar d'Harry c'était une jeune mouette svelte, aux plumes soyeuses couleur d'argent.

Quand des touristes visitaient le bazar, suivant les instructions de Colonello, elle restait tranquille parmi les oiseaux empaillés, faisant semblant d'être l'un d'eux. Mais le soir, quand le musée fermait et que le vieux loup de mer se retirait, alors elle se promenait de sa démarche maladroite d'oiseau de mer, dans toutes les pièces, s'émerveillant devant les mille objets qu'il y avait là, tandis que Jesaitout cherchait et cherchait dans tous les livres la méthode pour que Zorbas lui apprenne à voler.

– Voler consiste à pousser l'air vers l'arrière et vers le bas. Ah bon! Voilà quelque chose d'important, marmonnait-il, le nez fourré dans ses livres.

— Et pourquoi je dois voler? demandait Afortunada, les ailes bien collées contre le corps.

— Parce que tu es une mouette et que les mouettes volent. C'est terrible! Terrible que tu ne saches pas le faire! répondait Jesaitout.

— Mais je ne veux pas voler. Je ne veux pas non plus être une mouette. Je veux être un chat et les chats ne volent pas, protestait Afortunada.

Un soir elle s'approcha du comptoir de l'entrée et fit une rencontre désagréable avec le chimpanzé.

— Ne viens pas faire caca par ici, espèce d'oiseau! glapit Matias dès qu'il la vit.

— Pourquoi vous dites ça, Monsieur le singe? pépia-t-elle timidement.

— C'est tout ce que savent faire les oiseaux. Caca. Et tu es un oiseau, répéta-t-il, très sûr de son affirmation.

— Vous vous trompez. Je suis un chat et un chat très propre. J'ai la même caisse que Jesaitout, pépia-t-elle en cherchant à gagner la sympathie du chimpanzé.

— Ah! Ah! Cette bande de sacs à puces t'a convaincue que tu es un des leurs. Regarde-toi: tu as deux pattes, les chats en ont quatre. Tu as des plumes, les chats ont des poils. Et la queue? Hein? Où est ta queue? Tu es aussi folle que ce chat qui passe son temps à lire et à miauler: Terrible! Terrible! Espèce d'oiseau idiot! Et tu veux savoir pourquoi tes amis te cajolent? Parce qu'ils attendent que tu grossisses pour faire un grand banquet! Ils te mangeront tout entière, avec tes plumes et tout! glapit le chimpanzé.

Ce soir-là, les chats s'étonnèrent que la mouette ne vienne pas manger son plat préféré : les calamars que Secrétario chapardait dans la cuisine du restaurant.

Inquiets, ils la cherchèrent et ce fut Zorbas qui la trouva, abattue et triste parmi les animaux empaillés.

— Tu n'as pas faim, Afortunada? demanda Zorbas. Il y a des calamars.

La mouette n'ouvrit pas le bec.

— Tu n'es pas bien? Tu es malade? insista Zorbas inquiet.

— Tu veux que je mange pour que je grossisse? demanda-t-elle sans le regarder.

— Pour que tu grandisses et que tu sois forte et en bonne santé, répondit Zorbas.

— Et quand je serai grosse, tu inviteras les rats pour me manger? cria-t-elle les yeux pleins de larmes.

— D'où sors-tu toutes ces bêtises? miaula énergiquement Zorbas.

Retenant ses sanglots, Afortunada raconta tout ce que Matias lui avait glapi. Zorbas lécha ses larmes et s'entendit soudain miauler comme il ne l'avait jamais fait auparavant.

– Tu es une mouette. Là, le chimpanzé a raison, mais seulement pour cela. Nous t'aimons tous, Afortunada. Et nous t'aimons parce que tu es une mouette, une jolie mouette. Nous ne te contredisons pas quand tu cries que tu es un chat, car nous sommes fiers que tu veuilles être comme nous, mais tu es différente et nous aimons que tu sois différente. Nous n'avons pas pu aider ta mère, mais toi nous le pouvons. Nous t'avons protégée depuis que tu es sortie de ton œuf. Nous t'avons donné toute notre tendresse sans jamais penser à faire de toi un chat. Nous t'aimons mouette. Nous sentons que toi aussi tu nous aimes, que nous sommes tes amis, ta famille, et il faut que tu saches qu'avec toi, nous avons appris quelque chose qui nous emplit d'orgueil : nous avons appris à apprécier, à respecter et à aimer un être différent. Il est très facile d'accepter et d'aimer ceux qui nous ressemblent, mais quelqu'un de différent c'est très difficile, et tu nous as aidés à y arriver. Tu es une mouette et tu dois suivre ton destin de mouette. Tu dois voler. Quand tu y arriveras, Afortunada, je t'assure que tu seras heureuse et alors tes sentiments pour nous et nos sentiments pour toi seront plus intenses et plus beaux, car ce sera une affection entre des êtres totalement différents.

– J'ai peur de voler ! piailla Afortunada en se redressant.

— Quand ce sera le moment je serai avec toi. Je l'ai promis à ta mère, miaula Zorbas en lui léchant la tête.

La jeune mouette et le chat grand noir et gros se mirent à marcher. Lui, il lui léchait la tête avec tendresse et elle, elle lui couvrait le dos de l'une de ses ailes.

7

On apprend à voler

— Avant de commencer, récapitulons une
dernière fois les aspects techniques, miaula Jesaitout.

Depuis la plus haute étagère d'une bibliothèque,
Colonello, Secrétario, Zorbas et Vent-debout
observaient attentivement ce qui se passait en bas.
Là, il y avait Afortunada, debout à l'extrémité
d'un couloir, appelé piste de décollage, et à
l'autre extrémité Jesaitout, penché sur le tome
12, correspondant à la lettre L de l'encyclopédie.
Le livre était ouvert à l'une des pages consacrées à
Léonard de Vinci, et on y voyait un engin bizarre
baptisé "machine à voler" par le grand maître
italien.

— S'il vous plaît, vérifions d'abord la stabilité
des points d'appui (a) et (b), indiqua Jesaitout.

— Points (a) et (b) vérifiés, répéta Afortunada
en sautant d'abord sur sa patte gauche et ensuite
sur la droite

— Parfait. Maintenant vérifions l'extension des points (c) et (d), miaula Jesaitout, qui se sentait aussi important qu'un ingénieur de la NASA.

— Extension des points (c) et (d) vérifiée ! cria Afortunada en étendant les deux ailes.

— Parfait. Répétons tout encore une fois, ordonna Jesaitout.

— Par les moustaches du turbot ! Laisse-la voler une bonne fois ! s'exclama Vent-debout.

— Je vous rappelle que je suis responsable du vol ! Tout doit être parfaitement assuré car les conséquences peuvent être terribles pour Afortunada. Terribles ! rétorqua Jesaitout.

— Il a raison. Il sait ce qu'il fait, intervint Secrétario.

— C'est exactement ce que j'allais, moi-même, miauler. Est-ce qu'un jour vous allez cesser de m'enlever les miaulements de la bouche ? grogna Colonello.

Afortunada était là, sur le point de tenter son premier vol. Au cours de la dernière semaine, en effet, deux événements avaient fait comprendre aux chats que la mouette désirait voler, même si elle dissimulait très bien ce désir.

Le premier événement s'était déroulé un après-midi où Afortunada avait accompagné les chats prendre le soleil sur le toit du bazar d'Harry. Alors qu'ils étaient là à profiter des chauds rayons du soleil, ils virent planer au-dessus d'eux, très très haut, trois mouettes.

Elles étaient belles, majestueuses, se découpant contre le bleu du ciel. Parfois elles avaient l'air immobiles, flottant simplement dans l'air, les ailes étendues, mais il leur suffisait d'un léger mouvement pour se déplacer avec une grâce et une élégance qui donnaient envie d'être avec elles là-haut. Soudain les chats cessèrent de regarder le ciel et posèrent les yeux sur Afortunada. La jeune mouette observait le vol de ses congénères et sans s'en rendre compte étendait les ailes.

— Regardez ça. Elle veut voler, fit remarquer Colonello.

— Oui! Il est temps qu'elle vole. C'est maintenant une mouette grande et forte, approuva Zorbas.

— Afortunada. Vole! Essaye! suggéra Secrétario.

En entendant les miaulements de ses amis Afortunada replia ses ailes et s'approcha d'eux. Elle se coucha près de Zorbas et fit résonner son bec comme si elle ronronnait.

Le deuxième événement eut lieu le lendemain, tandis que les chats écoutaient Vent-debout raconter une histoire.

— ... Et comme je vous le miaulais, les vagues étaient si hautes que nous ne pouvions pas voir la côte et, par la graisse du cachalot, pour comble de malheur notre boussole était cassée. Nous avions passé cinq jours et cinq nuits en pleine tempête et nous ne savions plus si nous naviguions vers la côte ou si nous nous enfoncions vers le large. Alors, au moment où nous nous sentions perdus, le timonier vit un vol de mouettes. Quelle joie mes amis! Nous nous sommes efforcés de suivre le vol de mouettes et nous avons réussi à atteindre la terre ferme. Par les dents du barracuda! Ces mouettes nous ont sauvé la vie. Si nous ne les avions pas vues, je ne serais pas là pour vous miauler cette histoire.

Afortunada, qui suivait toujours avec attention les histoires du chat de mer, l'écoutait en ouvrant de grands yeux.

— Les mouettes volent les jours de tempête? demanda-t-elle.

— Par les tortillements de l'anguille! Les mouettes sont les oiseaux les plus forts du monde. Aucun oiseau ne vole mieux qu'une mouette, affirma Vent-debout.

Les miaulements du chat pénétraient au plus profond du cœur d'Afortunada. Elle frappait le sol de ses pattes et remuait son bec avec nervosité.

— Tu veux voler, jeune fille? demanda Zorbas.

Afortunada les regarda un à un avant de répondre.

— Oui, s'il vous plaît, apprenez-moi à voler!

Les chats miaulèrent leur joie et se mirent immédiatement à l'œuvre. Ils avaient longtemps espéré ce moment. Avec toute la patience dont seuls les chats sont capables, ils avaient attendu que la jeune mouette leur fasse part de son désir de voler, car la vieille sagesse des chats leur avait fait comprendre que voler est une décision très personnelle. Et le plus heureux de tous était Jesaitout, qui avait trouvé les principes du vol dans le tome 12, lettre L, de l'encyclopédie, et serait donc responsable de la direction des opérations.

— Prête pour le décollage? demanda Jesaitout.
— Prête pour le décollage! cria Afortunada.
— Commencez à avancer sur la piste en repoussant le sol à l'aide des points d'appui (a) et (b), ordonna Jesaitout.

Afortunada se mit à avancer, mais lentement, comme si elle patinait avec des patins mal graissés.

— Plus vite! exigea Jesaitout.

La jeune mouette avança un peu plus vite.

— Maintenant étendez les points (c) et (d)! indiqua Jesaitout.

Afortunada étendit ses ailes tout en avançant.

— Maintenant levez le point (e)!

Afortunada leva les plumes de sa queue.

— Et maintenant remuez de haut en bas les points (c) et (d) en poussant l'air vers le bas, repliez simultanément les point (a) et (b)! miaula Jesaitout.

Afortunada battit des ailes, replia ses pattes, s'éleva de quelques centimètres, mais retomba immédiatement comme un sac.

D'un bond les chats descendirent de l'étagère et coururent jusqu'à elle. Ses yeux étaient pleins de larmes.

— Je ne suis pas capable! Je ne suis pas capable! répétait-elle, affligée.

— On ne vole jamais du premier coup. Tu vas y arriver. Je te le promets, miaula Zorbas en lui léchant la tête.

Jesaitout essayait de trouver l'erreur en examinant encore une fois la machine à voler de Léonard de Vinci.

8

Les chats décident de briser un tabou

Afortunada essaya dix-sept fois de s'envoler, et dix-sept fois elle retomba par terre après avoir réussi à s'élever de quelques centimètres.

Jesaitout, plus maigre encore que d'habitude, s'était arraché les poils de la moustache à la suite des douze premiers échecs, et se disculpait avec des miaulements tremblants.

— Je ne comprends pas. J'ai consciencieusement révisé la théorie du vol, j'ai comparé les instructions de Léonard de Vinci avec tout ce qui se trouve à l'article "Aérodynamique", tome 1, lettre A de l'encyclopédie, et pourtant on n'a pas réussi. C'est terrible! Terrible!

Les chats acceptaient ses explications et toute leur attention se concentrait sur Afortunada, qui après chaque essai de vol manqué devenait de plus en plus triste et mélancolique.

Après le dernier échec, Colonello décida d'arrêter les essais, son expérience lui disait que la mouette commençait à perdre confiance en elle et c'était très dangereux si elle voulait vraiment voler.

— Peut-être qu'elle ne peut pas. Peut-être qu'elle a trop vécu avec nous et qu'elle a perdu sa capacité de voler, suggéra Secrétario.

— Si on suit les instructions techniques et si on respecte les lois de l'aérodynamique, on peut voler. N'oubliez pas que tout est dans l'encyclopédie, affirma Jesaitout.

— Par la queue de la raie! C'est une mouette et les mouettes volent! protesta Vent-debout.

— Elle doit voler. Je l'ai promis à sa mère et je le lui ai promis à elle, elle doit voler, répéta Zorbas.

— Et tenir cette promesse nous concerne tous, ajouta Colonello.

— Reconnaissons que nous sommes incapables de lui apprendre à voler et qu'il faut chercher de l'aide en dehors du monde des chats, suggéra Zorbas.

— Miaule clair, Zorbas. Où veux-tu en venir? demanda sérieusement Colonello.

— Je demande l'autorisation de briser le tabou pour la première fois de ma vie, miaula Zorbas en regardant ses compagnons dans les yeux.

— Briser le tabou! miaulèrent les chats en sortant leurs griffes et en se hérissant.

"Miauler la langue des humains est tabou." C'est ce que disait la loi des chats, et ce n'était

98

pas parce qu'ils n'avaient pas intérêt à communiquer avec les humains. Le grand risque c'était la réponse des humains. Que feraient-ils d'un chat qui parle ? Certainement ils l'enfermeraient dans une cage pour le soumettre à toutes sortes d'expériences stupides, car les humains sont en général incapables d'accepter qu'un être différent d'eux les comprenne et essaye de se faire comprendre. Par exemple, les chats étaient au courant du triste sort des dauphins, qui s'étaient comportés de façon intelligente avec les humains et que ceux-ci avaient condamnés à faire les clowns dans des spectacles aquatiques. Et ils savaient aussi les humiliations que les humains font subir à tout animal qui se montre intelligent et réceptif avec eux. Par exemple, les lions, les grands félins, ont été obligés de vivre derrière des grilles et d'accepter qu'un crétin mette sa tête dans leur gueule, les perroquets sont en cage et répètent des sottises. De sorte que miauler dans le langage des humains était un très grand risque pour les chats.

— Reste auprès d'Afortunada. Nous allons nous retirer pour discuter ta requête, ordonna Colonello.

La conférence des chats dura de longues heures. De longues heures pendant lesquelles Zorbas resta couché près de la mouette qui ne cachait pas sa tristesse de ne pas savoir voler.

Il faisait nuit quand la conférence prit fin.
Zorbas s'approcha pour connaître la décision.

— Nous, les chats, t'autorisons à briser le tabou une seule fois. Tu ne miauleras qu'avec un seul humain, et nous déciderons ensemble avec lequel d'entre eux, déclara solennellement Colonello.

9

Le choix de l'humain

Il ne fut pas facile de décider avec quel humain miaulerait Zorbas. Les chats firent une liste de tous ceux qu'ils connaissaient et les écartèrent l'un après l'autre.

— René, le cuisinier, est sans aucun doute un humain juste et bon. Il nous garde toujours une part de ses spécialités, que Secretario et moi dévorons avec plaisir. Mais ce brave René ne s'y connaît qu'en épices et en casseroles, il ne nous serait pas d'un grand secours pour notre problème, affirma Colonello.

— Harry aussi est un brave type. Compréhensif et aimable avec tout le monde, même avec Matias auquel il pardonne des abus terribles. Terribles! Comme s'inonder de patchouli, ce parfum qui a une odeur terrible, terrible! De plus il connaît bien la mer et la navigation, mais je crois qu'il n'a pas la moindre idée sur le vol, assura Jesaitout.

— Carlo, le chef des garçons du restaurant, affirme que je lui appartiens et je le lui laisse croire parce qu'il est gentil. Malheureusement, il s'y connaît en football, basket-ball, volley-ball, courses de chevaux, boxe, tous les sports, mais je ne l'ai jamais entendu parler de vol, expliqua Secrétario.

— Par les cils de l'anémone! Mon capitaine est un homme très doux qui, au cours de sa dernière bagarre dans un bar d'Anvers, a affronté douze types qui l'avaient insulté et n'en a mis hors de combat que la moitié. Par ailleurs il a le vertige sur une chaise. Par les tentacules du poulpe! Je ne pense pas qu'il puisse nous être utile, décida Vent-debout.

— Le garçon de chez moi me comprendrait. Mais il est en vacances. Et que peut savoir un enfant sur le vol? miaula Zorbas.

— *Porca miseria!* On a fini la liste, se désola Colonello.

— Non. Il y a un humain qui n'est pas sur la liste. Celui qui vit chez Bouboulina, indiqua Zorbas.

Bouboulina était une belle chatte blanche et noire qui passait de longues heures parmi les fleurs d'un balcon. Tous les chats du port se promenaient lentement devant elle, montrant l'élasticité de leur corps, le brillant de leur fourrure bien soignée, la longueur de leurs moustaches, l'élégance de leur queue dressée, ils essayaient de

l'impressionner. Mais Bouboulina paraissait indifférente et n'acceptait que les caresses d'un humain
qui s'installait sur le balcon avec une machine
à écrire.

C'était un humain bizarre qui, parfois, riait en
lisant ce qu'il venait d'écrire et d'autres fois froissait sans les lire les pages arrachées à la machine.
De son balcon s'échappait toujours une musique
douce et mélancolique qui endormait Bouboulina et provoquait de gros soupirs chez les
chats qui passaient tout près.

— L'humain de Bouboulina ? Pourquoi lui ?
demanda Colonello.

— Je ne sais pas. Il m'inspire confiance. Je l'ai
entendu lire ce qu'il écrit. Ce sont de beaux mots
qui rendent joyeux ou triste, mais qui donnent
toujours du plaisir et le désir de continuer à
écouter, expliqua Zorbas.

— Un poète ! Ce qu'il fait s'appelle poésie.
Tome 16, lettre P de l'encyclopédie, précisa Jesaitout.

— Et qu'est-ce qui te fait penser qu'un humain
sait voler ? voulut savoir Secrétario.

— Il ne sait peut-être pas voler avec des ailes
d'oiseau, mais en l'entendant j'ai toujours pensé
qu'il volait avec ses mots, répondit Zorbas.

— Que ceux qui sont d'accord pour que
Zorbas miaule avec l'humain de Bouboulina
lèvent la patte droite, ordonna Colonello.

C'est ainsi que Zorbas fut autorisé à miauler avec le poète.

10

Une chatte, un chat et un poète

Zorbas prit le chemin des toits pour arriver jusqu'au balcon de l'humain choisi. En voyant Bouboulina étendue parmi les fleurs il soupira avant de miauler :

— Bouboulina, n'aie pas peur. Je suis sur le toit.

— Qu'est-ce que tu veux ? Qui es-tu ? demanda la chatte en se levant.

— Ne t'en va pas, s'il te plaît. Je m'appelle Zorbas et j'habite près d'ici. J'ai besoin de ton aide. Je peux descendre sur le balcon ?

La chatte lui fit un signe de tête. Zorbas sauta sur le balcon et s'assit. Bouboulina s'approcha pour le sentir.

— Tu sens les livres, l'humidité, les vieux habits, l'oiseau, la poussière, mais on voit que ta peau est propre, constata la chatte.

— Ce sont les odeurs du bazar d'Harry. Ne t'étonne pas si je sens aussi le chimpanzé, l'avertit Zorbas.

Une musique douce arrivait jusqu'au balcon.

— Quelle belle musique! miaula Zorbas.

— Vivaldi. *Les Quatre Saisons.* Qu'est-ce que tu attends de moi? demanda Bouboulina.

— Que tu me fasses entrer et que tu m'amènes à ton humain.

- Impossible. Il travaille et personne, même pas moi, ne peut le déranger, affirma Bouboulina.

— Je t'en prie. C'est urgent. Je te le demande au nom de tous les chats du port, implora Zorbas.

— Pourquoi veux-tu le voir?

— Je dois miauler avec lui!

— Mais c'est tabou! Va-t'en! miaula Bouboulina hérissée.

— Non. Et si tu ne veux pas m'amener à lui, qu'il vienne. Tu aimes le rock, minette?

Dans l'appartement, l'humain tapait à la machine à écrire. Il était heureux car il était sur le point de terminer un poème et les vers lui venaient avec une fluidité étonnante. Soudain du balcon lui parvinrent les miaulements d'un chat qui n'était pas sa Bouboulina. C'étaient des miaulements discordants et qui avaient cependant l'air d'avoir un rythme. Ennuyé mais intrigué, il sortit et dut se frotter les yeux pour croire ce qu'il voyait.

Sur le balcon, Bouboulina se bouchait les oreilles avec ses pattes de devant et en face d'elle un chat grand noir et gros, assis sur son derrière, tenait dans une de ses pattes de devant sa queue comme un instrument de musique et de l'autre patte la grattait comme une corde de guitare, en même temps il poussait des miaulements exaspérants.

Remis de sa surprise, il ne put retenir son hilarité et au moment où il se pliait de rire en se tenant le ventre, Zorbas en profita pour se glisser dans l'appartement.

Quand l'humain se retourna toujours en riant, il vit le chat grand noir et gros assis sur un fauteuil.

— Quel concert! Tu es un séducteur original, mais je crains que Bouboulina n'aime pas ta musique. Quel concert! dit l'humain.

— Je sais que je chante très mal. Personne n'est parfait, répondit Zorbas dans le langage des humains.

L'humain ouvrit la bouche, se frappa la tête et s'appuya contre un mur.

— Mais tu... tu... parles! s'exclama l'humain

— Toi aussi tu parles et je ne m'étonne pas S'il te plaît calme-toi, conseilla Zorbas.

— Un... un... chat... qui parle, dit l'humain en se laissant tomber sur le sofa.

— Je ne parle pas, je miaule, mais dans ta langue. Je sais miauler dans beaucoup de langues, indiqua Zorbas.

L'humain porta ses mains à sa tête et se cacha les yeux en répétant "c'est la fatigue, c'est la fatigue, je travaille trop". Quand il enleva les mains de sur ses yeux, le chat grand noir et gros était toujours sur le fauteuil.

— C'est une hallucination. Tu es une hallucination n'est-ce pas ? demanda l'humain.

— Non. Je suis un vrai chat qui miaule avec toi. Les chats du port t'ont choisi parmi beaucoup d'humains pour te confier un grand problème et pour que tu nous aides. Tu n'es pas fou. Je suis réel, affirma Zorbas.

— Et tu dis que tu miaules dans beaucoup de langues ? demanda l'humain incrédule.

— Oui, tu veux une preuve ? proposa Zorbas.

— *Buon giorno,* dit l'humain.

— Il est tard. Il vaut mieux dire *Buona sera,* corrigea Zorbas.

— *Kalimera,* insista l'humain.

— *Kalispera.* Je t'ai déjà dit qu'il est tard.

— *Doberdan,* cria l'humain.

— *Dobreutra.* Tu me crois maintenant ?

— Oui. Et si tout ça est un rêve, quelle importance ? Ça me plaît et je veux continuer à rêver, répondit l'humain.

— Alors je peux en venir au fait ? interrogea Zorbas.

L'humain approuva, mais lui demanda de respecter le rite de la conversation des humains.

Il servit au chat une soucoupe de lait et il s'installa lui-même sur le sofa, un verre de cognac à la main.

— Miaule, chat, dit l'humain et Zorbas lui rapporta l'histoire de la mouette, de l'œuf, d'Afortunada et des efforts infructueux des chats pour lui apprendre à voler.

— Tu peux nous aider? demanda Zorbas lorsqu'il eut fini son récit.

— Je crois que oui. Et cette nuit même, répondit l'humain.

— Cette nuit? Tu es sûr?

— Regarde par la fenêtre, chat, regarde le ciel. Qu'est-ce que tu vois? demanda l'humain.

— Des nuages, des nuages noirs. Il va pleuvoir, observa Zorbas.

— C'est bien pour ça, dit l'humain.

— Je ne comprends pas. Je regrette, mais je ne comprends pas, reconnut Zorbas.

Alors l'humain alla dans son bureau, prit un livre et chercha dans ses pages.

— Écoute, chat. Je vais te lire quelque chose d'un poète appelé Bernardo Atxaga. Des vers d'un poème intitulé "Les Mouettes".

Mais leur petit cœur
— cœur d'équilibristes —
ne soupire jamais autant
que pour cette pluie bête

qui amène le vent presque toujours
qui amène le soleil presque toujours

— Je comprends. J'étais sûr que tu pouvais nous aider, miaula Zorbas en sautant du fauteuil.

Ils se donnèrent rendez-vous à minuit à la porte du bazar et le chat grand noir et gros courut informer ses compagnons.

11

Le vol

Une pluie fine tombait sur Hambourg et, des jardins, montait l'odeur de la terre humide. L'asphalte des rues brillait et les enseignes de néon se reflétaient déformées sur le sol mouillé. Un homme seul, enveloppé dans une gabardine, marchait dans la rue du port en direction du bazar d'Harry.

– Il n'en est pas question! Même si vous me plantez vos cinquante griffes dans le derrière, je ne vous ouvrirai pas la porte, glapit le chimpanzé.

– Mais personne n'a l'intention de te faire de mal. Nous te demandons une faveur. C'est tout, miaula Zorbas.

– L'horaire d'ouverture, c'est de 9 h le matin à 18 h le soir. C'est le règlement et on doit le respecter, glapit Matias.

– Par les moustaches du morse! Est-ce que tu ne pourrais pas être aimable une fois dans ta vie, macaque? miaula Vent-debout.

– Je vous en prie, Monsieur le singe! supplia Afortunada.

– Impossible! Le règlement m'interdit de tendre la main et d'ouvrir le verrou que vous, comme vous n'avez pas de doigts, sacs à puces, vous ne pourrez pas ouvrir, précisa malicieusement Matias.

– Tu es un singe terrible! Terrible! s'écria Jesaitout.

– Il y a un humain dehors et il regarde sa montre, avertit Secrétario qui regardait par la fenêtre.

– C'est le poète! Il n'y a plus de temps à perdre, s'exclama Zorbas en courant à toute vitesse vers la fenêtre.

Les cloches de l'église Saint-Michel commencèrent à sonner les douze coups de minuit et l'humain sursauta au bruit des vitres cassées. Le chat grand noir et gros tomba dans la rue au milieu d'une pluie d'éclats de verre, mais il se releva sans s'occuper des blessures qu'il s'était faites à la tête, et il sauta de nouveau sur la fenêtre d'où il venait de sortir.

L'humain s'approcha au moment précis où une mouette était hissée sur le bord de la fenêtre par plusieurs chats. Un chimpanzé se tripotait la figure en essayant de se cacher les yeux, les oreilles et la bouche en même temps.

– Aidez-la! Qu'elle ne se blesse pas avec la vitre, miaula Zorbas.

– Venez ici tous les deux, dit l'humain en les prenant dans ses bras.

L'humain s'éloigna rapidement de la porte du bazar. Sous son imperméable il emportait un chat grand noir et gros et une mouette aux plumes argentées.

– Canailles! Bandits! Vous allez me le payer, glapit le chimpanzé.

– Tu l'as cherché! Et tu sais ce que Harry va penser demain? Que c'est toi qui as cassé le carreau, affirma Secrétario.

– *Caramba!* Vous avez encore réussi à m'enlever les miaulements de la bouche, protesta Colonello.

– Par les crocs de la murène! Sur le toit! Nous allons voir voler notre Afortunada! s'écria Vent-debout.

Le chat grand noir et gros et la mouette étaient bien installés sous l'imperméable, ils sentaient la chaleur du corps de l'humain qui marchait d'un pas rapide et sûr. Ils écoutaient leurs cœurs battre à des rythmes différents mais avec la même intensité.

– Chat, tu es blessé? demanda l'humain en voyant des taches de sang sur les revers de son imperméable.

– Ça n'a pas d'importance. Où est-ce qu'on va?

– Tu comprends le langage de l'humain? demanda Afortunada.

113

— Oui. Et c'est un homme de cœur qui va t'aider à voler, lui assura Zorbas.

— Tu comprends le langage de la mouette? demanda l'humain.

— Dis-moi où on va, insista Zorbas.

— On ne va plus, on est arrivés, répondit l'humain.

Zorbas sortit la tête. Ils étaient en face d'un grand bâtiment. Il leva les yeux et reconnut la tour Saint-Michel éclairée par des projecteurs. Les faisceaux de lumière frappaient en plein la structure svelte recouverte de cuivre, à laquelle le temps, la pluie et les vents avaient donné une patine verte.

— Les portes sont fermées, miaula Zorbas.

— Pas toutes. Je viens souvent ici fumer et penser, seul, les jours de tempête. Je connais une entrée, répondit l'humain.

Ils firent le tour et entrèrent par une petite porte latérale que l'humain ouvrit avec son couteau. De sa poche il sortit une lampe et, éclairés par son mince rayon de lumière, ils commencèrent à monter un escalier en colimaçon qui paraissait interminable.

— J'ai peur, pépia Afortunada.

— Mais tu veux voler n'est-ce pas? interrogea Zorbas.

Du clocher de Saint-Michel, on voyait toute la ville. La pluie enveloppait la tour de la télévision

114

et sur le port, les grues ressemblaient à des animaux au repos.

— Regarde là-bas, on voit le bazar d'Harry. C'est là que sont nos amis, miaula Zorbas.

— J'ai peur! Maman! cria Afortunada.

Zorbas sauta sur la balustrade qui protégeait le clocher. En bas, les autos ressemblaient à des insectes aux yeux brillants. L'humain prit la mouette dans ses mains.

— Non! J'ai peur! Zorbas! Zorbas! cria-t-elle en donnant des coups de bec sur les mains de l'homme.

— Attends! Pose-la sur la balustrade, miaula Zorbas.

— Je ne voulais pas la lancer, dit l'humain.

— Tu vas voler, Afortunada. Respire. Sens la pluie. C'est de l'eau. Dans ta vie tu auras beaucoup de raisons d'être heureuse, et l'une d'elles s'appelle l'eau, une autre le vent, une autre le soleil qui arrive toujours comme une récompense après la pluie. Tu sens la pluie? Ouvre les ailes, miaula Zorbas.

La mouette ouvrit les ailes. Les projecteurs la baignaient de lumière et la pluie saupoudrait ses plumes de perles. L'humain et le chat la virent lever la tête, les yeux fermés.

— La pluie, l'eau. J'aime!

- Tu vas voler, assura Zorbas.

— Je t'aime. Tu es un chat très bon, cria-t-elle en s'approchant du bord de la balustrade

— Tu vas voler. Le ciel tout entier sera à toi! miaula Zorbas.

— Je ne t'oublierai jamais. Ni les autres chats, cria-t-elle les pattes à moitié au-dehors de la balustrade, comme le disaient les vers d'Atxaga, son petit cœur était celui des équilibristes.

— Vole! miaula Zorbas en tendant une patte et en la touchant à peine.

Afortunada disparut de leur vue et l'humain et le chat craignirent le pire. Elle était tombée comme une pierre. En retenant leur respiration, ils passèrent la tête par-dessus la balustrade et la virent qui battait des ailes, survolait le parking. Ensuite ils la virent monter bien plus haut que la girouette d'or qui couronnait la beauté singulière de Saint-Michel.

Afortunada volait solitaire dans la nuit de Hambourg. Elle s'éloignait en battant énergiquement des ailes pour s'élever au-dessus des grues du port, au-dessus des mâts des bateaux, puis elle revenait en planant et tournait autour du clocher de l'église.

— Je vole! Zorbas! Je sais voler! criait-elle euphorique depuis l'immensité du ciel gris.

L'humain caressa le dos du chat.

— Eh bien, chat, on a réussi, dit-il en soupirant.

— Oui. Au bord du vide, elle a compris le plus important, miaula Zorbas.

— Ah oui ? Et qu'est-ce qu'elle a compris ? demanda l'humain.

— Que seul vole celui qui ose le faire, miaula Zorbas.

— Je pense que maintenant ma compagnie te gêne. Je t'attends en bas. Et l'humain s'en alla. Zorbas resta à la contempler jusqu'à ne plus savoir si c'étaient les gouttes de pluie ou les larmes qui brouillaient ses yeux jaunes de chat grand noir et gros, de chat bon, de chat noble, de chat du port.

Laufenburg, Forêt-Noire, 1996

Table

Jeunesse
Livres illustrés
Co-éditions SEUIL / MÉTAILIÉ

Oscar COLLAZOS
La Baleine échouée
Illustré par Pierre Mornet

Michèle DECOUST
Mon oncle d'Australie
Illustré par Marc Daniau

Hans Magnus ENZENSBERGER

Le Démon des maths
Illustré par Rotraut Suzanne Berner

Les Sept Voyages de Pierre
Illustré par Blutch

Bernard GIRAUDEAU
Contes d'Humahuaca
Illustré par Joëlle Jolivet

Sybille LEWITSCHAROFF
Harald le courtois
Illustré par Sybille Lewitscharoff

Rasipuram Krishnaswami NARAYAN
Un tigre pour Malgudi
Illustré par Christophe Durual

Horacio QUIROGA

Contes de la forêt vierge
Illustré par Loustal

Lettres d'un chasseur
Illustré par Loustal

Le Tigre dévoreur d'hommes
Illustré par François Roca

Maria Mercè ROCA
Ça ressemble à l'amour
Illustré par Marc Daniau

Satyajit RAY
Deux aventures de Félouda
Illustré par Miles Hyman

Luis SEPÚLVEDA

Histoire d'une mouette et du chat
qui lui apprit à voler
Illustré par Miles Hyman

Le Monde du bout du monde
Illustré par Lorenzo Mattotti

Cet ouvrage a été composé par
Atlant'Communication
aux Sables-d'Olonne (Vendée)

Cet ouvrage a été imprimé en France par

à Saint-Amand-Montrond (Cher)
en septembre 2011

N° d'édition : 2483023 – N° d'impression : 112789/1
Dépôt légal : janvier 2004

STRAPPED

STRAPPED

A novel by
Laurinda D. Brown

Q-Boro Books
WWW.QBOROBOOKS.COM

An Urban Entertainment Company

Dedicated to the cast of *Walk Like A Man—The Play*
You mean the world to me.

ACKNOWLEDGMENTS

Thank you, God, for your blessings. Daily, I marvel at this gift and its ability to touch others. Thank you for also blessing me with the integrity and desire to unselfishly share my experiences with others and to help them achieve their dreams.

A multitude of thanks goes to my children and to Charlotte for enduring my long nights and temper tantrums when I demanded silence.

Thanks to my assistant, Shannon, for cleaning up my messes and attempting to keep me organized.

Thanks to Nikana for being that friend who tells me about life the way I need to hear it—rough and uncensored. Can you believe we've been out of high school twenty years?

To Tika and the MCCF correctional officers, thank you for all of your support over the years. I wouldn't be where I am if it weren't for fans like you.

A special thanks goes out to the cast of *Walk Like A Man—The Play*. Never in a million years did I think that writing a play for Vacation Bible School would turn into something like this. You are marvelous, beautiful women who have made my fantasies a reality. I love you dearly, and don't ever forget that.

MAMA MAY HAVE
Elise

A letter to my daughter
Part 1

My gay-ass daughter got that damn counselor from the group home, Mr. Dan, to ask me to write this letter to her, so if the Lord called me home one day, she would know how she came to be and why I treated her like I did. All of what I have to say might as well turn into a book, cuz I gotta lot to say 'bout all the drama in my life. True, she's come to me a few times with questions 'bout her background, but I ain't feel like talkin' to her 'bout it. I truly believe she's searchin' for somethin' in my past to blame for her issues. There's been times when we dun fought like pit bulls 'til we was both hoarse and full of snot. Child molestation, exactly what kind of shit is that? I ain't nevah heard of a child molester 'til Mr. Dan called me. Ped-pedi-peda-sure . . . peda-file. Whad da fuck evah. Honey, men will be men. Let 'em touch it, I say. That'll keep them from turnin' into faggots.

I grew up on the end of Bellevue where Jack Pirtle's Chicken House and Bellevue Park was. Oooo-wee, I sho as hell loved me some Jack Pirtle's chicken. My Mama taught me how to dip they French fries in the gravy before I even thought 'bout dippin' my biscuits and chicken in it. Now, that's some good eatin' I'm tryin' to tell ya. I remember in the summertime me and my friends used to walk to the Dixie Queen to get ice cream and then go and watch baseball games back at the park. We nevah knew who was playing. We just rooted for the team with the finest, bow-legged men. Long after the game was over, we'd all sit and talk to the ball playahs for as long as they wanted to hear us talk. I wondered who they was and where they came from, and sometimes asked if I could go back home with them. Hell, I didn't even know where home was for those cats, but anywhere had to be better than Memphis.

One scorchin' hot afternoon, back in '77, my friend, Cathy, and me was sittin' in the bleachers suckin' on cherry freeze-pops while we was watchin' this game that seemed to go on forever. The August heat was swelterin', makin' our pops drip all over our thighs and flip-flops. Cathy would lean over, with her legs gapped wide open, and slurp the juice, tryna to lap it up as quick as it fell. Those drops she missed, though, was landin' on the heads of the ballplayers in the dugout beneath our seats. I thought it was funny cuz I'd actually caught they asses lookin' up our butts a time or two. I was kinda actually flattered that a man wanted to see what I had going on up there. Shiitt, I was sixteen and hot as a firecracker. I kept my thighs all greased up with Vaseline for a reason.

All my friends had been tellin' me 'bout their little fantasies, but I was ready to do 'em one better and go all the way with the first man who showed an interest.

Durin' the game, I heard them snickerin' and chucklin' like niggahs do when they up to somethin'. Every once and a while, I'd prop my thighs up from the old wood to shake the beads of sweat from them. Flies was all over, 'specially 'round me cuz I had cherry sugar water drippin' everywhere. I was screamin' and smackin' my thighs each time one of those damn things landed on me. I was actin' like I was really bothered, but I wasn't. I wanted one of those cats to notice me.

Late in the ninth innin', out of nowhere comes these sirens from the south end of Bellevue, and then there was police cars all comin' from every whicha way. Some was headed north and some was headed south. The ones headed north were goin' in the direction of midtown. We was so used to hearin' sirens that none of us really bothered to turn around, but I saw a few folks tryin' to get up and go see 'bout all the commotion. But then. . . . *CRACK!* "Eric Lee! Eric Lee!" the crowd chanted. That cat had split the wood on his bat when he'd smacked the ball clear out the park. Far as I was concerned, Eric Lee was a dirty ol' bastard cuz he was the main one looking up 'tween our legs. I didn't even clap for his ass.

"C'mon. Let's go, Cathy. I need to get in the tub." I just felt nasty and sticky all over.

By now, Cathy had finished her freeze-pop and was headin' down to the fence to shake Eric Lee's hand when he came from home plate. "Now?"

"Yes, now," I demanded. "These flies keep chasin' me." I glanced up and saw Eric Lee comin' toward home plate. He was wavin' his hands and cap at the crowd, but when he passed me, I rolled my eyes and turnt away.

"Now, that's no way to be toward a superstar." He smiled as he walked toward me.

"Niggah, you ain't no damn superstar. Ridin' up

herrh from wherever you come from in a beat up ol' school bus. I seent you the last time with that same grass stain on your pants. Ain't you got nobody at home to wash your clothes?" I was loud when I said that, and you could see the red piercin' through his ebony, sun-baked skin.

Laughing at me while trying to hide his embarrassment, he replied, "No, I ain't got nobody to wash my clothes."

"Hmph," I snapped. "You nasty!" The crowd busted out laughin' at him, and for a minute, he was even laughin' right along with them.

"What's yo' name, little girl, with all that mouth?" he asked.

A man was askin' me for my name, and everybody was lookin'. "Elise is my name, and don't wear it out."

"OK, OK, Miss Elise." Eric Lee stood there while everybody else had gotten back into watchin' the game. He looked me over from head to toe before he said anythang else to me. I ain't know what he wanted from me, but I knew what I might be willin' to give. "G'on home to yo' Mama. I ain't got time to be nursin' nobody's babies." That niggah call hisself tellin' me off in front of everybody, but ain't nobody give him no dap for it.

When I got back to the house later that evenin', Mama told me Elvis Presley was dead. "Bet he O'deed, but we ain't gonna ever know 'bout it," she said. "White folks probably gonna cover that up. They coulda waited until after *Days of Our Lives* went off before they interrupted everythang. That shit'll probably be on all damn day."

Mama hardly ever went to work. She did hair down

to Miss Janice's beauty shop, and they ain't get along too good. Miss Janice had issues with Mama watching the soaps all day while she was supposed to be doing hair. Mama would get to cussing out Marlena and Stefano nem like they had dun cheated her outta some money in the back room at the pool hall. The ol' ladies got to complainin' all the time to Miss Janice, and she made Mama choose. For a minute, she did hair in our kitchen 'til one day Granddaddy found some hair in his food. He laid Mama out. Called her all kinds of lazy heifers and such. After that, Mama soaked up her pride and went on back down to Miss Janice's and just took a lunch break in time to see her show. Best to say she simply left for the day at 12:30, cuz she hardly ever, if ever, went back to the beauty shop.

I sat down next to Mama to watch some of the news 'bout this White man who they say used to move his hips like they was rubber and had a voice so cool that the White women was fallin' out all ovah the stage and shit. I ain't see no black folks out in all those crowds unless they was carryin' or holdin' somethin'. White folks was carryin' on worse than I ever seen anybody act over a dead man. Whatcha wanna be like that over a dope-head for? Yeah, I said it. A dope-head. Mama, while she was shucking corn for dinner, watched the TV for a minute, even stoppin' to listen 'bout how his ex-wife and little girl foundt out. I didn't even know who that man was until Mama had said somethin'. The only famous person I knew lived in Memphis was Isaac Hayes cuz every time we was on the bus and rode past his house right off South Lauderdale Mama would say, "Look, Elise, there go Isaac Hayes's house." I thought I was the shit since I knew where a real celebrity lived. That's the one thing I always hated 'bout

Memphis. Everybody always claimed to know a real
somebody when they really ain't know nobody. I even
fell into that trap with Eric Lee.

A couple of months later I saw Eric Lee again, but
this time he was at Mr. Luther's corner store over on
Wabash. By now, it was the middle of October, and fall
was creepin' up on us. The whole neighborhood had
been buzzin' 'bout Eric Lee's last-minute homerun that
made the Bellevue Stars win the championship game.
I ain't go to the game, but Cathy did and she was tellin'
me 'bout all the hussies runnin' up behind him after he
crossed home plate. Oh, I ain't tell you how good-
lookin' Eric Lee was. I think he was 'bout twenty-four
or twenty-five at the time. He was 'bout six feet tall
with dark eyes and thick, bushy eyebrows. His skin
was like hot fudge to me, and every since the first day
I seent him, I dreamt 'bout runnin' my fingers through
his hair. And man, did he have some good hair. It was
all wavy and shit, and when it was pressed under his
baseball cap, all his curls stuck to his head like a white
boy. Anyway, right as I crossed the threshold of the
store, he grabbed my arm.

"You ain't gonna speak?" he asked. His breath smelled
like old beer, but it ain't do nothin' to take away from
his pretty-ass smile.

I was runnin' to the store to get a sour pickle and a
peppermint stick befo' school. That was the best taste
in the world to me—that strong vinegar mixed with
sugar and a hint of mint. Mama usually gave me fifty
cents for lunch, but I always took ten cents and bought
a pickle and peppermint for breakfast every morning.
Mr. Luther got to the point where he always had it ready
for me. This particular day I was runnin' late and didn't
have time to stop and talk.

"You coulda spoke. Let my arm go," I yelled.

Removin' his grip, he was like, "Hold on, hold on, I ain't tryin' to hurt you. I just want to talk to you for a minute." By now, he had followed me into the store and was right up on me while I was payin' for my pickle.

"What is it?" I sassed. I could feel his smile all over me. With my back to him, I did everything I could to hide my joy.

"Why you always so mean? Either you're like that all the time, or you tryin' your best to keep me from likin' you."

I glanced up at the clock Mr. Luther kept on the shelf with the cigarettes. It was 7:45, and the late bell was going to be ringin' soon. I could either risk gettin' in trouble at school, which would only amount to havin' to wash tables after lunch, or I could spend a few extra minutes with Eric Lee so he could see that I wasn't mean at all.

Mr. Luther looked over the rim of his glasses at me. That meant he was goin' to tell my Mama on me. "Look, I really got to go. Will you be here after school?" I slid ten cents on the counter for Mr. Luther.

"I can be if you want me to," Eric Lee said. The sound of his voice was like my naked ass runnin' up against the velvet on Mama's bedspread—smooth.

Mr. Aaron Luther, with his shiny bald head that you rarely saw cuz he always had some kinda cap on, and my family went way back. Mama was seventeen when she had me, and Granddaddy Pop ain't nevah let her forget she made him a granddaddy before he was forty. From what I'd heard, Mr. Luther and him was the same age. The two of them was in the male chorus together, so he was old enough to be—well, my granddaddy—but a younger lookin' one if you ask me. I always made sure I was actin' right whenever I saw him cuz I knew he'd tell on me like he dun one time when we was up at the church.

One Sunday durin' altar call, me and Cathy snuck out the back door to go watch Pastor Sneed's wife, Lolly, and her lesbo friend, Tanika, doin' it in Room #12 at the Dew Drop Inn. The curtains was too raggedy for them to close all the way, so we always got a good view. They was both moanin' like they was getting dick from a pimp. I don't know what they was thinkin' when they put a church house right next to a ho-motel. Mr. Luther caught us comin' back in and ran his ugly-ass mouth to my granddaddy. Funky bastard. I couldn't answer Eric Lee in front of him even though I wanted to take the risk of an ass-beatin' at my age. He sure was worth it.

As Mr. Luther put my goods into a small, brown paper bag, I stole an opportunity to take a look at Eric Lee. Now, I understood what old folks meant when they say somebody was like a cool drink of water. I wanted that man, but I knew I ain't had no business with him. I was sixteen, remember? Reachin' for the bag, I slyly dropped my head to see if I could see the print of his dick . . . a bulge or somethin'. Right then, he snatched my bag.

"This is to make sure you come back to see me." He took off out the door.

After school, I went up to Mr. Luther's store, and just as he said he would be, Eric Lee was standin' right outside the door.

"Where my shit at, niggah?" I snapped.

Taking a drag from his cigarette and a swig from his

paper bag, Eric Lee replied, "You sho got a lot of mouth for you to be so young."

I was fire hot. "Yeah, muthafucka, I sholl do. And I got a big-ass foot to go wit' it, and unless you want me to plant my foot 'tween your legs, you need to gimme my fuckin' bag!"

Just as I was 'bout to kick his ass, I heard somebody screamin' my name from up the street. It was Mama. Her hair was tied up in a doo-rag, and she had on them metallic gold house shoes she'd got from Woolworth's. They was all scuffed up on the toes and so run-over she'd worn a hole on the outsides of both of 'em. You'd never catch her without her white crew socks on. She wore dem bitches mornin', noon, and night, winter, spring, summer, and fall.

The day she got her first gold tooth it took me a minute to get used to lookin' at her. It had a star in it, and all she bragged 'bout was gettin' her next one. When she did, Granddaddy Pop talked 'bout her so bad that she went to the dentist to see if she could get it taken off. All the women in our family took a lot of shit off Granddaddy, and sometimes he got cussed out. With a family full of women, he was all 'bout respect in the house and outside the house. Mama, though, did everythang she could to keep him happy. She ain't get the gold tooth removed, but she did make sho' she kept her words to Granddaddy at a bare minimum.

I was in mid-swing as Mama walked up. "Girl, what the hell you doing?" she asked, steppin' 'tween me and Eric Lee. I knew that bitch, Mr. Luther, had called her.

"Nothin.' He got my pickle and candy."

Mama checked Eric Lee from head to toe. She was unpredictable so I braced myself for the worst. "You ain't got nothin' else to do but mess 'round with this young girl? You been out here holdin' down your job as Mr. Luther's drunk-ass doorman drankin' beer like you at the all-day happy hour down on Beale Street. You need to go and get a real job." As if she could talk 'bout somebody not having a job.

Eric Lee ain't make too much of a fuss 'bout it. He kindly gave me my bag, but not without spittin' fightin' words with Mama. As he took his last sip of Colt 45, with his eyes bloodshot like Blacula, he whispered just loud enough for me to hear. "You got a fine-ass daughter there, Miss Viola Mae. You better watch out before she end up spoiled like you."

Even though all Eric Lee did was lean up against Mr. Luther's store all day with no desire or incentive to find a job, the two of them found plenty of time to do what men has a tendency to do. They gossiped all day long like two old church hens and talked 'bout anybody and everything. So I'm pretty sure Mr. Luther had told him 'bout Mama and her tendency to nevah know one niggah from the next cuz she dun fucked 'em all.

Mama cussed and fussed all the way back home, but I ain't paid her no attention. I was right back up at Mr. Luther's two days later flirtin' with Eric Lee. I started wonderin' though, how come Mama hadn't been runnin' up there to embarrass me and bring my ass back home cuz hell, I had looked Mr. Luther dead in the face a couple of times when I was trying to push up on Eric Lee's dick. I wanted that thang in the worst way. I wanted it in my mouth, my ear, my ass, my pussy—anythang with a hole in it. Couple of weeks later, I got my wish. I foundt myself in this empty old house across the street from Mr. Luther's store lyin' on on an old, wet blanket with Eric Lee's dick in me. Feelin' 'round on him, I saw he ain't have but one nut. I wanted to ask him 'bout it, but I ain't want to seem dumb or nothin'.

The place used to belong to Miss Willa, one of the sweetest, kindest ladies you'd evah know. There was holes all in the house cuz it had been ambushed by some people who thought Miss Willa's nephew was in there. He owed them money and kept hidin' out at different relatives' houses. There was 'bout two hundred holes in the walls of that house. Miss Willa's nephew wasn't there, but she was. Bullet straight to her head in her sleep. I heard she ain't feel a thang. Errhbody was scared to go over there and clean up the house, so it just ended up rottin'. Whatevah the dope-heads ain't steal, the rats ate up.

That ain't what I thought my first time would be like, but I was with the man of my dreams. I hadn't got my period yet, so I was good and ready to do this as many times as I wanted. Eric Lee grunted when he was doin' me like he was takin' a shit or somethin', and I made little weak-ass noises. He was big down there, kinda like the size of a cucumber. He struggled gettin' hisself in me sometimes, but I would just lay there and let him handle his business. I wasn't sure what I was supposed to be feelin'. I wasn't sure if my pussy was supposed to be feelin' like my heart felt 'bout Eric Lee. It burned sometimes when we did it, but I took it in stride. One time when we was doing it, I started bleedin'. I just knew he had busted my cherry, and I wasn't no virgin no more. When he got up off me, he saw the blood on the blanket and asked me if I evah got my period. I said, "No," and he went on with this air 'bout himself like he did when he smacked them homeruns.

"You know we gonna have to stop this when you get your period. I ain't tryin' to have no babies with you."

Cathy had told me she got her period when she was eleven, and we was both always wonderin' if I was evah gonna have one. According to what Cathy said her Mama told her, I was normal and was just a late bloomer.

Later that evening when I got home, I realized the bleeding didn't stop. I went to Mama, and all she did was give me a wad of toilet paper and told me to put it in my panties. We ain't talk 'bout nothin'. All she said was, "You betta watch yourself." Instantly, I called Cathy and told her 'bout what was happening. She started askin' me all these questions 'bout what the blood looked like and all that disgusting stuff. We both concluded I'd finally become a woman. Once I told her Mama had only given me a bunch of toilet paper, Cathy told me she'd be right ovah with some pads. The last thing she said to me before leaving the house was to be careful and that Eric Lee could make me pregnant if we was still having sex.

"Elise," she say. "You better make that niggah use a rubber. His old ass knows what that is."

"I'll tell him the next time," I smiled as I walked her to the door.

Toward the end of November, Eric Lee broke my heart by tellin' me he was leavin' Memphis to travel with another baseball team. We was standin' outside Mr. Luther's store when he broke the news. I know Mr. Luther heard us talkin' cuz he kept walkin' his nosy ass right by the door.

"Baby, I gots to go do this. I want to do this so I can buy you all the pickles and peppermint you want. Don't you want that?"

I was young, remember, so that shit sounded romantic to me. I cried and carried on for a minute befo' I answered in a baby voice. "Yeah, I want that."

"Tell you what. Lemme take you to the drive-in tonight."

I told Mama I was goin' to Cathy's house to do homework. Instead, two hours later, I had my leg propped up on the face bowl in the women's bathroom at the Bellevue Drive-In with Eric Lee inside of me. We was supposed to be watchin' *Which Way Is Up?*, but never really got around to it. Once he got that first nut out, I, with the tips of my fingers pressed against his back, got up and ran over to lock the door. I turnt to find him still standin' there with wood in his hand.

"I want you to do me from the back," I told him. I'd nevah asked him for anything, and this was what I wanted my last memory of him to be. Eric Lee bent me over the sink and spread my cheeks, gently rubbin' his finger along the crack of my ass. When he glided his finger across my butthole, I shivered. He'd hit that spot. He felt me pop and all that did was make him rub it harder. My clit felt strange. It stood at attention, but I ain't nevah had the urge I had then. He stuck his dick in and blew my back out. The closer he got to cummin' the harder he pounded. Just as I knew I was 'bout to cum, he pulled out and shot his juice all over my back and kep on doin' it, spraying shit all over the folks' mirror. That set me off, and I made some joy juice of my own.

Eric Lee was gone 'bout two days befo' I realized how much I really missed him. I ain't know what to do with myself. I hung with Cathy some, but what she had 'tween her legs was a far cry from what my man had. So it won't really the same. On that third day, I went to

Mr. Luther's store to get me a pickle and a peppermint stick. When I got in the store, I ain't see Mr. Luther.

"Hello?" I called.

The bell on the door jingled as it always did, but nobody came from the back. I walked through the aisles and was kinda puzzled cuz in all my years of going there Mr. Luther was nevah not there. I made my way back up the can good aisle toward the front to see if I was the only one in the store, but I felt like somebody was watchin' me. I turnt and went down the cereal aisle which was right by the front door. The door was closed, and the bell was took off. *What the fuck?* I thought. I made it my bidness to get the hell up outta there, but just as I was makin' a mad dash for the front door, somebody grabbed holdt of my arm and slammed me to the ground.

"Don't you say shit," he mumbled as he snatched my panties down. All I could smell was stale licka and musk. I tried to wiggle, but he was too heavy and had both of my arms pinnedt down. For a minute, I thought it was Eric Lee tryin' to be funny since I'd told him I liked it from the back. But the more violent those minutes got, the more I realized Eric Lee wouldn't a done that to me. "Like it from the back, huh?" he growled, ramming his dick in my butthole and not my pussy. My lip was bleeding pretty bad from where I'd dun hit the floor. Each time I tried to turn over, my head was smacked back down against the tiles. I nevah knew somethin' that big was meant to be in there, and from the pain I felt, I really don't think it evah was. His dick slid in and out like raw wood with splinters, tearin' flesh as it went along. The last jab he tried missed and ended up in my other hole.

"If you ever say a word to anybody," he growled

softly, "I'm going to tell your Granddaddy how fass you is and what you did at the drive-in and over at Miss Willa's." Then he released himself and left just as quietly and quickly as he snuck in. I wasn't sure what had just happened to me. Who on earth woulda done such a horrible thing to me?

SHAME
Elise

A letter to my daughter
Part 2

Since Mama nevah talked to me 'bout fuckin' and what happens to you when you do it after you dun got your period, I ain't know why my stomach was growin'. I mean, Cathy had told me I could get pregnant, but I ain't nevah thank it could happen so fast and that errhbody could tell it 'cept for me. It took Miss Janice to say somethin' to Mama one day when I came in the beauty shop to get some money for a pickle and some peppermint.

"Viola Mae, is Elise pregnant?" she blurted out in front of all they customers. "She sholl is a little thick 'round the waist. Face all puffy."

"Elise, you been fuckin'?" Mama asked me that in front of all dem people.

I ain't know what to say. I ain't nevah tell nobody 'bout what happened that day at Mr. Luther's. I'd kept on goin' in there for my pickles and candy and for anythang else I was s'pposed to get. Mama ain't know how to be discreet 'bout nothing. All dem womens was lookin' at me with fire in dey eyes.

"No," I answered. What else was I s'pposed to say?

Day by day, my stomach was getting bigger, and every day Mama asked me if I'd been fuckin' and every day I was tellin' her no. I could feel, though, somethin' movin' inside of me like a big butterfly or bird wit wings ticklin' the walls of my belly. We was 'bout in sprang when I come home one day to see Granddaddy Pop sittin' in the dinin' room talkin' to Mama.

"Good evening," I said befo' I headed to my room. Granddaddy had always told us to speak when we entered the room even if the folks we speakin' to ain't speak back. Nobody in the room spoke back. Mama's eyes was all red and puffy, and Granddaddy looked pissed off with the world. On the table was a bus ticket and I saw two suitcases sittin' by the door.

"Don't go in there," Granddaddy said. "Come over here and sit down." He nevah laid his eyes on me, staring down at the orange vinyl placemats Mama had got from Woolworth's. He was just spinnin' his thumbs 'round each other like a ferris wheel.

There was nevah an argument when it came to doin' what he said, so I sat down at the table 'tween him and Mama. "Yes, suh?" I asked.

When he raised his eyes, he looked dead at Mama, and she, as she'd learned to do, looked away from him. "Uh, you can't stay here lookin' like that," Granddaddy Pop said.

"Suh?"

Wipin' his eyes, he said calmly, "You heard me."

I could feel the tears comin' but I held 'em back. "Granddaddy Pop, I mean . . ."

"It's obvious somethin' was going on 'tween you and that Eric Lee boy, and ain't no way you can tell me any diff'rent. I don't need folks in the street runnin' back to me tellin' me you been screwin'. At fust, I didn't believe it. I couldn't believe it. Then I started noticin' you was lookin' diff'rent. I got six gurls and one granddaughter, and outta them, you and yo Mama dun disgraced me and my name. You can't stay here."

I looked over at Mama, waitin' to see if she was gon' say somethin'. "Mama?" I asked, weepin'. "You gon' let him do this? You gon' let him ship me off? Don't you love me?" I got up from my chair and walked ovah to her. I started kissin' and huggin' on her, but she ain't return my affection. "Mama . . ."

"You lied, Elise," she said hoarsely. Clearin' her throat, she continued, "I asked you over and over if you been fuckin', and you kept tellin' me no."

Mama acted like she ain't want to take the blame for any of this. I was shocked. The only thing I could do to defend myself was to put it all back on her. I took my seat and said shouted, "You ain't nevah told me nothin' 'bout havin' babies. You ain't nevah tried to explain this could happen!"

Granddaddy Pop fiercely slapped his hand against the table. "Stop it! Stop it! You ain't gonna talk to your Mama like that in front of me. Yeah, she fucked up. Yeah, she shoulda told you 'bout life, but she didn't. It ain't the place of a sixteen year old to tell her that! That's what I'm here to do. Since she ain't doing what she need to do, I'm sending you to my sister's house in Atlanta."

"What?"

I got his backhand after that. "Now, get your shit and come on befo' you miss your bus."

I wanted so bad to tell him I wanted to see my friends, Cathy and nem, but I ain't even bothah. Mama got up from the table and went to the bathroom and closed the door. She ain't even say good-bye.

All the way to Atlanta, I wondered who coulda told on me. It was probably Mr. Luther's ass. Probably.

I painfully gave birth to you only a couple months after I got to Atlanta. I called for my Mama when your little head popped out. Auntie Diane was there instead. She was holdin' my hand the whole time and kept tellin' me thangs would be all right. Spite what she'd been told 'bout me and my situation, she nevah spoke bad to me or 'bout me. I admitted I knew how to make a baby, but I ain't understand how. Instead of goin' through all the details, she simply bought me a book and said to let her know if I had any questions. She taught me how to use a pad and took me to the clinic to get on the pill. I told her 'bout me and Eric Lee, and all she said was thangs had happened the way God wanted them to. I asked 'bout an abortion, but Auntie ain't even answer me—gave me a look I ain't nevah forget.

I ain't know anythang 'bout takin' care of a baby other than what I used to doin' with my doll babies. It was kinda the same thing 'cept I couldn't drop you, and I had to feed you real food. Auntie Diane bought clothes for you and made sure you looked like a doll all the time. She always said "What your child looks like out in public is a reflection of you." So all of my life I tried to make sure you liked somethin' when you left my house, and that's why I can't believe you walkin' 'round lookin' like some ol' thug now. As you can see, I dun been through enough in my life where I had to worry 'bout what peoples thought of me, and now you puttin' me through it again.

Anyway, Auntie never had any kids, and she and

Granddaddy Pop were really close. After you turnt three months old, she told me he was askin' 'bout us all the time but ain't want us to come back to Memphis. He was ashamed of what I done, and to spare him further humiliation wanted me and you to stay away. Sometimes I wish I coulda had one of dem abortions, so I coulda got my life back and so I coulda went back home.

Inside of me, I was still keepin' that secret from that day at Mr. Luther's. Most of the time I blocked it outta my memory and went on like it ain't nevah happen. To this day, I don't know who it was that done them awful thangs to me. But, then I got to thankin' 'bout what that book Auntie Diane gave me said 'bout how you make a baby. It got me to thinkin' really hard.

On your first birthday, we was all out in the backyard havin' a cookout. I was workin' a little job and had saved up four paychecks to buy food and get you some hair bows, a coupla dresses, and your first pair of Mary Janes. We had hot dogs, smoke sausages, hamburgers, ribs, chicken, baked beans, watermelon and plenty of licka. We had Rose Royce, Parliament, and Rick James spinnin' on the turntable. We was blastin' sounds through the speakers all through the day and on into the night. You passed out right after you finished tearin' through your cake, and since all the food was gone, errhbody started leavin'. Them niggahs was so drunk they forgot the words to "Happy Birthday." I went into the house lookin' for Auntie so she could help me put out the fire on the grill and found her sittin' on the piano bench with her head buried in her hands sobbin' somethin' terrible.

"What's wrong, Auntie?" I asked, comfortin' her with gentle pats on her back.

"Your granddaddy is dead. My brother is gone," she said, pattin' tears from her eyes.

Auntie was an educated lady. She'd gone to Spelman, worked as a schoolteacher, and was nothin' like your great-Granddaddy Pop. He was the type of man that believed women oughta be trained on how to take care of a man and his needs. No matter what wrong your man did, it was your job as his woman to cook, clean, and let him hit it when he wanted. Grandmama gave him six gurls: Nellie, Penny, Sandra, Warene, Barbara, and your granny, Viola Mae. For some reason, he gave your granny the hardest time of 'em all, and he always tried to control her life. Henrietta, your great-grandmama, let him get away wit that. Now, wit him gone, I went on back home to raise you.

Niggahs from all ovah the city of Memphis was at Granddaddy Pop's funeral. He had folks there from the pool hall, the car wash, the lodge, the strip club, the shoeshine parlor, and the dog track over in West Memphis. Cars was lined all up and down the street cuz the church parking lot was overflowin', and peoples really ain't have no place else to go.

When I walked in the house to wait for the funeral home's cars, errhbody was lookin' at us like we won't s'pposed to be there. Grandmama come ovah first to pick you up, and then your granny came ovah. Viola Mae sprayed kisses on both of us like we been away for-evah.

"Ooohhhhhhh, look at my granbaby!" she said. "You look just like your ol' daddy." And you did look like Eric Lee. Had his hair, eyes, legs, and all.

Once we got to the church, peoples was still filin' in

like ants on a twinkie. Most of the folks Granddaddy
Pop knew was probably just comin' to get a free meal
afterwards. Remember what I said 'bout people claimin'
to know somebody when they really ain't know nobody?
That was the case here. Walkin' up the aisle I spotted
peoples I ain't nevah seent before 'cept when I come
eye-to-eye wit Eric Lee standing next to this woman
holding a baby. He looked the same, and when he saw
you, he just smiled and smiled. I realized maybe he
did care a little somethin' 'bout me cuz he was there.
While we was fillin' in the pews, I made sure to sit on
the end so I could look back and see him from time to
time. I wanted him to be able to see you and how much
you looked like him.

The male chorus came in the sanctuary from the side
door cuz of all the peoples out front. They marched
'cross the front of the casket so they could see him one
last time. Mr. Luther, walking in all cool and shit, was
leadin' the way hummin' "Hush, Somebody's Callin'
My Name." That was Granddaddy Pop's favorite. As
they walked by, you could smell Aramis mixed with
the aroma of the fried chicken from where they'd been
hangin' out in the fellowship hall. They took the choir
stand and loaded us up wit 'bout three or four more
songs. Mr. Luther came down to the podium and said
some words and so did a few other folks.

Later that day after the burial and long after we'd
finished up with dinner at the church, Eric Lee stopped
by the house wit that lady and the baby—his little family—to pay his respects. They was sittin' on one side of
the room, and me and you was sittin' on the other.
Mama broke the ice.

"Niggah?" Errhbody she ain't like was that to her. "I
see you got yourself kinda in a tight spot here. You
dun walked up in my house with a wife and another

baby. The last piece of pussy you got before you left here must notta been a nuff for you," she said, rolling her eyes at me.

"Viola Mae, your daddy ain't even in the grave good, and you want to start some shit with me and mines," Eric Lee said.

"You and yours?" she snapped. "What 'bout this . . . ain't that yours sittin' over there?"

Eric Lee looked at me wit those gorgeous eyes of his and quickly cut his eyes at his wife and other baby. Now what come outta his mouth next caused a whole lotta trouble in my house that day. "How do I know that's my baby?"

Mama dug through her purse lookin' for her Salems. At least that's what I hoped she was lookin' for. She kept a little pistol in there and ain't nevah hesitate to use it when she was threatened. She and I ain't nevah talk 'bout what was happenin' 'tween me and Eric Lee. All she knew was what Granddaddy Pop had been tellin' her and what she was seein' wit her own eyes. She'd nevah come to my defense 'bout anythang, so I was expectin' her to light her cigarette and blow smoke up my ass by actin' like she really cared. "Niggah, please. Don't come in here with that bullshit," she said flickin' her lighter 'til a flame burst up and singed the tip of her cig. Swiftly turnin' her head to the side and spewin' smoke to the left side of the room, she crossed her legs and leant back on the couch.

"I knowed you that baby's daddy just cuz I seent you sniffin' up behind my chile since she was sixteen. Ran your ass outta here like you some big-time ball playah and shit. If you so high and mighty, why you sittin' here with that scratchy-ass lookin' gal over there? You pulled up here in a damn Pinto . . . not a Caddy like folks do when they got a little somethin'. You won't 'bout shit when you was screwin' Elise, and you, for damn sho, ain't 'bout shit now!"

Eric Lee wasn't the type to raise his voice, but he ain't let nobody make him look bad neither. "Viola Mae, what do you want from me? I ain't got nothin' to give nobody. I'm barely providing for my family as it is."

Just as Mama was 'bout to go stupid on him, I softly spoke up. "Mama, I don't need nothin' from him. I been doin' fine by myself. I don't see how you can talk 'bout him not doin' anythang for me. Durin' all the time I been away from Memphis, you ain't done nothin' for me neither. Nevah even called."

Mama took another draw from her cig. "You bettah watch yourself, girl."

"I'm almost eighteen now, and I got a baby. I can take care of us." Grandmama was standin' in there and so was Penny. Ain't netha one of dem say a word. "I'm goin' back to Atlanta with Auntie Diane."

Eric Lee's little woman nevah said a word durin' that whole time, but she did manage to wank her eye at me. Guess that meant we was cool.

I went back to Atlanta with you and Auntie Diane 'round a week after the funeral. She lived over in West End, not too far from Spelman.

"Elise, have you ever considered going to college?" she asked one Sunday after church. "I think you'd make a fine college student."

"Well, no ma'am. I ain't nevah thought 'bout that, 'specially since I got a baby."

Auntie looked at me and smiled. "Having a baby shouldn't stop anybody from getting an education. I'd help you out with her."

I'd finished high school, but was likin' my job at the supermarket. I got free formula and baby food for you and always had somethin' extra to help out Auntie Diane. She ain't need it, but it was the thought that count. The main reason I ain't want to leave the store was Tevin—the hunk of man workin' the meat counter in the evenin'. He was always comin' to the front of the store to smile in my face, and on breaks we'd meet in the alley. I'd kissed that boy so much that my spit even tasted like his sometimes.

"Lemme think 'bout it, Auntie Diane."

The next day I called Aunt Penny, Mama's sister that was three years older than her, and asked her what she thought. Ain't none of the women in the immediate family but Auntie Diane evah been to college, but Penny sho carried herself like she did. Penny was like, "Is she going to pay for it?"

"I guess so. It sounded like she was."

"Elise, I would go. I mean, you would be able to get a better life for you and the baby. Something you know you aren't 'bout to get here." Penny ain't nevah lied to me.

I enrolled that fall and fell in love with it. I was taking up journalism and got in a basic English class where I was learnin' how to speak right and get my thoughts together. I could tell the hell outta a story. Auntie let me keep my job on the weekends so long as I kept my grades up. One Saturday night in the middle of the semester, Auntie told me she was going over to her church member's house to work on finishin' up their pastor's new robe they were giving him for his anniversary. She would be gone for 'bout three or four hours and was going to take you with her since I had to work late.

Earlier that afternoon, when I walked past the meat counter goin' to the stockroom, I winked at Tevin and patted my ass. Next thang I know, he done followed me into the stockroom and twisted the lock on the door. I wanted him in the worst way and needed to satisfy that urge I'd been having, but something was holdin' me back.

"What you gonna do, babygirl?" he asked as he rushed to take off his apron.

This was strange for me. A locked door—in a closed off place. Only this time I knew who was in the room with me. With him reachin' for my waist, I stopped abruptly shakin' my head.

"Wait, I can't do this." The memories of that day fell on me like a ton of bricks.

"What you mean 'wait'?" he asked.

I was too embarrassed to say somethin' else. My pussy had been hot for this man since I first laid eyes on him. Six-foot-two with a rock hard gut and big ol' feet and hands. He was a little rough 'round the edges wit the dirt under his nails and dingy white T-shirts he was always wearin'. I didn't care 'bout that too much, but I thought I was ready.

"Hold on, Tevin." Wit each step he made toward me I took one away from him. There was no way I was gonna tell him what had happened to me, but I had to say somethin' to keep him from pushin'up on me. The walls started closin' in. I was fightin' his movement wit e'rything I had, but he kept on comin'. "Tevin, please, wait!" Then I snatched a can of corn from the shelf.

Tevin threw on brakes and was like, "Whoa, Elise, what's wrong with you? I'm not tryin' to hurt you."

I started cryin'. "I'm sorry. It's just that . . ." I tried to get it out but couldn't. "This is all my fault. Teasin' you like this."

Tevin straightened up his clothes and pulled me to his chest. "You not teasin' me. It's gonna be fine."

Snifflin' and carryin' on, I hugged him, smellin' his strong body odor of red meat and swine. My pussy wasn't hot no more, but I still wanted him.

Kissin' my forehead, he asked, "How 'bout I take you up to The Varsity tonight for a burger and shake?"

"I'd like that."

We sat at The Varsity laughin' and talkin' for an hour or so befo' I realized that maybe, just maybe, I could let somebody love on me again. I could see his face. I could hold him. I could stop him if it got too rough. I could see him when it was over. Most of what I liked 'bout Tevin was he made me laugh even when shit wasn't funny. We flirted all day long at work, and sometimes we'd sit outside the store for hours and just act silly. Sippin' on my last drop of chocolate shake, I leant over and gave him a peck on the cheek. It was in my own time, and it felt right.

"Damn, baby girl, that felt kinda right even though your lips all sticky," he laughed.

"I'm sorry!" I giggled. Eric Lee didn't make me laugh like that. I looked into his eyes and found a place where I could run and tell my troubles to. I was feelin' like I'd found home. I closed my eyes and laid the softest kiss on his lips. Of course, he kissed me back, and it was on like a pot of neck bones! "You wanna go to my house?" I asked. "Ain't nobody there."

I was expectin' him to say no. "Yeah, let's do that."

Well, we didn't quite make it in the house. We rode up I-20 wit his hand in my pants. He had that finger action goin', and I didn't want it to stop. By the time we got to Auntie Diane's driveway, I had pulled my pants off and was bare ass naked on the seat of his Dodge Charger. I climbed over the gearshift and straddled his lap. He was ready for me cuz it went right in. I rode and rode until I felt like pee was runnin' down my leg, and wit e'ry stride he was right there wit me. Tevin had my titty in his mouth tuggin'on it like a piece of beef jerky. I tried so hard not to scream, but I couldn't help myself. Tevin was palmin' my ass like a basketball, slammin' me against his groin. He leant me away from him, so he could see what he was doin'. Our hairs were meshed together, our skins was wet with sweat. I guess in all that heat we didn't see Auntie Diane standin' on the front porch with her arms folded.

I hope you nevah have to find out what's it's like to carry a baby on the Greyhound. While I was outside gettin' my freak on, Auntie Diane was in the house packin' our shit. Judgin' by the way things were just stuck e'rywhere, she was highly pissed off at me. She didn't even fry us no chicken to take wit us. I'd fucked up royally and was pretty sure by the time I got to Memphis e'rybody was gonna know what had happened.

We got on the bus, and 'cause she didn't waste no time getting us to the station so we could make the last dog out, we ended up with the only two seats left, the ones next to the bathroom. All night long you were whining in your car seat, and I cain't blame you. E'ry time somebody came back there they just looked at me and rolled their eyes. When we finally got to Memphis, I struggled with you and our bags, and spite all them niggahs lookin' at me, ain't none of 'em try to help.

Right as I was 'bout to drop you and all your bottles, I saw your granny comin' at me. She wasn't smilin' or nothin'. I thought she was gon' reach out and hug me, but she didn't.

"Just can't keep them damn legs closed, can you?" she said.

You was close to 'bout three years old when that itch started settlin' in—you know, the I-shoulda-nevah-had-no-baby itch. I was tired of bein' tied down to you and your needs all the time. I didn't like bein' at the house all the time, and I hated bumpin' into my friends from back in the day 'cause they all got a chance to have a diff'rent life than what I did. Even my girl Cathy had gone off to school somewhere and hardly evah came home. To get away, I dropped you off at Penny's a lot so I could be free.

"Why didn't you just have an abortion?" Penny asked me one time.

I was like, "If I knew I coulda done that, I sho the hell woulda."

You were old enough to hear me and to repeat it when you was talkin' wit your little playmates. Tangie's Mama was the first to ask me 'bout it, and I denied it like Judas.

Mama kept her distance for the most part, and I'm glad she did. She had a tendency to make me feel like shit all the time. What she didn't understand was that the apple didn't fall too far from the tree. She had no cause to be mad with nobody but herself for me being who I was. The one thing I did know was that I could be and was a good Mama. I had my issues—we all do.

I was lookin' forward to the day you grew into a young lady so we do the things my Mama and I nevah did. I was workin' ovah at Purina Plant and was makin' a few dollahs. We wasn't hurtin' for nothin'.

One afternoon when you were 'round six, I sent you down to Penny's house to get the straightnin' comb.

You looked all pretty with your little white hair bows, white polo shirt, and white mini-skirt on. You had on them white bobby socks with the lace along the edges and a pair of white Mary Janes. I heard your feet slappin' the concrete from halfway down the street. "Stop runnin', girl, befo' you fall and scratch up them shoes," I yelled.

Huffin' and puffin', you took the straightnin' comb outta the bag and put it on the table. I saw there was somethin' else in it. "That man down the street, Momma, told me to give this to you."

"What man?"

"That man that live in that house by where that old store used to be. You know—the candy man."

I opened the bag, and there was a sour pickle with a stick of peppermint. "He gave this to you?"

"Yes, me and Tangie. We was walkin' from Aunt Penny's house, and he was out working in the yard. He asked us if we wanted some candy, and we said yes."

"What I tell you 'bout takin' candy from strangers?"

"Aunt Penny saw him. She said it was all right. He was like family."

I actually thought Mr. Luther had died. Nobody had said a word 'bout that man in years. It was so nice of him to remember me like that. Thinkin' 'bout him made me think of Eric Lee. I hadn't seent him since Granddaddy Pop's funeral. Even wit a touch of high blood pressha, a sour pickle wasn't gonna hurt nothin'.

"Next time you see Mr. Luther, be sho to tell him I said thank you."

Mr. Luther was the only man in my lifetime that gave me somethin' wit-out me askin' for it. I was on his mind when he wasn't on mine. For as I long as I knew, Mr. Luther hadn't nevah hurt a soul.

MO

It happened at a time when there was no such thing as a sex offender. There were simply dirty old men who could have their way with little girls and dared them to tell anybody. Nobody did time, nor did anyone get counseling. Bribed with money, candy, toys, and whatever else didn't come easy, almost every girl in the neighborhood had touched Mr. Luther's dick. I, myself, had seen it, kissed it, smelled it, and touched it more times than I cared to think 'bout.

My reflection in the floor-length mirror was disturbing at first sight. Blood was running down my legs, soaking through my white stockings. My pretty pink sundress, stained with dirt, blood, and his secretions, was torn at the shoulder straps, and the buckles on my Mary Janes were broken. I'd run from the railroad tracks as fast as I could, never looking back to see if he were catching up to me. When I got to the house, I bolted the front door and dashed down the hallway to the bathroom. There, I found some sense of security. On this blistering, hot summer's day, I'd had it. Oh, by the way, to my family and friends, my name is Monique.

At ten, I was a small girl—a little chunky in places—but for the most part, I was like the other girls my age. My areas of thickness were my breasts, my cheeks, and my rear end. My moms made me wear dresses every day with some type of matching bow in my hair. She refused to let me grow up and wear things more appropriate for my age. I had the Bobbie socks with the lace around the ankles, and my moms made sure my legs were shining from the clumps of Vaseline she slapped on my calves and thighs. To coordinate with all of my dresses, I had a pair of Mary Janes I wore with tights, necklaces, earrings—the whole nine yards. When Mary Janes came in style for pre-teens, she bought me some of those, too.

Moms and I lived alone in a two-bedroom house that we rented from some folks who went to church down on the corner. We weren't rich, but Moms made sure that I was neatly dressed whenever I stepped out of the house. She says it came from years of her playing with doll babies, imitation Barbie dolls, and those spooky-ass doll heads. From as early as I could remember, Moms never asked anyone for anything when it came to taking care of me. I met my dad once, one Friday after school, and was terribly disappointed because he wasn't this fine, debonair Black man that Moms had made him into whenever she sat on the porch cackling and gossiping with her girlfriends. Personally, I thought he was some ex-con looking for a handout. His beard was knotted up against his face, his teeth were yellow with white shit all between them, his corn-rowed hair had pieces of lint sticking out, and the stench from the stale liquor lingered in the house for days after he had left.

"Monique, this is Eric, your father. Come give him a hug," she ordered. There was no way in hell that I was going to let that man touch me. I took two steps back instead of any ones forward. "Get over here, Monique! Now. I know you ain't gonna disrespect your father. Don't let me have to beat your ass!"

All I have to say is that was the worst beating I ever got because after having never seen me, tucked me in bed, or kissed me on the forehead, she let him spank me, and none of his licks hurt more than the pain and hurt I felt toward Moms. When he was done, I saw his hands trembling as he lit a cigarette and walked down the hall to her bedroom. I went to my room, closed the door, and fell down on my bed, sobbing for hours. Throughout the whole weekend, I made my way to the kitchen and bathroom without ever being seen. Devastated, I realized that Moms could care less about me right then because her man was at home. Closed up in my room with my music and my dolls, I was content if I never saw him again—and I didn't.

Most of my life I knew Moms hadn't really wanted to have babies. She used to tell my Aunt Penny that she'd have an abortion in a minute if she had the money, but she wasn't going to stop fucking and wasn't going to use no rubber either. Apparently, she didn't have the money when she got pregnant with me. Most of my early years were spent at Aunt Penny's house on the weekends. Moms would drop me off on Friday evening and wouldn't pick me up until Monday after she got off work. At least, I was told she'd been to work. When we returned home, there was always this stale liquor smell in the house, and the sheets on her bed were a mess and smelled like ba-dussy—a dreadful combination of ass and pussy. I never questioned her about any of it cuz that was grown folks' business. Moms made sure I had what she felt I needed, but for herself, the only thing she did was to make herself available to whatever man came along. My granny believed that a woman's place was to cook, take care of the children, and be a freak in the sheets, and that's exactly how she acted. So did Moms.

Up the street from us lived this man named Mr. Luther who was like the candy man for our neighborhood. He sold twenty-five-cent sodas, freeze cups, pickles, candy, cookies, Popsicles, potato chips, and ice cream cones. Every day before school, for as long as I can remember, my cousins and I stopped by his house to buy cookies to go in our lunch.

"Here, Li'l Miss Monique, take this here to your mother. She likes my sour pickles," he'd say, and I'd put it in my lunch box and give it to her when I got home from school.

I liked Mr. Luther because he was always so nice, especially to us girls. Sometimes he was like the father many of us never had. Every day he asked how we were doing in school and if we were learning anything. Back then, if needed, Mr. Luther had this unspoken permission to knock us on our asses if we got out of line. I only heard about him doing that to a couple of the boys on our street but never to any of the girls.

By the time I was thirteen, I was still wearing the Mary Janes, but Moms had stopped making me wear dresses all the time. It was embarrassing for me to look like Little Orphan Annie even though I was a teenager. Now I had some say in my wardrobe and wore mostly jeans and nice frou-frou blouses. I had some corduroys and a couple of pair of khaki pants that I dressed in from time to time, too. Sometimes I'd wear a dress just to change up for a bit. On one of those occasions, I bumped into Mr. Luther at our school's playground.

We shared the play area with the adjacent park, so it wasn't unusual for folks to be sitting on the benches near where we played. At this point in my life, I'd started noticing the boys, and they'd started noticing me, too. I made sure I was cute every day, and I smelled sensational. Mr. Luther would always tell me how good I smelled when he saw me, and he told me in such a fatherly way that I never thought about anything being wrong with his comments.

That afternoon, however, he'd been sitting there watching me and some of my friends gossip about the boys in our class. We'd had a special program that morning, and most of the girls had on dresses. I ignored the glazed look in his eyes and the demented smile on his face. Hell, this was Mr. Luther, the candy man, and he could do no wrong.

"Mr. Luther, what are you doing here? Were you invited to our program today?"

Looking around to see who saw him, he replied, "No, I wasn't at your program. I came up here to drop some sodas off to your principal."

"Oh, OK." I smiled. "I'll see you later."

Winking at me, Mr Luther asked, "Why don't you come by after school and get a pickle for your mother?"

"Yes, sir. I will."

Since I was in middle school and class started much earlier, I didn't have time to stop by in the mornings like I used to. As I laughed and played that afternoon with my friends, enjoying my youth, it didn't dawn on me that sodas weren't allowed in our school. Later, after school, my friend Tangie and I headed toward Mr. Luther's place, but when we got there, she refused to go inside.

"Girl, what's wrong with you? You acting like you seen a boogeyman or something. It's just Mr. Luther."

Tangie's face had this look I'd never seen. Suddenly, she burst into tears. I reached for her arm, but she yanked it back. "Noooo. My momma told me to not go in there." She took off running down the street.

Nothing was going to stop me from getting my moms's pickle. She loved those things even though they gave her high blood pressure. I opened the screen door and walked into the kitchen where Mr. Luther kept the goodies.

"Mr. Luther?" I called out.

There was no answer. As I walked around the table that held the pickles, peppermint sticks, and penny candy, I noticed a stick of incense burning in a nearby plant. Just as I peeped around the corner into the living room, Mr. Luther came out of nowhere.

"Hey there, Li'l Miss Monique. I thought you wasn't going to make it. I was just about to get a fresh jar of pickles for your mother. Those are dill pickles in there. The sour ones are back here in the other room."

That was strange. I swore the jar read SOUR on the front. "OK," I answered and followed him to the back room.

Once in there, the door unexpectedly closed. But I wasn't worried because this was Mr. Luther, the candy man. I stood in the corner behind the door while he fumbled with some boxes. Nervous, I stood gawking at the tons of shit in that room. There was enough stuff to start a small convenience store. When Mr. Luther turned around, he had his penis in his hand, and it stood out like a flagpole.

"Li'l Miss Monique, would you help Mr. Luther and touch his little friend for him?"

I was repulsed. "No, Mr. Luther, I can't do that. I just came for my momma's pickle." He asked again, and I rejected him again. "I think I better leave."

"Oh, Li'l Miss Monique, just do it this one time for me. I won't tell nobody. It'll be our little secret. I'll give you a brand-new twenty-dollar bill and all the pickles you want for your momma."

I couldn't resist that. My moms loved those pickles, and I could use the twenty dollars to go to the mall with Tangie later.

At fifteen, I was a brickhouse. I still had a small frame, but I had curvaceous hips and voluptuous breasts. I'd gotten enough money from Mr. Luther to buy a new bike, a pair of skates, a *Seventeen* magazine subscription, and a few pretty gifts for my moms. One night when Tangie and I were having a sleepover, she sat up on my bed and looked at all the nice things I had around my room. "How much of this stuff did Mr. Luther buy?" she asked playfully.

Shocked, I swiftly got up from the floor and closed my door. "What are you talking about, Tangie?"

"Don't play dumb. Everybody on this street knows you been getting money from him, and you're not the only one."

"That's not true."

"Monique, your momma works at the same plant as my momma, and they don't make that much money.

There's no way your momma can afford all this stuff you got."

"Why you all up in my business?" I couldn't believe I was getting mad about this. I knew Mr. Luther was wrong, but he was giving me money, and I was able to afford a lifestyle my other friends didn't have.

"This is me, Monique. Quit trippin'."

I started crying. "Do you realize how much money he has given me since this started? Like hundreds and hundreds of dollars."

"All for you to do what for him?"

Ashamed, I began rattling off each act, none of which included him sticking it in. "Tangie, all I've done is touch it mostly."

"Monique, you need to tell your momma."

The tears began to pour. "I tried to . . . last year, and she didn't believe me. She thinks the man walks on water. Just the other night she was talking about us going to North Carolina with him, so what's the point?"

"Monique, it's only a matter of time before he asks for something else, and are you going to take money for that, too?"

I knew what she was talking about. I'd tried to stop the whole thing, but Mr. Luther threatened to tell my friends about the dirty things I did with him. I couldn't risk that and become the laughingstock of the neighborhood. "I'm going to stop it before it gets that far. I promise."

Soon after that weekend, things changed. My moms was assigned new hours at work, putting her on back-to-back shifts, which left me at home in the evenings and overnight. She got in just before it was time for me to go to school. One morning, as I prepared my lunch, she surprised me with some horrible news. "Monique,

I asked Mr. Luther to look in on you before he goes to bed."

I stopped dead in my tracks. I started trembling and felt light-headed. I was going to faint. "What? Momma, I don't need—"

"Hush your mouth. It's already done. He's going to start coming by tonight."

"But, Momma . . ." I was taking this chance to try and tell her again 'bout the unspeakable things he'd been doing to me. "Mr. Luther, he—"

"Monique, it's done."

Maybe I should have been more forceful about trying to get her to listen. Maybe life would've been different had I done that.

That night, just as I had nestled into my bed, there was a knock at the door. I figured he'd go away if I didn't answer it. Had he been watching the house to see my bedroom light go out? He rapped at the door again, but this time I heard the lock turn. Moms had given him a key. I lay there in bed, heart pounding and unmoving, as if I'd been asleep for hours. The next thing I knew Mr. Luther was sliding into bed next to me. His dick was hard as steel when he rubbed it against my back. He stroked it up and down the middle of my spine to the tip of my underwear, and then he stopped. His breathing became heavier and his movements more swift. When he shot off, it hit my skin like hot acid. I didn't budge.

"Thank you, Li'l Miss Monique," he sighed and walked back out the way he had come.

This went on for weeks, on the days when Moms worked. I'd told Tangie that I wanted to run away, and she told me they'd only find me and make me come home. She offered to let me stay with her and her momma provided that I tell her momma what had been happening. There was no way I was going to do that, so I sucked it up and dealt with it, day in and day out.

On our last day of school, the teachers and staff gave us a dance where we were asked to wear our best. Since it was sweltering outside, the boys didn't have to wear suits, but they did have to wear ties. All of the girls were expected to be in dresses. My grandmother Viola Mae had made me this pink chiffon-and-taffeta sundress with spaghetti straps. It was supposed to be for church, but I convinced her to let me wear it to school first. I had on my first pair of sheer white stockings, and some brand-new Mary Janes that had a silver butterfly on the top of each shoe. Moms knew she wouldn't be home when I got in from school, so she told me to make sure I kept the dress clean for church that coming Sunday.

"Make sure you put it back on the hanger, too, when you take it off," she yelled down the hall as I dressed that morning.

Walking home from school, I decided I wanted a Popsicle from Mr. Chu's, the Korean store on the other side of the railroad tracks. He sold the red, white, and blue firecracker bomb pops that I loved. Tangie had gone straight home because she was leaving to spend the weekend with her father and needed to pack.

Crossing the railroad tracks, I saw there were puddles of mud and oil along my path, so I took a detour through the field. I'd walked through it before and never had a fear of running into a rat or an old dog. Just as I opened my Popsicle, someone grabbed me from behind, covered my mouth, and dragged me through the weeds over rocks and broken glass. Kicking and wrestling with my captor, I realized that my screams were muffled, and no one could hear me. I was pushed face first into the ground and didn't have to try very hard to figure out who was attacking me. I could smell the incense in his clothes and the liquor on his breath. It was Mr. Luther trying to snatch the last bit of innocence I had. I tussled with every ounce of strength a fifteen-year-old could muster, but he overpowered me, ripping at my underwear and stockings.

At one point, Mr. Luther snarled and growled at me, but I didn't have time to be scared. His upper body was lying on my legs while his arms had my upper torso pinned to the ground. He grabbed my crotch and rubbed it so hard and rough that it felt as if it were on fire. Then he thrust his fingers into my vagina and stuck his thumb in my butthole. I struggled to scream but my mouth filled with dirt. He flipped my frail body over and covered my mouth with one of his hands before I had a chance to call out. With his other hand, Mr. Luther released his dick and rammed it between my legs. My eyes bulged from their sockets as excruciating pain tore through my body. He wiggled his way deeper into my private part with no compassion or mercy. I managed to free one of my hands as he moaned and grunted, and I reached for a piece of broken glass that was strewn about the ground. When he lifted himself from me, still erect, I, in one fierce swing, sliced him across his dick. As he fell to the ground and rolled to his back, I jabbed him in his balls with the shard of glass one final time.

Standing in the mirror, I was faced with something I'd come to know all too well—fear. I was afraid Mr. Luther was going to come bursting through the door to finish his business. I was afraid I was going to jail. I was afraid my moms wouldn't love me anymore because I'd done this horrible thing, and I was afraid someone would know that I'd hurt Mr. Luther.

I removed my pink dress and placed it back on the hanger. I hung it in the bathroom with me as a reminder of what hell had been like for me. I turned on the hot water and contemplated whether I should take a bath or a shower. Taking a bath would force me to sit in my filth and allow it to soak further into my soul. I didn't want that.

As the water beat against my back, I watched the blood run down the drain with the dirt and the pain I'd experienced for years. I leaned against the tiled wall and thought about what I had allowed myself to get into. The hair bows, the dresses, the Mary Janes— all of those things made Mr. Luther like me and made him want me. I shed tears for every girl in the neighborhood at that moment. As I observed the suds swirl down the drain, I watched a part of me disappear, too.

I went to the bedroom and packed a bag with jeans, T-shirts, a jacket, and some tennis shoes, then I returned to the bathroom and pulled out a pair of scissors and cut my hair off down to the scalp. I took some wave pomade from the cabinet, spread it in my palms, and rubbed it into what was left of my straight black hair. In the sink was the femininity I was prepared to leave behind. Next to the pomade were two Ace bandages. I took them and wrapped them around my bosom until I was flat. I put a T-shirt on with a pair of jeans and borrowed a pair of Mom's work boots. I returned to the bathroom and revisited myself in the mirror.

In that moment, I'd made up in my mind that I wasn't going to stay around any longer to deal with anything that reminded me of Li'l Miss Monique. I didn't care if that bastard bled to death out there in the field. No more dresses, no more hair bows, and no more Mary Janes—ever.

I snatched up my shit and headed for the back door. Oh by the way, I'm now that niggah they call Mo.

STRAPPED
Mo

My moms didn't know I was packing heat. I got it from my boy, Jamal, when I was at the teenage runaway shelter. His ass had two of them because he'd run away from his stepdad who had been molesting him and beating his mother. I couldn't blame him for that because I was living proof that muthafuckers is crazy. Once I told him what happened to me out in the field that day, he told me he'd heard that the candy man had been in the hospital for a few days and that he had reopened for business. That bastard had a limp, but he was going to live. If that son of a bitch Mr. Luther even looked like he was stepping my way, it was really going to be all over. The nightmares would stop, and I'd be free to dream again.

The counselors called Moms within forty-eight hours of my arrival and told her what happened. The first time she came to visit she had problems looking at me, especially with the way I'd cut my hair and all. She hated the way I was carrying myself, and she detested the name Mo.

"Where did you get this Mo crap from? Your name is Monique."

I sat at the table carving my initials in the table with my fingernails. I was more into that than I was her visit. "I know they told you why my name is that."

"Why couldn't you come to me with this?"

I wanted to gouge her eyes out. "I did try to tell you, but you chose to ignore me."

Moms seemed like she was getting annoyed with me and started rushing me with my answers. "Why did you cut all your hair off, and why are you wearing your clothes like that?"

I wasn't liking Moms too much right then. "I . . ."

"Don't you hear me talking to you?"

The counselors were watching her and decided they'd had enough. One of them came from the back office and asked her to leave.

"I'm trying to talk to my daughter or whatever the hell she is."

"Ma'am, she needs her rest. Maybe you should come back when you've had some time to gather your thoughts. Your behavior isn't helping the situation."

Moms sat there, shaking her head. "Lawd Jesus. Help me, Father," she cried. She collected her things and got up from the table and stared at me like I was the villain. "Well, call me if you need me."

I didn't need her. I hated her, and instead of rising with her to embrace her, I tearfully turned and departed for my room.

To prevent further humiliation, I dropped out of school and spent my days and nights at the shelter. In the evenings, some of the boys and me would hang out on the corner by the Kitty Kat Club and watch the perverted folks go in and out. I wondered if Mr. Luther's ass ever went up in there. If I saw him, I would kill him, and my partners would back me up, too. He wouldn't even know it was me.

I'd been gone for almost two years, and Moms was still too ashamed to tell folks how I was doing. What was she gonna say, "Oh, Monique, she doing all right down there in that juvie home for crazy runaways?" She was too proud for that. I'd found a barber who cut my hair for me exactly the way I liked it. I'd actually let him cut me bald one time, but the fellas said it didn't look right on me because my face was too round.

The shelter had an arrangement with the deli next door to hire kids who were old enough to work. That's where I got my first job as a stock boy. They paid us under the table, so there was no papers to fill out and shit. As I requested, everybody called me Mo. One day while I was stocking the canned collard greens, this young lady approached me and asked me if we carried Glory food products. She was a nice-looking woman wearing denim capris with a tight yellow shirt to match. Other than that I didn't pay no more attention to her than I would have anybody else.

"Naw, we don't carry Glory stuff. We got Sylvia's, though."

"Oh, well, that's OK. I was looking for Glory." She turned to walk away but kept looking over her shoulder at me.

Later that evening, my partners and I was hanging out in front of the Kitty Kat Club when a group of ladies walked past us. Bringing up the rear was the same girl I'd seen at the store that day. When she got up closer to where I was standing, she stopped in front of me, leaned in, and asked, "So, this is your night job?" She had to have felt my piece tucked inside of my jeans.

I cracked a smile and said, "Nope. Just hangin' with the fellas." I looked over to where they were standing because they knew what was up. I was pretty sure they'd have jokes when we got back to the shelter.

"Oh."

"You cook dem greens?" I laughed.

Blushing, she responded, "Yeah, I did actually. Found some Glory greens at Mr. Habib's store." Her friends had stopped and gave her that bring-yo'-ass-on look. "I have to go."

Jamal was standing there chuckling when the girls finally went into the club. "Uh, you gonna handle that, Mo?"

"What you mean, playa? It's all good."

"A'ight, it's all good. You better watch yo'self."

That Friday, which was also payday, I was walking down past the club and found this novelty shop that sold rubber dicks and other freaky shit for the bedroom. Jamal had gotten me a fake ID, so I strolled in like I knew what I was looking for and was prepared to flash that bitch if I needed to. The dicks were in all shapes and sizes, colors and varieties. There were some that could squirt shit in you and some that vibrated. I merely wanted one that would look real beneath my zipper. The salesperson, who'd been busy when I first came in, approached me and asked if there was anything in particular I was looking for.

"I want something simple that I can wear all day long and be comfortable in," I told her.

The people who worked in those kinds of stores had to be some all-time freaks because her ass knew exactly what would work for me. She reminded me of those ladies who work in the fancy department stores who help women get fitted for bras.

"Now for the first few days you're probably going to look like you got your hands on some Viagra, but the way you fix that is to buy you some men's bikinis. Boxers might even work for you."

I tried it on, and I looked great. "I'll take it." I bought the harness and shit to wear with it, too. When I got back to the shelter, I locked myself in the bathroom so I could put on this new part of me that, as far as I was concerned, was permanent. I was sure I could wear it even while I was on my period, wearing it over my panties. My transformation was complete.

On the corner that same night, Miss Gurl and her friends walked by going to the club. I was looking pretty fresh with some new Timbs, new jeans, and a flannel plaid shirt. I'd thinned out quite a bit since high school, so everything hung off me. "What's up, Martha Stewart?"

The whole group busted out laughing because they knew she liked to cook, and although she appeared slightly embarrassed, she started laughing herself.

"You know you wrong," she said as she pressed her body against mine. She had to feel that bulge in my pants. "My name is LaQuita."

"My bad. LaQuita Stewart then."

"You're funny."

"I try." I felt like I had much game that night, and despite Jamal's evil looks every now and again, I was determined to holla at LaQuita.

"Look, I'm late for work. Can I come by and talk to you at the store tomorrow?"

"Yeah, you can do that. I get off at three."

"OK, I'll see you then."

As soon as I walked out of the store, I saw LaQuita standing across the street smoking a cigarette and holding a brown paper bag. I'd developed this trot like my partners and had even learned how to hold my dick while I was doing it. " 'Sup witcha?"

"Nothing much," she smiled. She smelled like vanilla and sugar.

"What's in the bag?" It had a big grease spot on the bottom, so it had to be food.

"Something for you. Compliments of LaQuita Stewart."

I opened the bag and saw a plastic container full of greens. On top of it was a piece of corn bread wrapped in Saran Wrap. I hadn't had greens and corn bread since I was at home with Moms. "Dayum, baby girl, you hooked a niggah up, didn't cha?"

"And they ain't from the can either. I made 'em this morning. I figured you don't get stuff like that in the shelter."

"How you know I'm at the shelter?" I was defensive.

"Everybody knows you guys are from the shelter. Calm down. It's not a big deal."

If she knew that, then I wondered what else she knew. "A'ight then, since you know sumthin' about me, tell me sumthin' about you."

"What do you wanna know?"

"You work at the Kitty Kat Club?"

"Yeah, I do," she said, taking a drag from her cigarette.

"What, you a dancer or sumthin'?"

Hesitating before she answered, LaQuita flicked her cigarette to the ground and replied, "Yeah, I'm a dancer. You got a problem with that?"

"Naw, do ya thang. You let dem men feel all over you?"

"Unh-unh. They not allowed to touch."

For some reason, I was relieved. LaQuita and me walked a few blocks to the basketball courts and sat there and talked until it got dark. She seemed cool but not cool enough to know my secret yet. I walked her to her apartment and told her I'd see her later. Couldn't define when later was, but I knew it would be soon.

Jamal was sitting on the steps of the shelter when I came in. "You been with that girl, Mo?"

I wasn't ashamed about it. "Yeah, why?"

Jamal had been like a big brother to me. He knew about the shit with Moms, he knew about my pain, and he knew my secret. "Look, if that girl ever finds out that you walking around with a plastic dick on, she's gonna have your business all out in the streets. Are you ready for that?"

"Mayne, I don't know. We just talkin'. Ain't nobody tryin' to get wit' nobody. I ain't never said nothin' about likin' chicks no way."

Jamal was an intelligent brother who could have had a lot of shit going for him if he ever got his head on right. Word had gotten back to him that when his mom tried to divorce his stepdad, the punk-ass bitch beat her into a coma. Jamal slipped into the hospital one night to see her, and it took everything in him to keep from going to bust a cap in his stepdad's ass. He cried like a baby on his mom's bed until the morning came.

"You know why that niggah beat my mom?"

"No, why?" I asked, taking a seat on the step below him.

"I had this aunt named Yvonne that wasn't really my aunt. She used to be my mom's girlfriend. I was crazy about her because she could cook and shit. I ain't never seen my mom so happy. Then, one day, out of nowhere, Yvonne just up and left. No phone calls, no letters, no nothing. Next thing you know I came home one day, and my mom was laying up with that fool. He was all right for a minute. About two months after he'd been living with us, Aunt Yvonne called and wanted to come back home. Mom tried to put Stanley out. She even fessed up and told him why she wanted him to go. That's when the beatings started. He grabbed me by the neck in front of her and made me suck his dick while he held a knife at my throat. That shit didn't have to happen to me but once before I knew I needed to leave. He told me if I ever told anybody he'd kill her."

"What about your aunt?"

"You remember that body they found in the river a while back?"

"Yeah, the woman who had been shot in the head."

"That was Yvonne." Jamal, the hardest fool in the shelter, was crying. Wiping his eyes, he whimpered, "I don't want you to end up like her. I know he did it because he said he'd kill her if she ever came around again. Mayne, you couldn't stop the bond she and my mom had." He looked off into the distance, shaking his head. "He caught them one night sitting in my mom's car. Soon after that was when Yvonne disappeared. That almost killed my mom, and to look at her in pain and in fear all the time, I couldn't take it, so I came here."

There was a time when I felt that no one could possibly hurt as badly as I did, and after hearing Jamal's story, I still felt that way. I understood why he packed heat. He was waiting for the perfect time to catch

Stanley alone. I could tell, though, Jamal had worked through his anger because when I first met him, he was spending every day running streets looking for Stanley. Then, he'd found more productive ways to occupy his time.

"Jamal?" I said.

"Yeah?"

"What do I do if I'm gay?"

He started laughing. "Don't do shit. But you need to tell that girl you ain't no niggah. If she cool wit' it, then work your magic and pop that coochie. It's about time you did that anyway."

"I mean, how am I supposed to know what to do?"

"Oh, you'll know. Trust me."

LaQuita and I chilled a lot after that. I'd saved up enough money to get me a little apartment that the counselors helped me find. They asked me if I wanted Moms to have the address, and I told them it was OK. I hadn't seen her in months so I knew she would never come to visit anyway. The place wasn't much, but it was mine. Outside of Jamal, I didn't have many friends. That made me enjoy LaQuita's company even more. As a housewarming gift, she bought me a leather loveseat and a television. One evening while we was watching TV, somebody knocked at the door like they was the po-po. *Who the fuck?* I'd been in the apartment for two months, and the only visitors I'd had were Jamal, LaQuita, and one of the counselors. With each knock, my heart raced and the thought pounded through my head that Mr. Luther had finally come to seek his revenge.

"You invite somebody over here, Quita?"

"No." She sat up on the loveseat, just as startled as I was.

I pulled out my nine-millimeter, released the safety, and walked slowly toward the door. Whoever it was had become impatient and was trying to turn the knob with one hand while pounding fiercely with the other. I was ready to blast his ass. "Who is it?" I yelled.

"It's your Mama. Now open this door."

I stood there contemplating what to do. Moms wasn't going away, especially since she knew I was in there.

"A'ight, hold on."

LaQuita, still sitting on the loveseat, was all geeked and excited. "You ain't never said nothin' about your momma. I can't believe I finally get to meet her."

There wasn't another room for me to send LaQuita into, and the closet had too much junk in it. Besides, Moms was going to come in and look through the place anyway.

"Before I open that door, I need you to know I love you . . . no matter what."

"OK," she said then smiled curiously.

Shoving the gun back in my pants, I opened the door, and Moms barged in, spitting fire like she was on the war path. "What the hell took you so long to open the door?"

"I thought it was somebody for the folks across the hall."

"You a damn lie. Who is this?" she asked, glaring at Quita as she took a seat next to her.

"Uh, this is my friend LaQuita."

Moms rolled her eyes and continued her tirade. "Monique, why couldn't you bring your ass back home to stay instead of movin' into a dump like this?"

I was fucked. She'd called me Monique. LaQuita's

gaze turned toward me, but she didn't move or say a word. Since motor mouth was telling everything, I saw no reason to hold back. "I'm more comfortable here."

"Monique, Moesha, Mo . . . whatever you callin' yourself, you too young to be livin' on your own."

I had to stop her. "What don't you get? I don't want to live with you. You want to blame somebody for me being like this then blame yourself. I tried time and time again to tell you that bastard was doing some awful shit to me, and you ignored me. Yeah, I tried to slice his dick off, and every day I wish I had. Because of that, I don't want shit to do with no man. I don't want no man touching me or kissing me or even looking at me. That's why I look like this."

Moms sat there conspiring against me. I didn't know what she had for Mr. Luther because she never tried to protect me from him. It was all about what I had done. She mean-mugged LaQuita again.

"So I guess you dykin' now?" she asked.

"What?" I cried.

"This tramp you got here."

I pulled my nine from the back of my pants. I'd had enough. "Get out." Her eyes were like tiny balls of fire. Through them, I saw the woman I used to get pickles for—the one who I wore the dresses, hair bows, and Mary Janes for. And I hated her.

"Oh, so now you bad cuz you call yourself bein' strapped? Well, lemme tell you somethin'. You goin' to hell. All this shit you dun brought on yourself ain't gonna do nothing but get you a first-class ticket to hell," she screamed at me.

By now, LaQuita had gotten up from the loveseat and was standing by my side with her hand resting on my arm. "Give me the gun, baby. Don't do this."

Pulling a gun on Moms was something I never thought I'd do. But as I looked at her, I felt nothing— no love, no compassion, no connection to her at all. If the gun had accidentally gone off, I probably would have dragged her body into the bathroom, cut it up Tony Soprano style, and put all the pieces into a big trunk and tossed her in the river. There wouldn't be no love lost either. "I hate her, Quita," I wept as I knocked her hand away from my arm.

"I know, baby, but give me the gun."

Moms was like a pit bull. She just wouldn't stop. She kept at me, hurting me more with every word. "You must still have some girl in you cuz you standin' over there cryin' like a ol' bitch." With that said, she stormed past LaQuita toward the door, slamming it when she left.

"You should've let me kill her," I said, handing my girl the gun.

"No, I wasn't going to let you do that. No matter what she says or how she acts, she's still your mother." LaQuita took me by the arm and guided me back to the sofa. Then she went into the kitchen and brought me back a glass of water. "So, when were you going to tell me about Monique?" she asked as she plopped down in the seat next to me.

"Never. As far as I'm concerned, she's dead." LaQuita felt my pain. My tone had changed, and it was clear that we'd never talk about Monique again. "I'm sure you want to get out of here, considering you know the truth now."

Sitting there kissing my muscles I worked hard at the shelter to get, LaQuita took me by the hand and said, "Actually, I thought I might hang around to get to know you better." With those words, LaQuita, the twenty-one-year-old dancer who'd never let any man at the club touch her and who could cook greens better than Moms ever could, and who'd kept me from ruining the rest of my life (because I was going to kill Moms's ass), made love to Mo that night and rescued me from my nightmare.

BEAUTY AND THE THUG
Mo

Although I walked around with my pants hung low over my boxers and a rubber dick dangling against my thigh, I couldn't figure out my place in the world. It had only been a few years since the attack, and no matter how much I did to run away from it, there was always something around to remind me of it. For one, there was Moms. All I wanted her to do was just listen. Dan, my counselor, said it would take time for her to come around. He must not've known Elise Cummings. Then I told him about me and Quita making love. "How did that make you feel, Mo?" It had only been a couple of days since it'd happened.

"When Quita started kissing me that night, I didn't know what I was supposed to do. My breath was all pasty with stale cigarette smoke and Schlitz Malt Liquor. I tried so hard to push away, but I couldn't. She kept telling me to act like it was my first time."

"Well, did you?"

Dan was educated but dumb sometimes, and we'd started these sessions at my house to keep me from being late for work all the time. My boss was riding my ass about coming in ten minutes late twice a week.

"Dude, this was my first time with a woman. I had never kissed a girl let alone lick a pussy, and I ain't even trying to do that yet. It was my first real sexual experience. I've tried to block that shit out with Mr. Luther, but it's hard."

"Mo, you've got to learn how to separate your emotions about the rape from the emotions you have for LaQuita. Those are truly not the same things. What happened to you with Mr. Luther was abuse. What you have with LaQuita could really be love."

The main thing I wanted to accomplish with my therapy was understanding, and to a degree, I felt Dan was rushing me. Just because this female was attracted to me didn't make me gay. I mean, I was like feeling the way Quita and me was digging on each other, but I wasn't sure if I was ready for the other stuff.

Quita fucked that dick like some shit out of a porno. The kissing was cool. The fondling was cool. That part made me want her. My pussy wasn't spitting fire or nothing like that, though. To me, she was fucking the dick and Mo. Not Monique. By now, I was furious.

"Dan, I'm not gay, and I don't want you sitting here treating me for that. I don't like pussy that way. We're at this point because of Mr. Luther."

"Exactly!"

Our session ended just like that. Personally, I was more confused about everything than I was when we got started. I was a man! I wanted to hide that desire Mr. Luther preyed on. Why couldn't anybody understand that? I went on to work as usual, and once I got into the store, I saw Quita waiting for me on the dog food aisle. "Wassup?"

She was standing there dressed for work in a black trench coat and red vinyl platform boots. She towered above me in those four-inch heels. "Nothin', babe. How was therapy?"

"It was a'ight. You know . . . same shit different day."

Quita smelled ravishing. She was wearing something that had snuck up my nose and sat its ass on my nostrils. I didn't know what was happening to me.

"Hey, what kinda perfume you got on? You smell wonderful," I said softly as I reached to hug her and kiss her on the neck.

"Red Door by Elizabeth Arden. You really like it?"

"Hell, yeah." As the scent intensified around to the back of her neck, I made myself step away. "All I gotta say, girl, is meet me outside when you get off work."

When her shift was over, Quita met me out front as I'd asked. I had a cheeseburger from Dixie Queen with a cherry freeze waiting for her. We stopped at the store to get her a 7-Up, and I picked up a bag of Cheetos for myself. At the apartment, I took a seat on the sofa and watched Quita begin to undress. She was wearing this red halter dress that matched her boots perfectly, and I thought she looked beautiful in it.

Slowly, as if giving me my own private show, she slid the dress off and onto the floor, revealing a red garter and red thigh highs. I was playing a tune or two in my head to help with my imagination as she unsnapped the garters. When she got down to her panties, she asked if I wanted to help, and after I thought about it for a hot second, I said yes. Still in her boots, she strutted over to me and stood in front of me, tossing her pussy right in my face but then drew back. "I hate to do this to you, but I'm going to take this on to the shower." It was like she got some sick pleasure out of teasing me. It was all good, though, because I knew Quita was about being fresh after coming in from work. "Care to join me?"

"No," I replied. "But what you can do is allow us to start where we left off." And that's exactly what she did.

With her thighs still moist and sticking to the lining of her boots, I pulled them down quickly and leaned back in my seat on the sofa. The hair on Quita's pussy was shaved to form a single line from the top of her hairline to the tip of the split. It was cute and all, and I guess she did it for her performances. I'd heard she was butt-ass naked on stage.

"Well, whatcha gonna do with it, playah?" she asked.

What? I thought. She brought it closer.

"You got all this in front of you, and all you can do is just sit there?"

Honestly, I was confused. I didn't know I was supposed to do anything. "Well, uh, Quita, what is it you want me to do?"

She straddled my lap with her pussy spread over my thighs. Quita was starting to breath heavily as she worked her hips into mine. Then, in one swift movement, she lifted herself enough for her pussy to once again be right in my face. "Mo, I want you to eat me," she moaned erotically. I think it was more *neurotically* because she'd lost her damn mind. "I want you to make me cum."

In an instant, I picked Quita up off me and put her on the other side of me. "Babe, we gotta talk."

Seemingly bothered but even more so concerned, Quita asked, "What's wrong?"

Finding the words was easy. Getting them to make sense was something else. "What do you want from me?"

"What do you mean, sweetie?" She'd slid back against the other end of the sofa and had pulled a blanket over her.

"Maybe I mean more like why are you attracted to me? The other night we had sex, and basically, you fucked Mo . . . not Monique."

"Right, right."

"But just now, you wanted me to eat you like a lesbian would, and I'm not that."

Quita sat silent for a couple of minutes before she answered. "So, you're saying you're not gay?"

"Yes, that's what I'm saying. I like you and everything, but it's not that kind of like. In my mind, I'm a young man. I wear my clothes like one; I kid around with my pardners like one; I take on the world like one. Answer me this . . . why did you start coming on to me outside the club?"

"Mo, I knew you were a girl. Believe it or not, you have the softest eyes. Now, I wasn't about to bust you in front of your boys. I figured you'd tell me in your own time. Now, if you want me to love Mo, then I'll love Mo, and if you want me to love Monique, I'll love Monique. Either way, it's up to you."

I was slightly comforted. "So you like the thug in me?"

"Hell, yeah," she said throwing back her blanket with her legs spread wide open. "Now, come show me the nucca you really are."

Unzipping my jeans, I whipped out my Master D and worked it on her. I raised her legs to my shoulders and plunged inside of her walls. Quita massaged the back of my neck with her fingertips as we met eye-to-eye, soul-to-soul. Right before I felt this surge of energy rush through me, I stopped and pulled out. The jerk startled her. "What's wrong, baby?"

Relaxing her legs to the sofa, I asked, "Do you still want me to eat you?"

Quita chuckled like a little school girl, "Yeah, but only if you want to."

The smell of her made me want her. The gentleness of her touches made me want her. The love in her eyes when she looked at me made me want her. Using my imagination, I could do this.

"OK," I replied.

I slid down between her legs and first rested my head on the inside of her right thigh. I leaned in and kissed every inch of her skin until I had run out of space. I slowly moved to the other side and repeated my moves. My kisses extended downward to the bottom of her ass. I was loving this shit. Gliding my tongue from the bottom of her ass to the bottom of that split was nothing but joy for me. I entered right at the point of insertion, and she melted in my mouth like ice cream on a hot summer's day. I imitated Master D's movements with my tongue and made stutter steps through the walls of her pussy. Quita was literally quivering all over.

"Do you want me to stop?" I asked.

"Oh, God, no," she whispered. With my tongue now vibrating her clit, I entered her cavern with four of my fingers. "Ooooh, Mo, give me another one, please, baby, please!" she shrieked. I already had over half my hand in her. The only thing I knew to do was make a fist and go for it. "Ooooooooohhhhhhh, yes! Ooooooooohhhhh-hhh, yes, Mo! Fuck me, baby! Fuck . . . me . . . fuck . . . me!" Quita was shuddering like she was in convulsions. Next thing I knew, she was fast asleep.

TWENTY-ONE
Mo

My twenty-first birthday couldn't come quick enough. Quita and I had been together for close to three years, and I was feeling a whole lot better about who I was. I enjoyed walking through Southland Mall with her on my arm and watching them other niggahs roll they eyes at me. I'd blaze a fool in a minute, and Quita knew it so she made me leave me heatah at home. The deli bought some more shelves and knocked a few walls and became Liberty Supermarket. I'd gotten a little promotion and was able to move us into a better apartment out in Whitehaven. With the kinda money Quita was making, we could've moved sooner, but I was supposed to be taking care of *her*. Nuff said.

The day before my birthday, Quita says, "You still ain't told me what you want for your birthday."

I couldn't tell her this, but the only thing I was looking forward to on my birthday was to finally be able to go inside The Kitty Kat Club!

"Baby, you know you don't have to get me anything. I told you that," I responded.

In previous years, she'd always gotten me a Dickie shirt, a pair of Timbs, and some cologne. This year was probably not going to be any different, and I was cool with that. My idea of an extravagant dinner was a Dilly plate with an extra piece of meat from Piccadilly's. I wasn't that hard to please.

"Well, I figured you tell me that so I planned a special night out for us. I took off tomorrow night . . ."

Damn, so much for The Kitty Kat Club.

". . . and we're going to The Half Shell out in East Memphis. Then I got tickets for us to go see Mary J. Blige at the Pyramid, and after that, I got a big surprise for you."

"You takin' me to The Kitty Kat Club?" I jived bouncing up and down on the bed.

"Uh, no. You don't need to be goin' in there. It's something else way better than that."

My spirit was broken, but the agony would pass. I surely thought since I'd been too young to get in the club before, Quita would be anxious to finally get me in there. That damn security guard was worse than immigration. He knew about how old I should be because I was hanging around with the other cats from the shelter. I couldn't wait to blast his ass with my I.D.

"Uh, Quita, I know we ain't about to take the bus to all these places."

She cackled at me, "No, silly. We're not takin' the bus. I rented us a car." Now, I forgot to mention Quita was two years older than me so I found out in our second year together. She'd told a lie or two so she'd be able to dance at the club.

"Oh, shit! For real?"

"Yeah, baby. I got us a Crown Vic. We goin' in style for your birthday." She was more excited than I was.

At this point, there was nothing that could ruin my day. Well, almost.

I was scheduled to work on my birthday, and I didn't make a deal about it because I could use the extra money. In my new position, I was a cashier and was pretty good at what I did. My hair had grown into a short natural that I got touched up weekly at the barbershop. I was a regular customer at Gus's shop but never offered too much in conversation. I respected Gus because the first time I went in there he asked me if I wanted the works which was a cut, wash, shave and facial treatment. I was like why not. I was wearing a black hoodie, some black cargo pants, and a pair of black Lugz. He asked me to take off my hoodie so it wouldn't get wet in the shampoo bowl. I was a'ight with that and was adequately prepared with a black T-shirt on underneath. Gus gave me the cut and led me to the shampoo bowl. I reclined in the chair and stretched my neck back. He had his back to me while he was talking to another barber and was basically treating me like the rest of the clients. By the time he turned around, my eyes were already closed, and I was ready for him to come on with the come on so I could go on about my business. The water was running and periodically splashing against my face. I opened my eyes shocked to see Gus staring at me but more directly at my elongated neck and the apparent absence of an Adam's apple. I pleaded with my eyes for him to not judge me. *Just do your job, man*, I prayed. I didn't say a word, and neither did he. Obviously, I wasn't going to need that shave. In all these years, he has yet to utter one word about it.

Anyway, I had rang up this old lady with her turnip greens and vinegar when I thought I saw a black shadow walk past the lane. Suddenly, I got this eerie feeling and became a little sick to my stomach. "Young man, are you all right?" she asked. "You look like you just saw a ghost or something."

"Ah, yes ma'am, I'm fine. You have a good day."

I looked up in the booth for Al, my manager, to ask if I could take a break, but he wasn't there. The longer I stood there the sicker I got. I saw Terry, the assistant manager, and asked if I could step out for a minute.

"Well, Mo, I can't spare you right now. Can you wait another twenty minutes until Octavia comes back from lunch?"

I couldn't wait that long. "I really need to step out a minute."

All the lanes had lines of customers, and in their reality, I didn't need to leave. In mine, I needed to get the fuck out of there. Terry hadn't even waited for me to answer her. She'd disappeared into the crowded aisles. I was peeking over folks, literally jumping up and down so I could find her.

"Can you ring this up for me?"

I froze. I couldn't move my feet, and I couldn't look up. I felt the knot in my necktie tightening around my neck. I recognized the voice and tried my best to not lose it.

"No, sir," I said. "I'm closed."

I felt the old man look around to try to understand why I would say such a thing when my light was on and a line of people was behind him. "You sure about that, son?"

Terry had suddenly appeared and overheard me telling the old man I was closed. She knew I never caused any trouble and seemed curious as to what made me click like that. I believe the steady stream of tears gave it away.

"Sir, she can take you on number six," Terry said. She turned my light off, took me by the hand and led me to her office in the back of the store. "Mo, honey, what's going on with you?" she asked, patting me on the thigh. "Take a seat."

Terry was a short, frumpy old White woman who always wore the same pair of brown polyester pants with elastic in the waist. I guessed she considered it her uniform or it was truly the only pair of pants she owned. Whatever rules Al had made, it was her job to find a way to bend them.

I wept quietly, and if she didn't know I was a girl by now, then I'd mastered the game. "Uh, I can't tell you that," I said gently. "I know I wasn't professional out there, and I'm sorry for that."

I'd been working at Liberty Supermarket on Lamar for a good while, and no one had ever discovered my secret.

"No, it wasn't, hun. Best be glad Al wasn't here because he would've fired you on the spot."

Sniffling, I replied, "I know."

Terry understood me not wanting to share what was wrong and offered to send me home. I accepted, and when I got on the bus, I stayed on it until they told me I had to get off because they were taking it back to the hub.

Walking down Lamar, I took a turn on Bellevue and headed toward Whitehaven. I had a hellified walk ahead of me, but I needed it. As I got closer to the apartment, I stopped at the Mapco and picked up two forties. I didn't have to worry about I.D. because the cashier and I were cool like that. I got to the complex a few minutes later, but instead of going home, I went and sat by the pool. With one of the forties in me, I was ready to dive in and sink straight to the bottom. I popped open the other one, and in two long drags, I emptied it. I put my head on the table and sobbed like the woman I had been reminded of earlier the day before.

"Where the fuck were you?" I heard faintly, and those words were accompanied by a smack across the head. "Mo, do you hear me?" Quita yelled.

I was too dazed to respond and too drunk to raise my head. It was the beginning of an overcast day with the sun nowhere to be found. I knew she was angry with me for disappearing on her like I did, but I had no choice. I sat upright in the chair that was full of dirt and cobwebs and cleared my eyes.

"Mr. Luther came in the store yesterday."

Quita's demeanor quickly went from I'm-gonna-fuck-you-up to baby-I'm-so-so-sorry. "Oh, my God, Mo. How . . ."

"I don't know, baby. He was like right there in front of me. I had my heatah on me, but I couldn't do nothin'. I was helpless. It literally took the breath out of me."

"Did he recognize you?"

"No, he didn't."

"Good. What do you need me to do for you?"

"Really, I just need you to hold me."

Quita pulled up a chair and put my head to her chest.

Back at the apartment, I helped Quita clean up the balloons and streamers from what was supposed to have been my late night surprise party. I felt a little bad about missing it, but she said everyone had a good time—without me. In the bedroom, I found a man's tailored black pantsuit laying across the bed with a note attached stating, FOR THE MAN IN MY LIFE."

The malt liquor had my stomach a little upset, and I ran to bathroom. It was coming out of both ends, and after puking and shitting my guts out, all I wanted to do was sleep. Quita came in about 5:30 that evening and told me she was headed to work. "Are you gonna be here all night?" she asked. The light in the room was blinding me.

"Probably so," I mumbled into the pillow. "Can you close the blinds, please?"

"Baby, they already closed. Get you some rest, and I'll see you when I get home."

The minute I heard the door lock, I hopped out of bed and into the shower. When I was finished, I called Jamal and asked if he was ready.

"Damn, skippy, I'm ready," he said loudly through the phone. "I told you when you was ready, I was gon' be ready."

Jamal had actually turned twenty-one three months before I did but wanted us to go to The Kitty Kat Club together.

There was a line when we got there, and that wasn't unusual. We just fell in with the rest of the fools trying to get a peep at the kitties. Bustah the security guard had already spotted us in the line and was waiting on us to get up front so he could bust us out in front of everybody.

"Here we go," he said. "Y'all azzes know you ain't about to get up in here. So just turn your happy azzes around and bounce."

I was like a little kid who couldn't wait to show off his new shoes. "Bam! I'm twenty-one, nucca!"

"Bam! Me, too, punk!" Jamal chimed in.

Bustah snatched the I.Ds and went through them with a fine-tooth comb. He checked the pictures, four or five times. Reluctantly, he handed them back to us and he frisked us. I'd left my heatah at home.

"So much as a peep out of you two, and I'm calling the cops. Understand?"

"Whatevah," Jamal said as he tossed a wad of spit against the brick column Bustah was holding up.

Ass everywhere. On the tables, on the bar, on the poles, on the stage, on the chairs. To me, it was like a chocolate festival—milk, white, dark, thick, hot. All of the above, dammit! Jamal's eyes were bucked, and his mouth hung open so long gnats had started landing in it. We took a seat at the bar, and our dumb asses didn't even know what to ask for.

"Uh, uh, gimme a wine cooler," Jamal requested.

I, like the bartender, was stumped. "Niggah, you up in here with the grown folks and all the ass you can digest in a single sittin', and you orderin' damn Kool-Aid?"

"Shit, I ain't nevah ordered no drink from a bar before. I . . ."

"Pardner, give this fool a double shot of Hen, and I'll take one, too. And keep'em comin'," I requested.

The room was packed with men, old and young. I was shocked at the number of women in the club, though. They had they own tables across the front, and there was even peepshow for just the ladies. I wondered what that was all about because the room for it was so packed you couldn't even get through the aisle on that side.

"This y'all first time in here?" the bartender asked as he slid our drinks to us.

"Yeah," I answered.

"Well, just so you know, you look like it, too." He laughed. "I can give you a tour right here from your seats if you want."

"That's cool with us." Jamal grinned. I swear his ass was acting like a twelve-year old boy who had just got his first nut and was ready to take on the whole cheer-leading team.

"OK, over there to right is the VIP section. By the looks of y'all, ain't neither one of you gonna ever be over there so no need to tell you about it. Back behind that partition is the entrance to the peepshows. You gotta pay to go in there. It's fifty dollahs for ten minutes. On the left is the private rooms for lap dances and whatever else you want. That's one hundred dollars and up. Your broke asses ain't gonna never be able to go over there neither. Then right here, just off the bar is the For Women Only Section. You have to go down the stairs and through another hallway to get to it. That's two hundred for the lap dances, three hundred for the peepshow for ten minutes, and a one-night pass is one thousand dollars. With that, you get all access—all night long. But, you ain't got to worry about that because what? You ain't women."

"You can't even get to the stairs to get down there," I said complaining.

"Son, what you worried about it for?" the bartender inquired. "It ain't for you. I will tell you this, though. There's a chick down there named Miss . . ."

"Excuse me, bartender," a well-dressed dude summoned. "I want to place an order, please." The cat must've been a regular because the bartender dropped the conversation and scurried over to the other side of the bar.

* * *

Me and Jamal had taken down maybe three drinks and an eyeful of tits and asses before he started asking me the kinda questions Dan should've been asking me.

"Man, what's up with you and Quita?"

"What you mean?" I tossed back another drink.

"You know, how y'all workin' out considerin'?"

"Aw, man, we good. Had a little scare yesterday, though."

"Yeah, I bet she blasted yo' ass for not showing up last night."

Staring at myself in the mirror behind the bar, I never even responded to the comment. "Mr. Luther came up in the store yesterday, and I lost it."

"What? Did that fool know who you was?"

"No, he ain't say nothin'. I was pretty fucked up behind that the rest of the day."

"Shit, no doubt, no doubt."

I was discreetly glancing over my shoulder checking out the booties to see which one of them belonged to me. There were white ones, black ones, yellow ones, but I didn't see my honey-colored tan one. Right as I had decided to get up and take a stroll, the bartender came back.

"Sorry about that fellahs, but he tips very well, and you two don't know squat about being up in da club," he kidded. "Now, where was I?"

"You was about to tell us about somebody down there in the ladies' part," Jamal said.

"Oh, yeah, yeah. My bad. Miss Q is her name, and the women love her to death. The bitch is bad."

"Dang, we can't get to see her? Just a peek?" I asked.

"I'm gonna do this for you this one time since you're still wet behind the ears and need to be broke in. I'm about to go on my break, and I'll sneak you down there."

In unison, me and Jamal said, "Bet!"

"Meet me over by the exit sign in five minutes."

Our asses was there in two minutes. My heart was racing, and Jamal had wood. "Man, can't you do somethin' with that?"

"I'm tryin'!" he snapped, wobbling from side to side.

"See you gon' be the reason we don't get down there."

Soon as the bartender walked up, he spotted Jamal's issue. "Look, you gonna have to do somethin' with that before I take you down these stairs. You ain't about to be the reason I lose my job."

"I'll be right back," and Jamal ran off to the restroom.

"My name's Mike by the way," he said, giving me a handshake.

"Mo—nice to meet you."

Anxiously watching the clock over the bar, Mike added, "So you ain't been to the butt-naked club."

"No, I ain't. Just turned twenty-one yesterday."

"Oh, OK," he laughed. "That explains a lot." He took a quick look up the hallway. "Speaking of that, here comes the two-minute brotha."

Mike led us down the long staircase that stopped at a huge wooden door. There was three deadbolts on it and a padlock. The only door I'd ever seen like that was at my old apartment.

"What's down here?" I asked.

"Liquor, baby, liquor. And that's why it feels good to be the only niggah with the keys," he said, dangling the ring in front of our faces.

We walked through the stockroom that was full of boxes and plastic containers with glasses and bar supplies in them. The closer we got to the other side of the room you could faintly hear music. There was another big door like the one we'd just came through. "What do you use this room for?"

"Well, obviously, for storage, but on occasion, the dancers cut through here because they can't get in through the other entrance."

"Oh."

The music was louder now as Mike opened the door. "Now, you about to see some shit on the other side of this door that's gonna blow your mind. Please don't touch the dancers. If you do, you'll find security on your ass like flies to shit, and you'll be banned from the club for life. The main rule for us is don't touch the dancers anywhere on the premises. Are we clear?"

"Crystal," Jamal and I chimed in graciously.

There had to be about two hundred women tightly packed into the room throwing money toward the stage like candy pouring from the sky in a Skittles commercial. Mike let us stand in the back of the room.

"Now this girl here is about done. Miss Q comes on after her. I want you to watch what happens when she takes the stage."

Before we knew it, the number of women in the room seemed to double. Where would all these women fit? Late-comers were plum shit out of luck, and we even struggled with our view. The lights went up and then down again. Ladies started screamin' and yellin' "Miss Q! Miss Q! Miss Q!" One girl had passed out and had to be carried out before the show got started. The minute Miss Q entered the stage I was ready to leave. She was completely nude. The money flooded the stage like falling rose petals. Quita was droppin' it like it's hot for a room full of dykes.

"Uh, Mike, man, we can go." And I really didn't want Jamal seeing this.

"What! You wanna leave now? She ain't even. And then she's gonna. What about the . . ."

Jamal was feeling me. "Pops, this scene ain't for us. We can roll out."

I left the club with a huge chip on my shoulder and ran right home to get my heatah. I wasn't going to do nothing with it, though. I was angrier than I thought I'd ever be about Quita's dancing. I knew she was a dancer, but I had thought she was dancing for the men. They could only fantazize about her. The women? That was different. Me and about seven other dudes from the shelter was standing across the street when the back door of the club opened and the dancers filed out. "Come on, y'all. I'm going over to see if I can get a autograph tonight from one of the new ladies." Yeah, I was frontin'. I was trying to get next to Quita.

They all jumped on the bandwagon. "Yeah, we wanna get one, too." One thing I'd learned about niggahs that don't have nothing to do with their lives is that they quick to fall in and do stupid shit together.

From the jump of our relationship, Quita told me about the inner workings of the club. Everybody on the block knew what time Bustah started locking the place down. I'd watched Bustah step away to go to do a final sweep of the bathrooms and the stairwells.

"Wassup, Quita?" I asked, rolling up on her like a gangbustah.

"Hey, Poo-Poo. What you doin' here this time of night?" She stopped just beyond the entrance to the club. "Aren't you supposed to be at the house restin'?"

My boys was standing under the awning laughing at some hookahs passing by in red and blue wigs. "Uh, I decided I was going to come up here and surprise you."

"I see. I told you there was nothin' here for you to really see."

"Yeah, you did, but you ain't tell me you was dancin' for women up in there." That Hen I'd had earlier was still heavy on me.

It was a bit breezy outside, and Quita pulled the belt of her coat tighter. "Mo, can we talk about this at home? It's freezin' out here."

"No, I want to talk about it right here, right now, at the scene of the crime."

"Scene of the crime? You've been drinkin' and aren't makin' any sense. Let's go home."

I grabbed at her arm as she tried to pass me, but I missed. "Quita! Don't walk away from me."

"Mo, look, let's go home. We can talk there."

"No, let's do it here," I insisted.

"OK, you know what? You win. What is it?"

"How can you go in there and show your body like that in front of all of those women?"

Quita blew a gasket. "You're crazy. Those *women* in there have paid me enough money over the past three years to help take care of your ass. Those *women* in there want to be entertained and not fucked. Those *women* in there respect me while the jackass men in there make sickening faces at me waggin' their damn tongues at me like I'm a piece of meat. And last I checked, despite what *you* say, you *are* one of those *women* in there! Now can we go home?"

The nerve. I reached for Quita's arm again and right as I caught it, Bustah's big ass, walked out. "What I'd tell you, niggah?"

Even though she was mad as hell at me. Quita stepped up, "Bustah, I got this. Don't worry about it."

"Unh-unh, rules are rules, and that punk knows it. The folks on they way."

"What! This is my business, Bustah. Not club business."

"Yeah, you might be right. This is your business. But where you standin'? On the premises of the K-I-T-T-Y K-A-T C-L-U-B! I'm through with it." Bustah got on his two-way and called the peoples on us saying we was trespassing and harassing the dancers.

The po-po must've been right around the corner because they asses was there in a split second. And they brought the fuckin' wagon. Me and my situation, I couldn't say nothin'. Quita looked at me with tears in her eyes, pleading for me not to run. Three of my homeboys who knew the folks was looking for them took off runnin' and got away. I didn't put up a fuss or a struggle. When I was asked to place my hands above my head, I did so, revealing the top of my heatah.

"Put your hands up!" they ordered. "Get on your knees!"

I did what I was told and in a matter of seconds my life was changin' . . . again. Quita reached out for me, but was pushed away by Bustah and Mike. I was thrown to the ground with a knee to my back and handcuffed. We were all loaded into the wagon and taken downtown. During the ride Jamal whispered in my ear, "Try your best to not say a word. If they find out about you, it can get worse."

The ride took about ten minutes and me and the others were taken to the intake side of 201 Poplar. We walked through what was a short tunnel before we saw a deputy. "You get one phone call. Choose it wisely," he said.

Standing in line for the phone, I ran down the short list of people I could call. When my turn came I said a prayer hoping the phone would be answered. "Hello?"

"Hey, it's me. I'm in jail and I need you to come get me before . . ."

"I know. I know. Oh Jesus, I know. I'm on my way."

The five of us were first moved into a five-by-ten holding cell with seven other men. There was a nine foot steel bench, a toilet, and a sink. The cell smelled like a combination of weed, whiskey, musk, and cheap cologne. Jamal stayed close to me as if to protect me from the others.

"Man, why did you have the heatah on you? You ain't have it when we was at the club," Jamal stated.

"Man, I don't know. I was so mad at Quita I went home and got it. I don't like being without it."

"Mo, do you know how much trouble we could get into right now?"

"We? Um, I was the one with it, not you."

"Yeah, but where'd you get it from?"

I guess I wasn't really thinkin'.

Intake was fingerprinting and mug shots. I watched them carefully to see how they listed my gender, and from what I could tell, everything said "male." Nobody ever asked any different. In processing, Jamal was right behind me. After that it was off to the medic.

"Open your mouth, please." I opened my mouth as wide as I could, and for first time in my life, I was ashamed of my bad breath. "Thank you. How much do you weigh?"

"About one hundred and fifty pounds."

"How tall are you?"

"About five-seven."

It was really stupid for her to sit and ask me all these questions when they had all that shit to determine your weight and my height right there in front of her face. Lazy bitch. We went through about ten more rather intrusive questions before I was sent to some kinda counselor. Nobody ever said who these people actually were. You just assumed by the shit they were doing to you what their job might be. This broad looked like they just called her ass at the house, she got out the bed and came right on to work.

She approached me. "Mr. Cummings, do you know why you're here today?" *Mr.?* I thought.

Jamal was standing there guiding me through my answers. This time he told me to nod my head. She wrote something down and asked another question.

"I hope you're aware that your friends will likely go home and return for court later in the morning."

Jamal didn't tell me what to say behind that. I beefed up a little. The lady was looking at me like she was waiting for me to say something. "What?" I asked.

"Young man, do you realize the trouble you could be in?" She sat there flipping through papers like she had something on me. I know it wasn't shit in there.

"I mean, what you want me to say? I ain't dun nothin'." I was scared as hell, but I refused to let her see it.

"Look, it's your first arrest, so you might be able to go home with your friends, but just like them, you're going to have to come back tomorrow morning. They got you down here charged with disorderly conduct and possession of a concealed weapon. Get you a good lawyer, and they might dismiss it."

"Whatevah," I mumbled.

Jamal and I were led to another slightly larger cage.

The guards in the watchtower could see every move we made, and if they wanted to, they could hear every word we said.

What was supposed to only be a couple of hours I was told ended up being a few hours. Niggahs who got there after me was already being sprung. Jamal was more patient than me and knew how to handle the stress.

"Dude, you can't be up in here trippin'. This is the last step right here. When they let you outta here, you on your way home. Who'd you call anyway?" he asked.

Sitting there laughing at myself for believing she'd really come to help me, I blurted out, "My moms."

Jamal couldn't believe his ears. "Your moms? Mayne, you woulda been bettah off calling Quita or Dan. It's been what three, four years since y'all talked?"

"'Bout that, I guess." It was coming up on noon, and my stomach was growling. "Ay, when y'all gonna feed a niggah?"

"Mo! Stop it, man! This is bad, real bad." The deputies kept walking past, looking at me and shaking their heads.

A couple of minutes later a dude came by in a blue jumpsuit with a meal cart. There was sandwiches on it wrapped in wax paper, and this huge tub of orange-colored liquid.

" 'Bout time. Y'all about to starve a niggah up in here," I said, fussing. I was handed the wax square with no napkin. Jamal opened his first. He took a look and closed it back up.

"What's wrong?" I asked.

"Peanut butter and honey? Who the hell eats that, especially on this hard-ass bread? Bread so hard feel like crackers."

I took my chances and ate mine. "Ay, if you ain't gonna eat that, hand it here." Jamal tossed his over to me, and I demolished it. "Can a bruh get some more of that orange Kool-Aid?"

Again, Jamal got his first. He turned his nose up at it. "I can't drink that."

Then it hit me. "Yo' ass got a hangover. Ah, you got faded and can't handle yo' shit. Lemme have yours," I said as I guzzled mine.

Seconds later, a deputy came to the cage with a clipboard. "Stevens and Cummings?" he yelled.

"Yeah," we both answered.

"Come on, let's go." He unlocked the door and told us to wait while he signaled to the gatekeeper behind the big window that he could buzz us out. "You need to stop by window twenty when you get to the end of the tunnel."

When the buzzer sounded, we broke like we was running the hundred-meter dash. I got to the window first. "Which one are you?" dude asked.

"Uh, duh? Don't you have the mug shot?"

The man had on coke bottle thick glasses and jacked up teeth. "Look, you ain't far enough away from that door down there to not be sent back."

"Whatevah. I'm Mo." He gave me a shit-load of paper to sign, and I was that funny niggah. I signed everything with a X. Dude told us we was being released on our own recognizance as if I ain't know.

"You must report to Division Nine at 9:30 in the morning. Don't be late, and you need to have an attorney with you."

"A'ight."

Jamal had to go to court, too, but not the same courtroom, and he didn't say nothing about having to get a lawyer. I ain't care. I was glad to be out the joint.

Busting out the door, Jamal said he was going back to the crib to take a shower, and I wanted, for some silly reason, to see Moms. I took the bus over to Castalia and walked across the tracks to Person. Making my way to the corner of Person and Cooper Avenue, I stood there looking up Cooper as if it were my life story. It had been years since I'd been over there. The days of running through the playground at Magnolia School; the days of swinging on the monkey bars in my dresses and Mary Janes; the days of trotting back and forth to the candy man with Tangie. All of that was staring me right smack in the face. I jetted up Cooper past Wabash and the schoolyard and made the right turn onto Turner Avenue. Moms lived in the last house on the street at the end of the cove. When the trains passed by, it was like they were on top of our heads. Granny Viola Mae lived three houses up the street, and Aunt Penny lived across the street from her. None of them had seen me since I became Mo, and there was no telling what moms had told them.

I was still wearing my clothes from the club—a Sean John pullover shirt, some jeans, and Timbs. The front door was open when I walked up the steps, and I heard Moms on the phone, cackling like she was on a comedy show or something. She had the radio blasting some O'Jays and didn't even notice me at the door. I yanked at the screen, but it was locked. "Moms," I yelled.

She scooted over to the door in her house shoes, unlatched it, rolled her eyes at me, and kept on talking.

"Damn, you ain't even gonna get off the phone for me?" I slammed the door and put the lock back on. Moms was frying some chicken, baking a cake, and picking peas all while she held the phone between her ear and her shoulder. It smelled like the chicken house, but I ain't want to eat shit out of there. "Moms!"

Wearing a black moo-moo and a pair of Fila shower shoes with some of her tracks missing, she reluctantly got off the phone. "What the hell is it, Monique?"

"Why ain't you come get me out?"

Taking a drag from her Newport, she said, "I don't know."

"But you said you was comin'."

"I got tied up, Monique, shit," she commented while turning chicken. "Besides, everybody I called wasn't even at home."

I got up and walked over to my elementary school pictures on the wall. Damn hair bows, dresses, and Mary Janes. She didn't have no pictures of me as Mo even though I'd sent her one or two over the years.

"Well, I ain't need you no way. They lemme out."

"Good," she said flicking ashes in the dishwater. She never left the kitchen. "Want somethin' to eat?"

"Naw, I'm good." I was lying my ass off. That chicken smelled so mutherfucking good! "Uh, I got to be in court in the mornin'. You gonna come down there?" I tried every which way I could to reach out, but she would just knock me down.

"I doubt it. Got somethin' to do." I hated her. Since I'd been with Quita, she stayed away. "Where's that gurl you live wit?" I knew that was coming. I remembered a time when you could damn near eat off my mother she was so clean. I don't know what happened to her.

"I guess she at the house. I ain't seen her today."

"Oh, well," she said, contaminating the air with her cigarette smoke. "She oughta be there wit-cha."

I gave up. I didn't need her, and I was on a mission to prove it. "Did you ever talk with Dan?"

Pulling her lemon pound cake from the oven, she frowned in the face of the heat. "No, was I supposed to?"

I know she knew she was supposed to talk to him. I was sitting right in front of him when he called her. I heard him ask her if she was going to at least come to one meeting with him, and she agreed. He's never mentioned anything to me about it.

"I guess not. I'll see you later."

It had started raining outside, so I took a short cut and ran across the school playground over to Castalia. Granted, I was pissed off with Quita, but right now, she was my refuge.

A CALL FOR HELP
Elise

I got Monique's call 'bout three in the mornin'. When I heard her voice on the other end, I knew I could rest easier just cuz I heard from her. I didn't care where she was or who she was wit then. I'd missed her birthday cuz I didn't have nothin' to give her. I tried to borrow a little piece of money from Mama, but she didn't have it. I didn't get paid 'til the end of the week, and, while people thought I was makin' a lot of money workin' at the Purina Plant, I wasn't makin' shit. They was layin' off folks and cuttin' back on hours. I had got caught up with a few no count niggahs that was robbin' me blind. Monkey, in particular, set me back cuz he was sellin' dope outta the house I used to live in, and, when the landlord foundt out, I had to move. It was in the dead of winter, and Penny's boyfriend's pick-up broke down in the rain wit my shit on it. Ruint everythang. The last big piece of money I had I gave to Eric Lee for some operation he was needin' to have. I'm paying the IRS back cuz I was filin' taxes on Monique while Eric Lee was claimin' her. I think he payin' back, too, cuz she was filin' them on herself with that little job she had.

Lotsa bad things went through my mind 'bout her being down at 201, and I wished none of it on her. First, I tried to call her daddy, but his phone was cut off. Then I asked Penny and them other broke-ass sistahs of mine and ain't netha one of 'em had it. Next, I called Dan and asked him what I should do.

"Wow, she called you instead of LaQuita?" He sounded surprised. "That's odd."

"Look, Mister. I *am* Monique's Mama."

Dan got quiet on his end. "Ms. Cummings, please don't take offense, but I thought you'd be the last person she'd call. You two don't exactly have the greatest relationship. In a situation like this, she should've called someone she knew would help her. Then again, it might be her way of trying to reach out to you."

Well, I took offense. The fact somebody that don't even know me realizes I'm a bad mama was embarrassing. I started cryin'. "Look, suh. I love Monique. She's just hurt me so bad with this change she made. Do you know how folks look at me when I'm out in the street? Do you know what they say?"

"Ms. Cummings, it was my understanding nobody knows 'bout Monique and what she's done. Nobody you both know at least. Are you sure you're not just paranoid?"

"Mr. Dan, you seen her? Walkin' 'round wit her pants hangin' off her ass showin' her underwear. She don't look right."

Dan pondered the choice of his next words. "What I'm confused about is why you have such a great interest in what other people think about you? Not Mo. You."

"That's personal. Mind yo' bidness."

"Sorry. Well, ma'am, Mo is doing well because she believes in who she is. She's put the attack . . ."

"Oh, and that's anothah thang. What you know 'bout that?"

"I know a lot. Tell you what. Come down to my office so we can talk, and I'll tell you what you want to know about everything. I already have Mo's permission to talk to you. She figured I'd never have to use it."

I thought 'bout it for a minute. I didn't nevah think I was gon get to talk to a shrink. I wasn't for it when all the trouble started up with Monique, but, now, after all this time, I needed to talk to somebody. "I don't know if I'm ready to do this." I was so full inside. My heart was heavy with so much pain.

"Ms. Cummings, can you write pretty good?"

"I do all right. Why?"

"Write a letter to Mo as if it's the last time you were going to talk to her. She's always wanted that from you. Tell her everything she needs to know about you. Then you and I can talk about it. How's that?"

"OK, OK. I can do that." I hung up the phone and got to writin'.

MEANWHILE, ON THE SAME SIDE OF TOWN
Cassie

Fifth period was the only part of the school day I hated. It was P.E., and I was self-conscious about wearing my gym uniform. My shirt was just long enough to fit over my shorts that were wayyy too revealing of my butt and thighs. I'd complained about it to my teacher, and all she'd say was to tell my mother to buy me another size and to remember that if I didn't dress out it was an automatic ten points off my daily grade.

Typically, it was the boys making fun of my butt— "Cassie got a big ass, Cassie got back"—when I wore my Angel jeans and a nice baby-doll tee. I took it in stride because I did have a banging body I inherited from my mother. In the mornings before school, I'd stand in the mirror and admire my developing curves. At first I was little shy about them, but both my parents taught me to love it. My mother picked out my clothes, and my father, a funeral home director, made sure we had the money for my mother to do so.

I wanted to go to Forest Hill High because my father

met my mother there. All of my aunts and uncles went there, and it had the best band in town. I wasn't in the band, but I always thought it was cool to go to a school where the games would be live on account of the drum sections showing out at half-time.

When the school year started, I noticed this new girl that hung around the boys all the time. Not in the sense of liking them—being fresh—but like she was one of them. We were in the same homeroom, had the same lunch period, and had gym together. Before I knew it, she'd developed a little clique. Unika, Tiffany, Beatrice and Charity all started hanging out with her. It wasn't long before this girl, Tristina, was running the eleventh grade hallway.

Her hair was cut in a natural, and she wore boys' clothing. I didn't understand it and never really wanted to until the day I closed my gym locker and she was standing right next to me. I looked, and her little posse was snickering on the other side of the locker room.

"What's up with you, baby crypt keeper?" Tristina's breath smelled like old Funyuns.

"Excuse me?" I walked off and headed toward to the sink and mirror to comb my hair. Tristina was right behind me and stopped at the sink just as I did.

"Why you always act so stuck up?" she asked, glancing over at her crew for their approval of her gradual humiliation of me. I had never acted that way with her. In spite of my parents' tendency to be that way, I vowed to do just the opposite.

"I'm not stuck up, Tristina. That's just your imagination. Oh, do you even have one of those?" I joked.

Tristina didn't take it that way. "Bitch, what?"

"You heard me. Why don't you go somewhere and find a boyfriend—well, just anybody—and get laid?"

She slammed my face into the mirror, twisting my

jaw with her rough hands. "You know what? I just might do that."

Then she and the rest of them left the locker room, cackling at the top of their lungs. From that point on, Tristina, along with her posse—both boys and girls— teased me for no reason in P.E. The joke—"Cassie and Tristina sittin' in a tree K-I-S-S-I-N-G. First comes love, then comes marriage, then comes Cassie with a baby carriage!" It didn't make things any easier that Tristina was sending me love letters. Somebody else had been writing, CASSIE LOVES TRISTINA, on the bath- room walls. She was whistling me at me whenever I jogged by during laps, and she would walk up to me and smack my butt when we were playing volleyball.

Well, I hadn't seen Tristina or any of her peeps since then. I'd hoped they were all on the Basic English class field trip to see "Romeo and Juliet." I was looking for- ward to gym being quiet and actually pleasant for a change. There were only six of us in class—Muriel and I, and the other four were boys. Muriel decided not to dress out and used her extra credit points for a one- day pass. I'd already used mine, so after a very relaxed class, I decided to take a shower since I was the only person in the locker room.

While I was drying off, I heard the squeaky locker room door open. I didn't think much about it. Could've been the coach coming in to put the equipment away. When I walked over to where my locker was, I saw Tristina sitting down on the bench next to my row of lockers. I ignored her and proceeded to put on my de- odorant and lotion.

"Honey, I'm home," she mocked.

I ignored her and reached in the locker for my bra and panties. I knew I'd put them in there. "Looking for these?" she asked dangling the pair in front of me.

"Give those back, Tristina," I snapped. I lunged for them, but she began this game I didn't want to play.

"Or what, baby crypt keeper? You gonna tell?"

"Yes, I am."

Tristina took my underclothes and stuck them in the pocket of her Sean John shirt. "Well, good luck, because coach was called up to the front office a minute ago, and I had the door locked from the outside."

I didn't believe her. Immediately, I ran toward the door and realized she wasn't lying. She'd had someone to lock the door, and there was no other way out of the locker room. I stood there with my head pressed against the door and conceded to face my fate. I turned around, and Tristina, Unika, and Tiffany were right there, nude with smirks on their face. I couldn't scream because no one would hear me, and if someone did, she'd trained them all to look the other way.

"You said I oughta get laid. Well, let's see if we can make that baby."

NONI-YO-BIDNESS
Mo

Iwalked up to the apartment expecting my shit to be
sitting outside the door, but it wasn't. You know how
God be throwing you for a loop with rain one side of
town and none on the other? He was stone-cold trippin' this day. Sun was out and not a cloud in the sky.
I'd lost my keys somewhere and was going to have to
knock. I changed my mind about going in, turned
around, and walked over to Big Daddy's.

This joint, on the other end of Bellevue they re-
named Elvis Presley Boulevard, was always packed
with mo-fos who either didn't have no job, didn't want
no job, and/or had a woman who took care of them at
home. Big Daddy's was their hang-out until the work-
day was over. Sad to say, that bitch stayed crunk. There
was about twenty-something pool tables in there, ten
old school video arcade games, five skee-ball machines,
and a barbershop in the back. Up front, they had an
eat-in area where they served the best cheap food in
Whitehaven. To calm my nerves before I dealt with
Quita, I decided to shoot me a game of eight ball.

In spite of being locked up the night before, I actually felt pretty good. I'd spent the night as a man. That was so fucking cool. It was confirmed—I'd officially crossed over. I walked to the change machine and started digging through my pockets for a dollar. I pulled lint out of all of them except one, and in there, that's all I had, one dollar. "You sure you want to spend your last dollar at Big Daddy's?" a female voice said softly.

"Yeah," I said with a slight 'tude because the fucking machine wouldn't take my money.

"Maybe that's a sign you shouldn't," she said, seemingly walking away.

I wanted to tell that ho to mind her business, but I'd had enough drama with females lately. I looked around to ask her to stop choppin' and give me another dollar, but she was gone. I walked over to the counter and asked the waitress if I could have another dollar, and she said I'd have to buy something. "Miss, I'm trying to buy a game on that table over there, but the change machine won't take my money."

"Can't you read, boy?" she pointed. The sign clearly said no change without purchase.

I didn't want change! I just wanted a new dollar. "Miss, you mean you ain't got anothah dollah in yo' pocket?"

She was playing the cook, too, and had moved to the back flipping burgers. "Son, please get on outta here and stop worryin' me."

"Damn!" I wanted to blaze that ass right there, but good for her I didn't have my heatah on me. I was going to have to fix that, too.

I took my ass on outside to get some air and blow off some steam. I propped up against the window and proceeded to bite my nails. I hated hangnails. Right after I came out, this female followed. She was about my height with some sweats on and nice Nikes. Hair was tight, nails pretty, and she smelled like a dream. I was weak for a woman that smelled good and had pretty nails.

"You know there's no loitering out here," she said as she walked over to the trashcan. While there was nobody else out there, I didn't think she was talking to me, so I kept at what I was doing, spitting nail debris on the sidewalk.

"Oh, I see you one of *them*."

I looked around like, "You talkin' to me?"

"Yes, I'm talking to you," she said staring me down. "You know there's a nail shop back in the back."

Perplexed, I asked, "What do you mean, '*one of them*' and why I do I need a nail shop? It's just a hangnail."

She walked closer to me and got right up in my face. "Now, tell me. What does a *man* know about hangnails?"

With her all up in my face, I looked the other way. I wasn't feeling this kinda shit. "Miss, with all due respect, I'm gon' need you to get up out my face and go on about your day."

She stayed planted. "You need Jesus."

Wooooooooooo! What the fuck is going on with me today? Was this "Fuck with Mo Day?" I tried stepping to my right—she stepped to her left. If I stepped to my left, she stepped to her right. "Look, I don't like folks all up in my face. Do you mind?"

"What? You don't think you need Jesus?" She was cute in the face, but she was getting uglier by the second to me with this church shit. In this little game of hers, she managed to connect with my eyes, and that did it for me.

The best way for me to handle this was to flip it on her. "A'ight, look. You got a booklet or something I might could take home?" I'd softened up a bit. Anything to get this ho out of my way. Religious fanatics always had something for you to read—a booklet, a pamphlet, a mini New Testament—something.

"Sure, wait right here. You're going to wait, right?" She flashed a beautiful smile, but she had a gap a mile wide.

"Yeah, I ain't going nowhere."

As she crossed the street, I watched her ass jiggle like a bowl of Jello in those sweatpants. Hers wasn't as round as Quita's, but it had potential if I could just get to it. She had on a white T-shirt and a matching jacket. I started pacing, still trying to get that hangnail.

Slightly out of breath, she came back to the sidewalk. "Here you go."

"Oh, OK." I glanced through the pamphlet and said, "Thank you very much. I'll take a look at it when I get home. I'll read it during dinner time."

Her demeanor perked up some. "Dinner? I was just thinking about that myself." *Here it comes.* "If you want, we can have dinner together, so if you have any questions, I'll be right there."

Boo-yah! What kills me is the woman that wants you to think they walk this straight line, with Jesus no doubt, but the minute you catch them just a little bit off guard, they turn into the biggest freaks and shout all up and down in the aisle on Sunday asking for forgiveness.

We went down to China Star, maybe a block away, which used to be the old Red Lobster. These Chinks had some big black woman in the kitchen laying out serious soul food. The collard greens, right next to the pork fried rice, had ham hocks in them swimming in vinegar and red peppers. The black eyed peas, next to the seafood delight, had chunks of smoked turkey necks floating in them. The candied yams, next to the General Tso's chicken, were so full of sugar and butter you had no choice but to dip your cornbread in it. The egg rolls, next to the chittlins, had a hint of bacon grease, and the sweet tea was nothing but sugar and water with a hint of tea and a burst of lemon. I loved it there, and after I was finished eating, I was always ready for sex. Who ever knew soul food was an aphrodisiac?

Her name was Noni Richmond, and she had a pussy like hot butter. It turned out one of *them* rocked her world that night. After dinner, she offered to take me home, and I was cool with it. I could've very easily walked since it was only two blocks away, but I wanted to spend a little more time with her. When we pulled up to the apartment, I studied the windows to see if there was any movement inside.

"Can I use your cell phone real quick? I want to see if my cousin is at home to let me in," I said.

"Sure, no problem."

It was well after six o'clock, and I knew Quita had to be gone. I dialed the house phone but didn't get an answer. I called it again but hung up as soon as the voice-mail picked up.

"Shit, she ain't home."

"What time does your office close?" she asked.

"They closed at six. The maintenance man lives on the property, though, and me and him is cool. Can you take me 'round there real quick?"

Noni was rolling that green Honda Civic like she was at the Indy 500. Joe, whose nickname was Monkey, lived two buildings over near the back of the complex. Monkey had been in trouble with the law a few times and had to keep a steady job while he was on probation. It could've been a job shoveling shit at a stable, a gig at the bus station wiping scum out the toilets, or a stint at the mall scrapping gum off the floor. That niggah had to work! He had serious charges against him—intent to sell, intent to distribute, weapons possession, and some more shit. Heard the D.A. didn't want to send him to jail because they didn't have no room out at the penal farm. So he began working at the complex as the niggah you go to when you in a jam. He was supposed to charge eighty dollars, but he ain't charge me shit because we like that. I got out and left Noni in the car.

I knocked on the door so hard I found myself banging on it. "Monkey!" I saw the blinds move, and then I felt the footsteps on the other side of the door. I heard him pressing up against the door to check the peephole. Then the locks clicked.

"Whaddup, fool?" He gave me some love and invited me in. That niggah had that house crunk with weed and liquor.

"Nothing, mayne, you got it."

Sitting down on this brown couch that was full of cigarette burns, he said, "Heard you got in a li'l trouble last night at the club."

"Aw, shit, mayne, it's all good. Nothin' but a thang."

"Caught you a gun charge, too, I hear. When you go to court?" That fool knew everything about the system. I wouldn't be surprised if he was paying somebody on the inside to keep tabs on things. "Got a lawyer?"

"In the morning at 9:30. I ain't got no lawyer yet, though. Look, uh, I'm locked out, and Quita's at work."

Niggahs talk too much as it is, so I was trying to hustle on up out of there.

"Aw, aw, yeah. I'll come 'round there and let you in. Uh, you know it's a charge, right?"

No, he ain't. "What?"

"You know they got after me about not charging folks. Sorry, chief."

"OK, uh, I'll be right back."

I trotted down the steps and tapped on Noni's window. "Uh, he gotta charge me. I know you don't me like this, but any chance you got it on you? I'll give it back to you when we get in the house."

An apparent God-fearing woman who just happened to have a little freak in her, Noni didn't hesitate. "Sure, sure." She opened her wallet thumbing through layers of twenties. "Here you go."

I got back upstairs to see Monkey peeping out the window. "Who dat you got out there in the car?"

"Aw, that's a friend of mine." Monkey's phone rang, and he stepped into the other room.

"Mo, I'm gonna give you this here key. It's a spare for your place. Just bring it back when you get a chance. I'm gonna have to take this call."

"OK, cool."

Noni drove me back around to my place. "You wanna come in so we can talk about this pamphlet of yours?" I already knew the answer. A true wanna-be playa can spot a freak a mile away. She was hot for me.

"Sure," she said anxiously.

I hopped out the car ahead of her to make sure Quita hadn't come home. I ran to the backroom, the guest-room, and checked both bathrooms. By the time I got back to the front door, Noni was standing in the doorway. "Come on in," I gestured. "I ain't mean to run off like that, but I had to release some of that tea."

Laughing at my foolishness, she took a seat in the recliner and sat her purse on the table. "You have a cute little place here."

"Thanks. I ain't here much because I work a lot."

"Really? Where you work?"

I wondered what the chances of her stopping by my job were. At this point, pretty high. By the time, I finished with her? Through the roof. "I work at the Wal-Mart in Southaven. I work overnight stocking the shelves."

"Honey, I love me some Wal-Mart. You get a discount?"

"Of course, I do." Please don't ask how much.

"How much?"

"Not a whole lot."

"Any little bit helps. How much?" she asked, sitting there with her eyes all bucked out.

The only way I could get out of this was to abruptly change the subject. I plopped down on the couch and pulled out her little pamphlet. "So tell me about this paper here you gave me. I gotta go to work tonight."

Noni pulled one out of her bag. On the front it said JESUS SAVES and on the back it was a form to fill out and send in with a donation. "Well, I'm a member of Mountain Glory Church of Christ. I'm a missionary looking for more of God's children to bring into His kingdom. I saw you in the pool hall and felt your spirit call out to me."

"And you, uh, what was you doin' in the pool hall?"

"Duh?" she said, wiggling her fingers in front of me. "Getting my nails done."

"Oh, yeah, that's right." I dropped my legs open a little bit and saw her steal a glimpse of my bulge.

"So, uh, what questions did you have?" She was a little restless crossing and uncrossing her ankles every two or three minutes.

"Well, I gotta bad ear. You ain't notice me constantly saying 'What' and 'Huh' all evenin'?"

"Yes, I did notice that. You want me to come over there next to you?"

"That's on you, Miss Thing. I'm one of *them*, remember."

Noni ran her ass over to that couch so fast she tripped over her own foot and knocked over Quita's favorite plant. Adjusting her clothes, she sat down next to me. Our thighs touched. For someone who had been cool most of the evening, she was visibly shaken.

"So, uh." She turned blood red in the face. "I'm so sorry. I don't even know your name."

"It's Mo."

"Mo? Is that short for something?"

"No, it's just Mo."

"OK then, Mo. What questions do you have for me?"

I had to think fast. I hadn't read shit on that thing. I flung my arm around her. "Lemme see. Um. Why you say I need Jesus? I mean, you don't know me."

"I apologize. Maybe I went about it all wrong. I just started doing this ministry last week."

"That's wassup," I said.

"But to answer your question, you don't seem to have Jesus in you."

"And what is that supposed to mean?"

"You know how some people walk the walk?"

"Yeah, I guess. But some of those people are the biggest hypocrites. They talk the talk—like I believe you tryin' to do here with me, but I don't believe you walk the walk."

She was a little peeved, but I didn't care. Digging in the bag she brought in with her, Noni whipped out a Bible. "See, Mo, right here," she starts while flipping the pages. "It says . . . Hold on."

This going back and forth was over for me. It was time. "What's that fragrance you're wearing?" I asked, sniffing around her neck. She was still looking for that scripture. "It smells divine."

"Anais Anais. I'm sure you've never heard of it."

I kissed her neck, and I swear before God, she started shaking like she'd taken some of them earthquake pills that Wile E. Coyote used to try to give to the Roadrunner. "You smell really good, Noni."

"Thhaaannkk yyyoouuu," she said, still clutching that Bible. By now, though, she'd closed it.

I kept throwing kisses on her neck, one right after the other. She started returning them to me on any spot she could find. "I got another question," I managed between smacks.

"Uh, huh," she said, sucking through her teeth.

Sticking my tongue in her ear and circling the outside of it with my nose, I asked softly, "Why you call me one of *them*?" I never stopped my stride.

"Because," she moaned. "You're one of those people who wants the world to believe she's something she's not." She grabbed Master D, letting out a sigh like she'd found heaven.

"OK, well," I said, still massaging her upper body with my lips, "it's fair to say that goes both ways now."

And then I tugged at her sweatpants until I got them down around her thighs. She unzipped my pants and released Master D into her mouth, sucking it like a pro.

She held onto it, playing with it, snapping it between her lips. Slowly, I raised her head from me and bent her over the coffee table and mastered my game one step further by telling the church lady what she could do with her thoughts about me being one of *them*.

MISS Q
Elise

Callin' that girl—the one Monique called her woman—was the hardest thing for me to do. Didn't want to be 'round her. Didn't want to talk to her. And I sho as hell didn't want to see her. Nobody made me call her, but I'm sho she might be in a bettah spot to help my child. I tried callin' information to get their number, but it was listed as private. Folks be killin' me wit they numbers listed private like they somebody important. They can have your number, but you can't have theirs. Niggahs live in the bottom of the damn projects wit a private number! I ended up callin' Mr. Dan back to get their number ovah there.

"Quita?" I asked.

"Yes," she said. Then she a propah bitch at that. "Who's speakin?"

"This, Elise, Monique's Mama. How you doin' this mornin'?"

She act like she was scared cuz she didn't say nothin' right off. "I'm fine, Ms. Cummings, and yourself?"

"Blessed and highly favored, thank you. Monique called here this mornin'. You know she been in jail?"

"Well, yes, ma'am. I know."

"Say you do? Whyn't you call me?"

"I don't know, Ms. Cummings. I actually didn't think you cared. I've spent most of the day pulling money together to get her a lawyer."

"Did you get it?"

"Yes, ma'am. My cousin is a lawyer, and she said she'd take care of it."

"I see. Quita, I wanted to help her. I truly did, but I ain't have it."

That child ain't say much for a hot second, but when she did, her mouth ran so fast I could hardly keep up. "Ms. Cummings, your daughter needs you. I don't know what else to tell you. Simply put, she's hurtin'. She's got a potential weapons charge starin' down at her if she doesn't get the best help out there. My cousin is the best."

She did a fine job of makin' me feel useless. "I don't know what to say or what I'm s'pposed to say."

"I know it's hard to digest, but it's OK to admit our faults and fix them so we can move on."

I was startin' to like Miss Thang. "So what you think I oughta do?"

"Well, I have to run out to get the rest of the money my cousin needs. Do you have some time today for us to talk?"

"Later this evening maybe."

"I'll take off work tonight and bring some dinner so us ladies can chat."

"Naw, you ain't gon' bring somebody else's food up in here when I make the best fried chicken on the block. Get here about 6:30. Dinner's on me."

* * *

She got here on time, and it was a little uneasy for her just like it was for me.

"I brought you a picture of me and Mo."

I saw her lookin' 'round to see where she thought I might put it. "Just give it here, and I'll put it up later." I was gonna put it in a box with the other ones. Quita ain't no bad lookin' girl. I just don't believe in girls being wit girls. "Want somethin' to drink?"

"Yes, please. I'll have some water."

"Girl, what this look like? The Peabody? Ain't no water here. I gots some purple, orange, or red Kool-Aid. Which one you want?"

It kinda made her laugh. "I'll take the purple."

We ate dinner—fried chicken, peas, and lemon pound cake—and talked about stuff like Quita's job and her family. She was tellin' me her cousin, C.C., was from 'round here. I didn't even ask her nothin' 'bout that, cuz nobody I knew 'round here was smart enough to be no lawyer.

"I talked wit Dan this mornin' 'bout Monique, and he asked me to write her a letter."

"She'd like that. Um, are you going to court tomorrow?"

"No, I told her I wasn't gonna be there."

"You should rethink that. It would mean so much to her for you to be there."

Excuses was all I knew I had. I didn't have nothin' to do. Just didn't think I was no use to her. I got up from the table and ran to the mirror. "Look at this mess! I can't go nowhere wit my do lookin' like this."

"Calm down," she said. She pulled at my hair and some tracks fell out. I hadn't taken care of it like I used to. "If you want me to, I can fix it for you. It won't take long."

"Even if you fix my hair, I sill don't got nothin' to wear down to the courthouse."

"Excuses, Ms. Cummings. We'll check your closet and find something."

Quita played in my head 'til she was able to get all the tracks out. She washed it and kept saying Mo got hair like mine. Mo got hair like Eric Lee. I didn't want her to put no curls in it. I hadn't nevah had no perm and wasn't gon start. I told her I just wanted to wear it natural. I found a little bit of Spicy Cognac Jazzin' and asked her to put it in for me. Out of all the transformation, that's all I requested. We dug through my closet and found me a coupla outfits, but the moths had got to 'em. Quita stitched up both of 'em so I'd have some choices. I found a pair of shoes I used to wear to church that didn't make my feet hurt too bad. By this time, I felt comfortable enough wit her now to ask her 'bout some stuff wit Monique. We was sittin' in the livin' room drinkin' a coupla of wine coolers. "Quita?"

"Yes, ma'am?"

"Did Monique ever tell you what happened to her that day when she was comin' home from school?"

Water started comin' to her eyes. "Well, yes, she did."

"I ain't been wantin' to talk to her 'bout all that."

"It may help you to better understand why she is who she is. I know it was brutal. I know it was violent, and I know it still haunts her."

"I see."

"Honestly, though. I think you should ask her. It would be better for both of you if she told you."

"OK."

Quita began to get her stuff together. It was goin' on midnight. "Ms. Cummings, I need to get out of here.

Mo will be lookin' for me soon. You know, she's really a good woman."

"Is she?"

"Yes, she is. She knows how to make me feel special." She reached in her purse and handed me an envelope. "I would really like to see you and Mo fix things. Here is the money I have to pay my cousin. Take this in the morning to Division 9. C.C. will be there and will be calling out for Mo. That's what they do when neither of them have ever met. Go up to her and give her this envelope and tell her it's for Mo. Me being there would be nothing but a distraction. You two need this time. I know it would mean a lot to her."

The only thang I knew to say was thank you.

THE MONKEY ON MY BACK
Mo

Quita came through the door around 12:30 in the morning, which was kinda early for her. I'd gotten rid of all the evidence of the church lady including the pamphlet and the mishap with plant. The covers were pulled over my head, so she couldn't see my face. The light went on in the bathroom, and she closed the door. I'd taken about three or four showers to wash that perfume off of me and sprayed Money Blessing to get the scent out of the house. I went ahead and tidied up a bit so it wouldn't seem strange to have vacuum lines in just one part of the living room.

"You home early," I said when the bathroom door opened.

She came toward the bed and took a seat. "Mo, I wasn't up to it tonight. I left early." Her trench coat landed on the bed, and I heard her shoes hit the floor. "When did you get out?"

"Some time after noon."

She walked over to my side of the bed and pulled

the covers back. "Get up, I wanna see you. I was so worried about you."

"Stop, girl. I don't feel like it. I'm tired."

"How'd you get in? You know while you were actin' an ass, you dropped your keys," she said, dangling them in my face. I was beginning to wonder if she suspected something. Her questions had a niggah on edge.

"Monkey let me in. I gotta take the key back tomorrow."

"Oh, OK. Doesn't he charge now? Where you get money from?"

"Naw, he let me slide. I'll take it to him when I take the key back." I was very uneasy. I didn't like lying to Quita.

"OK."

She pulled covers back over me and started undressing for bed. I was a little puzzled about that because she always came in and took a shower before she got in the bed. "How was work?"

"Fine," she said softly. "What did they say downtown?"

"Nothing but I got to be in court. That's about it." Quita sat motionless for a moment. "Mo, I got you a lawyer. My cousin, C.C., is gonna meet you down there. You know they tryin' to slap a gun charge on you."

"Figured as much," I said nonchalantly. "Are you comin' with me?"

Again, she was motionless. "No, I'm not."

"What?" My heart hit the floor. "I'm gonna be by myself?"

Quita turned out the light and got in the bed. "I took C.C. the money earlier today. As quiet as it's kept, I'm still a bit pissed with you. Last night was foolish on your part."

"Oh, oh, a mayne can't not want his woman strippin' in the club?" I said, sitting up in the bed.

"It's not like that, Mo. Those women aren't touchin' me. They treat me like a real celebrity. Do you know that on any given night I can bring home $3,000 if I wanted to? You don't never seem to have problem with helping spend the money I make."

"Aw, hell, no. You not gonna make it seem like I'm livin' off you. Your money is your money. I ain't never asked you for shit. I don't say nothin' to you when you run your ass down to the casino with your stripper friends and spend your money and MY money."

"You know what? We don't have to talk about this anymore. Good night."

"Right, we ain't gotta talk about it no more because tomorrow when I get done in court we're goin' over there so you can quit." I yanked the covers toward me, rolled them around me, and slammed my head against my pillow. "If I got to work five jobs to keep you from workin' over there, then I will."

"Whatever, Mo. Make sure you listen out for the alarm in the morning. You don't wanna be late for court."

THE ZOO
Elise

Iarrived downtown at the Criminal Justice Complex
a little before nine o'clock. It was gon take 'bout
twenty minutes to get through the security line. Quita
had fixed a navy blue outfit and a black outfit for me. I
picked the navy blue one.

Downstairs is what they call The Zoo cuz it's so
many folks 'round there. There was folks in suits, jog-
gin' suits, dresses, jeans and anythang else you could
imagine. It was elbow-to-elbow niggahs down there
and could be a bit much for somebody not used to
bein' 'round a buncha us. Comin' down on the escalator, I caught a glimpse of somebody that looked just
like my friend Cathy that I hadn't seen since before I
went to Atlanta. When I got to the bottom, the herd
from the escalator pushed me out into the open floor. I
didn't know Memphis had so many folks wit issues.
I couldn't judge nobody cuz my child was one of 'em. I
got to Division #9 courtroom but didn't see Monique.
It was 9:20.

"Mo Cummings!" I heard a woman callin'. "Mo

Cummings!" she went again. I walked up on her, and I be damn if it wasn't Cathy.

"Cathy?" First she looked at me like I was crazy. Then she did a double look.

"Elise?"

"Yeah, girl. It's me!" I said, reachin' out to her to give her a hug. She had these bags and papers wit her.

"It's so good to see you," she said wit a big ol' pretty smile on her face. She had on a black skirt wit a matchin' jacket and a nice shirt. "What are you doing down here?" she asked me.

"Well, I'm down here for my daughter. She dun got herself in a bit of trouble. I thank I heard you callin' her name."

Cathy looked down at her paperwork. "I was callin' for a young man named Mo Cummings."

I was so shamed. "I know. That's my daughter. It's a long story. Your cousin told me to give this to you." I handed her the envelope.

"LaQuita?" she said, raisin' her eyebrow.

"Yes."

"Come over here and sit with me for a minute, Elise. We need to talk before Mo gets here." We walked over to a little sofa and sat down. "We have a few problems here."

"Quita said it was gon be simple. Just pay you and you'd take care of e'rything."

"Well, that was the idea until I got here and pulled the docket. That gun Mo had may have been used to kill a man three and a half years ago. I'm usually a little skeptical about matters like this. The ballistics process usually takes weeks, so I'm going to need to investigate this a little further. I don't want her facing any other unnecessary charges."

I couldn't believe what she was sayin' to me. It was comin' at me so fast. "So you sayin' Monique killed somebody?"

"No, no, I'm not saying that. Then there's that problem." Cathy pulled out Mo's file. "Mo is listed as a male on all the intake information. The D.A. believes whoever killed this man was young and stupid and was male. With Monique being Mo, I don't know how this is going to play out until I talk with her."

We waited until 9:28. I watched the top of that escalator like my sistah-nem watch for the mailman at the first of the month. Cathy told me she had to go on in cuz she had some other folks to see 'bout. After a few more minutes, I went in to at least see who the judge was.

There was 'bout thirty-to-forty people inside. I saw Cathy and walked close to where she was. E'rythin' was alphabetical and formal. When they called Mo, this gentleman got up and walked to the front where Cathy was. He reminded me so much of Eric Lee's style. That was my child lookin' like a young man now. I had nevah seen her that way.

"Your Honor, Cathy Crenshaw, for the defense."

"Go ahead, Counselor." The judge was a Black woman wit pretty hair. Look to be a little bit older than both me and Cathy. I wonder where I was when they were handin' out all these degrees.

"I need a few minutes to speak with my client, your Honor."

"That's not a problem." The judge started laughin' and talkin' wit all the official folks up there wit her.

Cathy took Monique to the side and said somethin' to her. Monique was shakin' her head. After a few minutes, Cathy approached the D.A. and the judge. Nobody knew what they were sayin'. All I know is when they got through, Monique and Cathy were ready to go.

"You look like your Mama," I heard her say softly as they were walkin' out.

"You think so?" Monique asked. She was wearin' a real nice black suit with a pretty pink necktie. Her hair looked she'd just come from the barbershop. She saw me and stopped dead in her tracks. "Moms? When did you get here?"

"She's been here," Cathy said openin' the door for us.

We got out in the hallway, and people were lookin' at you like you were somethin' out of a magazine. "I want you two to meet me at my office in about an hour. Can you do that?"

Monique spoke up sayin' "Dependin' on where it is and if MATA goes there."

Cathy started laughin'. "Oh, no, no. You don't have to go far. It's right down the street on Poplar. I'd take you down there, but I've got to run to my son's school and drop off his tuition." I was fine wit walkin' as long as Monique was, but then Cathy said, "You know what? We're family. You guys can ride with me out to the school, and then we can come back down here."

My girl from back in the day had a nice ride. One of them Black Men's Bentleys. Monique and Cathy seemed like they had more to talk 'bout than I would wit eitha one of 'em. We passed by a lot of pretty houses that I didn't even know were in Memphis. I'm thankful LaQuita did somethin' to my hair last night. 'Bout twenty minutes later, we pulled up to the buildings that looked like they was expensive. There was a football field and lotsa fancy cars in the parkin' lot.

"What school is this?" Monique asked.

"Briarcest."

Monique ain't say much to me nor Cathy after that. When Cathy got in the car, she askedt me how I'd been and where I had gone off to. My family ain't say nothin' to nobody 'bout any of it. It was like they were all shamed of me and what I'd done. Cathy told me after high school she went to George Washington University to study political science and stayed on up there where she met her husband, Dylan, and got into law school. They adopted a twelve-year old boy and lives out in Eads. He's a professor ovah at the college, and she do what she do for some big time firm in town.

We was comin' back down Poplar, and Monique saw the signs for the Memphis City Zoo. "Can we stop there? I've never been."

Cathy's mouth fell wide open. "You've never been to the zoo?" she asked.

Monique cut her eyes back at me, "No, I haven't."

In her skirt and all, Cathy turn up in the zoo parking lot and said, "Since Elise and I were best buddies growing up, you're the daughter I never had. Come on, let's get out and walk around for a while. I have some time. We can talk out here."

Cathy got her phone and reached in the back to get her tennis shoes from the floor. I got out while she changed her shoes, and Monique took off her jacket and necktie. This was diff'rent for me.

We walked around 'bout an hour befo' anybody said anythang 'bout what was goin' on. Finally, Cathy asked Monique somethin' that was burnin' my mind, too.

"Monique, what's up with the look?"

Monique ain't say nothin'.

Cathy looked ovah at me, and I shrugged my shoulders. "You don't have to tell me, but I'd like to know so I can better understand what's going on."

I was hopin' Monique wasn't gon say nothin' cuz I couldn't bear the shame. "I'm comfortable this way. That's all."

"Wow, you know if it ever comes out you're a woman, it would embarrass the hell out of the folks down at 201," she laughed. Cathy spotted a nearby table and waved her hand so we'd follow her. There was crums and flies e'rywhere, and she got to fannin' dem like she was too cute to sit down. Back in the day, the Cathy I know woulda just set right on down.

Monique was watchin' the peacocks walkin' 'round wit all them pretty feathers. I nevah knew they let them birds out like that.

"Well, let's hope for them that never happens."

"Right, right. Look, you want to tell me where you got the gun?" Monique locked up on Cathy. That gurl's mouth was sealed shut. "Monique, I'm your lawyer. Whatever you tell me is between you and me. I can even ask Elise to leave if you want me to."

Monique rolled her eyes at me, and I know Cathy had to see somethin' was wrong between me and her. "It's cool. She can stay."

"OK, good. Where did you get it?"

"My homie, Jamal Stevens."

"The young man that was arrested with you?"

"Yes, ma'am."

"Did he ever tell you where he got it?"

"No. I never asked. Why?"

"Forensics traced the gun they got off you and discovered it was used in a homicide three and a half years ago. An unidentified young Black male was seen leaving the scene. The police kept the investigation open as long as they could, but eventually the trail ran cold. Now how long have you been calling yourself Mo?"

" 'Bout that long. Three years or so."

Cathy shook her head. "You know, if the D.A. wanted he could pin that murder on you."

"The White man can try to do whatevah he wants to me. He ain't gonna win."

"Well, see, that's where we have a problem. The only lead they've had in almost four years is the gun they found on you, Mo Cummings. They don't know anything about a Monique Cummings . . . yet."

"What's that supposed to mean?"

"You were processed as a male. You sat in a Shelby County jail with the men. Right now as we speak, the D.A. probably has someone trying to put a wrap sheet together on you."

Monique got huffy. "I don't have other charges."

"Did you give your real birthday during intake?"

"Yes."

"Did you give them your place of birth as Memphis?"

"Yes."

"See, right there, we have a problem. You weren't born in Memphis. You were born in Atlanta at Grady Hospital." Cathy knew more than I thought she knew about me.

"What?" Monique gave me the evil eye . . . again. One day she would know e'rything.

"What's going to happen is this. The D.A. is going to run your name and birthday through the system. You, Elise, and I know he's not going to come up with a match. He's going to be like 'Hmmm, that's strange.' His next step is to check with vital statistics, and they're going to tell him that there was no Mo Cummings born in Memphis on your birth date. What will then happen is he will conduct a national search. With the way technology is, he'll eventually track you down. It might take him a minute, but he's going to pull it off. Then he'll be ready for court to prove that you're a liar. Let me ask you a question."

"Yes?"

"Did you give your real social security number?"

"Well, yeah. Duh?"

I saw why Cathy was a lawyer. "No, it's more like I should be saying that to you. You've all but given yourself away. You wanna-be gangstas kill me."

Monique turned to Cathy. "What you say?"

"I mean, you young people kill me trying to be all hard and street smart, but you're just as dumb as they come when it pertains to reality."

I swore Monique gave Cathy a look I can't describe. Her eyes started releasin' this rage that even the animals in that zoo couldn't match. "Do you wanna know why I'm like this?" Closin' in on Cathy, she asked her again. "Do you wanna really know?" Water was fillin' that child's eyes. "While growin' up moms kept me in all that girlie shit. That man, he started touchin' me with his filthy hands. Then he kept doin' these horrible things to me." Monique was cryin' so bad we could hardly understand her. "All I wanted to do was get moms her pickles."

Cathy had clued in to Monique's secret—to our secret. "Elise, is she talking about Mr. Luther?"

I got up from the table. I couldn't answer that, and I ain't want to hear no more details.

SAME SHIT, DIFFERENT DAY
Mo

A nd that right there is why I can't stand my moms'
ass. She never wanted to face reality! She never
wanted to hear what that monster was doing to me!
She never wanted to tell me why she blamed me for all
of this! All she cared about was me in them damn
dresses, hair bows, and Mary Janes. Let her keep her
ass over there. Hell, she could go on home for all I
cared.

I sat there talkin' to Cathy like I'd known her all my
life. I told her about Mr. Luther and what he'd done to
me.

"Monique, why didn't you tell someone?"

I pointed over to Moms like I was telling it on her. "I
did! I did! But she wouldn't listen. So I packed my shit
and I ran away. That's when I met Jamal. At the shelter."

Cathy was motionless.

"That man y'all talkin' about was his stepfather, and
he was doin' some bad things to him and his moms. If
you ask me, he deserved what he got. Shit, y'all gotta

prove he did it, and I know you ain't going to be able to do that."

"Technically, you're right. They may not be able to prove he did it, but they can point the finger at you since you had the gun. Of course, they'd be lacking a motive, but you're Black and supposedly a male. That's all that's going to count."

I was fed up with the games. "What you want me to do, Cathy? Give up my boy?"

"If you don't want to go to jail for the rest of your life, then you might want to consider that."

Shhiitttt, I didn't know what to say. "When do we have to be in court again?"

"Three weeks unless you do something stupid."

"Somethin' stupid?"

"Yes, like getting picked up again for fighting with LaQuita."

"See, y'all don't even know what y'all talkin' about."

Cathy started laughing at me. "I'm kidding. She told me what happened. That girl loves her some Mo."

The zoo was cool and all, but the smell of those animals was killing me. I thought we was done, but then Cathy had some more questions for me.

"Are you willing to give a statement about where you got the gun from?"

"I need to talk to Jamal before I give you that answer." I was watching the little kids running around with their friends laughing and playing like they didn't have a trouble in the world. "Do you know what it feels like to have your innocence stripped from you, Cathy?"

She was shocked a thug like me could ask something like that. "I can't say that I do."

Judging by her expression, the next words out of my mouth ripped through Cathy like a chainsaw. She listened to every horrible detail of that awful day. The more she listened, the more real it became for her. She began to understand why Mo wasn't a figment of my imagination. He was real. "Now, if I help you, Cathy, do you think you can help me?"

Drying the tears from her eyes, she said, "I'm going to do my best." Her cell phone rang after that, and she walked down the pathway toward the entrance. We'd had hot dogs and chips while Moms sat her ass off on a bench looking like she was waiting on the bus.

"Monique, come here," Moms said softly but firmly.

"What?" I said hatefully.

"What you go and tell her that shit for? That ain't none of her business."

I couldn't believe what she was saying to me. "You know what? No matter how many times I talk about this to someone, there's one thing that never changes."

Getting up off the bench she asked, "And what's that?"

"How much I hate you. I don't need you to be here for me if you're going to constantly act like this never happened."

"For your information, I . . ."

I was done . . . yet again with her. "I don't want to hear it. I don't want to hear it!" I yelled.

About that time, Cathy was trotting toward us. "Monique?" she asked breathing heavily. "Where were you yesterday afternoon?"

Behind that question, I know I looked about the face like Sylvester when he'd swallowed Tweety Bird. "Uh, I was at home. Why?"

"Is there anybody that can back you up on that?"

Oh, I wasn't touching that one. "Well, earlier in the day I was at Moms's house."

"What time was that?"

"Some time over in the afternoon. I left there and went to Big Daddy's and later had dinner with some friends."

"Where?"

"China Star."

"At any point during the afternoon were you running through Castalia?"

"Well, yeah, to catch the bus."

Cathy hesitated for a second and then started going through her phone. "That was the D.A. Apparently, yesterday afternoon a young lady at Forest Hill High School was sexually assaulted by a group of girls. The ringleader ironically fits your description. The D.A. and the SVU detective want me to bring you in for questioning."

"What? After what I just told you, do you honestly think I could or even would do something like that?"

"Monique, what did I explain to you not even an hour ago? He's been digging. The D.A. who thinks we all look alike wants to talk with you, and I've got to produce you. You were processed as a male. Sonny, the conservative D.A. from Collierville who could care less about Blacks and gays, wants someone to go down for this because this young lady's father is a well-known funeral home director who contributes major money to his campaign. Feel me?"

Where in the hell was all this coming from? Who was trying to ruin my life? "So what am I supposed to do?"

"Those friends you had dinner with? I need to talk with them."

Shit.

"Anybody who saw you yesterday needs to call me, and I mean anybody."

Shit again.

Cathy picked up her keys and drank the last of her water. "Let's get going. By the way, I need to talk to your friends and any other witnesses before the D.A. gets to them."

"And if I don't find them or they don't want to cooperate?"

"Then you, my dear, need to decide who you *really* are in order to save yourself."

Now what the hell was I going to do? The only two people that saw me was a crackhead and a sexually frustrated church ho. Cathy couldn't talk to Noni. The only way I knew to find her was to go over to her church. And Monkey? I didn't need him telling nobody he saw me with a woman other than Quita.

ALL GOD'S SINNERS
Cassie

I laid on the couch listening to Daddy rant and rave about this and that. "I told you Cassie shouldn't have been going to that ghetto-ass school! Didn't I tell you her clothes were too tight? I can't believe you didn't tell me they had lesbians over there!" he screamed at my mother. As usual, she paced the floor, looking for answers to why all of this was happening to her baby.

It was my plan to not tell anyone, but Unika, who broke rank, chickened out. Tristina had told her to hold my arms down, but she wouldn't. "Hold her fuckin' arms down or you're next!"

"Tristina, we shouldn't be doing this. We can get in a lot of trouble."

"We'll only get in trouble if somebody tells. Right, baby crypt keeper?"

The whole attack lasted all of five minutes. Tristina got her rocks off, and so did Tiffany. Unika turned her back and cried while I tried to fight them off. Next thing you know, Unika disappears. Then right after her, Tristina and Tiffany take off. I was left lying on the cold tiled floor with my nose and mouth bleeding from where they had punched me. I sat up against the lockers trying to put my underwear on but was too sore to do so. Seconds later, the coach arrived with a towel to help me up.

All Unika told them was that I was in the locker room and was hurt. She didn't call any names or describe what she saw. It was left up to me to say who it was, and because everyone knew that Tristina taunted me and was afraid of her, nobody at school said a word.

Daddy insisted the principal call the police. No one was going to rape his daughter and get away with it. He was warned, however, of the likelihood of the media getting involved and was asked if that were something he wanted. That's when he used his favorite phrase, "Do you know who I am?" The principal didn't care who he was. Her concern was negative exposure for her school. Well, the police came and tried to get answers, but, as I said, no one really said anything. They had an ambulance take me to the hospital, and for what? During those five minutes, Tiffany and Tristina took turns with me—one on top while the other held my hands down. I didn't fight with them. There was no use because it was two against one the whole time. Tristina, rubbing her naked body against my thin pelvis, was rough but gentle if there's such a thing. Trying to teach me lesson about my smart ass mouth was maybe what I deserved. Before she completed her last shot at pleasure, Tristina licked me down there and asked, "How does that feel, baby crypt keeper?" She kept stroking her tongue against me until I told her I liked it. Daddy would just die if he knew I'd done that.

Every time somebody asked me about what happened I shrugged my shoulders and shamefully looked away. The nurses were going in and out. I knew they were in the hallway gossiping about me and my loud-mouth-ass daddy. Mother came in and asked me if I was OK. I told her my only desire was to go home. She heard the disgust in my voice and saw the humiliation in my eyes. "OK, baby. I'm going to make it happen."

I got home and took the hottest bath I could stand. I was sore and wanted to soak all of the filth away. Getting out of the tub, I could hear voices in the kitchen. It was Mr. Dawson, the D.A. He and Daddy played golf together. They got along well because neither of them liked Black people.

"Ray, look, if Cassie doesn't identify this girl, then we don't have a leg to stand on." Mr. Dawson was a short man who'd grayed prematurely and whose legs were attractively bowed for a White man. His daughter and I used to play together, but when she started going to St. Mary's—the posh all-girl school of the east and I started going to Forest Hill, our tastes in friends, and each other, quickly changed. About twenty years ago, Mr. Dawson's family had a long-standing relationship with Quayle Funeral Home, but after some old debts came to haunt its owners, they sold it. Of course, the other White clients couldn't vacate fast enough when they learned that a Black man now owned their beloved institution. That was right around the time that Mr. Dawson first ran for office. Daddy financed his entire campaign provided the Dawsons remained clients. With money as the common denominator, they've been friends ever since.

"You mean to tell me that out of all those mug shots and fingerprints you got down there, you can't find one person to lay this on?"

"That's what I'm saying."

"I don't believe it." Daddy rose from the table, went to the refrigerator, and got them both a beer.

"It's complicated. I know you want some vindication. I would, too, if it were my daughter. The reality of the whole thing is that if Cassie doesn't speak up, then it's we have no case."

Daddy could be cold when he wanted. "OK, Sonny. I understand. When I think she's up to it, I'll talk with her. But I want you to remind yourself of that calendar," he said pointing to the one on the wall.

"What about it?"

"According to my calculations it's coming close to re-election time."

Mr. Dawson hated when Daddy kept it real like that, and he knew he didn't stand a chance. "All right, I'll see what I can do. In the meantime, you may want to get your daughter into counseling. She's going to need to show she's been doing that if we ever have to go to court."

"Not a problem," Daddy said.

I went to my room and closed the door.

A NEW SHERIFF'S IN TOWN
Mo

Cathy called me two days later. "Monique?" It was eight o'clock in the damn morning. I'd worked a double shift the day before and was tired as hell. Quita was laying on the other side of me knocked out. I wanted to kick her in her back so she could be up, too.

"Yeah," I said wiping the sleep out of my eyes.

"Can you come down to my office this afternoon? We have some developments I need to speak with you about."

"Uh, Cathy? Can we do it over the phone?"

"Sorry, we can't. I need you down here."

"OK, fine. What time?"

"One o'clock is good. Make sure you come by yourself."

"A'ight." I clicked the off button as hard as I could. This whole thing was beginning to get on my nerves.

I arrived at Cathy's office at one o'clock on the nose. Her secretary was a cute little White chick who kept looking at me like I was about to steal something. I sat back in my chair, legs hanging open like I ain't had no home training. To complete the picture, I still had my pick in the back of my head. Cathy came on out looking all fly and shit. It was hard to believe she and Moms grew up together. She gave me one of those momma stares like you dead-ass wrong for coming up in my job looking like that.

"How are you today?" she asked, passing me a bottle of water as she headed toward her desk.

"I'm cool."

"Quita?

"Oh, she a'ight. What's good?"

Cathy pulled out this big ass brown folder and laid it on her desk. "Monique, I'm going to let you know something.

"What's that?"

"I don't expect you'll be offended, but I'm sure what I have to say will shed some light on me and the kind of lawyer I am and how serious I take my job."

I shrugged with an attitude that stated "say what you got to say already."

"Where did you go the evening you were released from jail?"

"I told you. I went to Big Daddy's and went out to eat with some friends."

She opened the folder and threw some pictures at me. "I need you to know I'm not the one to fuck with. Those, *pardner*, are pictures of you at Big Daddy's, but you didn't leave on foot. These pictures, *pardner*, are of you in China Star with one friend not friendsssss."

What the hell could I say?

"Oh, and by the way, Monkey does tricks and has a way with words when you dangle jail or some weed in his face. And he'll never let on that somebody's asked him for info. Who's the girl?" Cathy leaned back in her chair.

Damn, she got me. "Where you get that stuff from, mayne?"

"First, you talk too much. Just from that one conversation we had at the zoo, I was able to get this information. Big Daddy's didn't want its license fucked with since everybody knows they have illegal gambling going on in the barbershop, China Star didn't want to be reported to the health inspector because of its many violations in the kitchen, and Monkey wants to stay out of jail. Who is she?"

"In legal terms, she's my alibi."

"I know. How in the hell could you cheat on LaQuita with some woman you met on the street and allowed to go home with you?"

"I don't know. I mean, it just happened."

Cathy was mad as hell at me, and I figured she had told or was going to tell Quita. "What pisses me off the most about this whole thing is because of our attorney-client privilege I can't say shit to Quita."

"Mayne, why you do this? I was gonna tell you."

"No, you weren't. Besides, I had to get it before the D.A. got it and destroyed it."

"Is he like that?"

"Worse. I told you we're not playing a game here. Ray Owens, the girl's father, is no joke. He doesn't like his own people and will do everything he can to bring another Black person down. I need that girl in here."

"I can't do that."

"Why not?"

"I don't know where to find her."

"Well, looking at these pictures of her coming out the nail salon, you at least know where she is once every two weeks."

"OK, I'll try to look for her."

I was ready to flush this toilet when Cathy brought up some more shit. "Have you talked to Jamal?"

"I plan to this evening."

"Am I going to have to step up and . . ."

"Naw, I got it. Are you done?"

"Yes, I am. Monique, we go to court in two weeks. We need to have this wrapped up before then."

Before I walked out of her office, I had only one thing to offer. "Cathy, you know if Quita finds out about what happened at the house, she'll leave, and well, she's all I got."

"You should've thought about that before you brought someone back to your house and fucked her."

WHEN TROUBLE COMES A-KNOCKIN'
Mo

Noni Richmond, that night at China Star, didn't say much about who she was. She was focusing so hard on stuffing her face that there was no time for talking. I'd never seen a woman eat like that. At one point I stopped her and asked, "Are you really that hungry?"

She said, "Oh-my-God, I'm so sorry. I must be eating like a dog if you had to ask me that."

"Well . . . yeah, you are," I said sarcastically.

"Oops! My bad. Since I've been working out, my metabolism is through the roof. I try to stay away from all-you-can-eat buffets because I tend to go a little overboard."

"A little?" That bitch needed a trough. "So how often do you work out?"

"Four times a week."

"That's wassup." On the way to the house, she was running down to me all this stuff about where she grew up, where she went to school, and some shit about her family. What bothered me is that she wasn't paying attention to the fact that I really didn't care. After I knocked that ass right out the ballpark, I considered the whole thing over just as quickly as it began. Never paid attention to the playah details—make sure she ain't got your number—make sure she doesn't remember where you live.

In the midst of all the other mess that had been going on, Sunday morning the phone rang about six o'clock. Me nor Quita budged. It rang again half hour later. We didn't answer. I got up to pee and didn't notice Quita reaching for the caller ID.

When I came out the toilet, she was sitting on the side of the bed. "Ain't there a law or somethin' about telemarketers calling on Sundays?"

"Hell, I don't know," I said scrambling back to bed. "Thank the Lawd for caller ID."

She then got up and made her way to the bathroom. Quita had a bad habit of talking to me while she was the on the toilet. Everything was an echo. I hated that.

"You know," she started. "One of the dancers is selling this stuff called Noni Juice and was asking me if I wanted her to stop by and let us taste it. I wonder if that was her."

I was laying there stiff as a board. Quita came out the bathroom. "Uh, what was you saying?" I asked.

"Noni Juice? My coworker wanting to bring us some . . ." she said in a little you-wasn't-listening-to-what-the-fuck-I said tone. "That's who was on the caller ID."

"Noni?" My heart was about to jump out of my chest, and I laid there with my back to Quita the whole time. "Why she calling so early?"

"Honey, knowing her she never went to bed. She's a hustler, and time is money." Quita got back in the bed and pulled the covers over her head.

I didn't know what to do. How the hell that girl get my number? I never wrote it down for her or anything like that, but then I remembered I used her phone and the heifer must've saved it. "Baby, can you go and get me some aspirin and some orange juice?"

"Yeah, what's wrong?"

"Oh, nothing. Just got a little bit of a headache."

"OK."

The second Quita hit the hallway, I flipped over and fell to the floor. I crawled under the bed, disconnected the phone and was back in the bed before she returned. Since she and Moms was cool now, we all had dinner at my place on Sundays. It was the same time, three o'clock, each week. There was no need to call. It was just understood.

"Here you go, baby," she said handing me the cup and the pills. "I hope you feel better." Quita had me spoiled like that, and I knew she was waiting for me to drink the last drop.

"Go ahead and get back in bed," I encouraged her. "I'll take it back." That way I was able to disconnect the other phones.

Early in the afternoon while I was watching the football game Quita came stomping through the living room in a panic. "I'm out of noodles."

"What?" I asked. The Cowboys and the Redskins were duking it out. Washington had scored a touchdown on the opening kick-off, and Dallas was storming back with the ball on the Redskins five-yard line. I heard her, but I never took my eye off the TV.

"Mo, I need some noodles for my lasagna. I need you to go the store."

"Now?" I asked. "Dallas is about to score."

With her apron full of tomato sauce and egg yolks, Quita walked her ass over to the TV and turned it off. "Well, you'll find out about it when you get back with my noodles."

Was I ready to fight or what? I snatched the keys from the counter and left for the store. At the bottom of the stairs, I met Monkey. "Wassup, niggah?"

Monkey, in his dirty green jumpsuit, was high as a fucking kite. "Aw, not a thang, not a thang. Where you off to?"

"Mayne, female in there wants me to go to the store. 'Bout to run over to Kroger."

"Look, I'm gonna stop by later and pick up that key. Yo' ass forgot to bring it back."

"My bad. I'll be back in a few. You can stop by in a coupla hours."

"Can't you go back and get it now while I'm right here?"

"And risk gettin' a pot thrown at me? Hell, naw. Just come get it later."

When I came back in the house, Moms was there. I hadn't been gone but fifteen minutes. I didn't even speak to her. That was her and Quita's thing. As far as I was concerned, shit hadn't changed between me and her.

Moms had been keeping herself up pretty nice since she and Quita started hanging out. Had on a little make-up, earrings, and nice clothes. She could be dressed like Tyra Banks or Judge Hatchett for that matter. I didn't care. I let those two females have at it.

Dinner was ready just in time for the second part of

the double-header: Indianapolis Colts versus Balti-more Ravens. Quita fixed my plate and brought it to me on my TV tray while Moms made me some red Kool-Aid. Females didn't seem to understand the need for a niggah's privacy on game day. I didn't want to talk about shit; I didn't want to do shit; and I for damn sho didn't want to go nowhere. If your ass wasn't plan-ning on watching the game, then you better keep your ass at home or bring you something else to do. Moms and Quita played Scrabble.

Now picture this. Ball is on the 23. Colts Ball. Third and inches. Colts down 14-12. There's the snap. Peyton Manning drops back. He's got time. Looking for a re-ceiver. Manning now under pressure. Finds Harrison. Looking to throw. What! He loses the ball and . . . ! Then the cable goes out. That's the equivalent of some-one stopping by and interrupting the game like Mon-key did that day. I opened the door.

"Sup, niggah?"

I was so fucking mad I didn't know what to do. "What, Monkey?" He was a tall, lanky fuckah with long arms that hung down past his thighs. After that whole thing with Cathy, I didn't trust him anymore.

"I came by to get that key off you." He heard Moms and Quita laughing and talking in the kitchen. "Quita in there?" he asked.

"Yeah, she in there with my Moms."

"A'ight then. Lemme go holla at her."

I went to the bedroom to get the key. With every-thing that had been going on, I'd forgot about it. Head-ing back to the front of the apartment, I heard "Niggah, where the fuck my money?" Then I heard, "Bitch, kiss my ass!" After that, "Muthafuckah, I'll cut yo' ass right here, right now! Quita, let me go!" I jetted down the hallway and broke for the kitchen. Moms had a butcher knife and was inches from Monkey's nuts, and poor Quita was losing the battle of keeping them apart.

"Whoaaa, what the fuck y'all doin'?"

Moms yelled, "Monique, what this sorry-ass-bag-of-shit doin' up in yo' house? Lock all yo' shit up and make sho yo' TVs and stereo locked down!"

"Bitch, fuck you wit yo' sour-ass pussy. Made my dick itch for months!"

"What!" Moms lunged at him again this time with an open palm. "Niggah, I'll smack the taste outta yo' mouth."

"Do it! You bad! Do it!"

I couldn't take any more. "Hold the fuck up, just hold the fuck up. This my house, and both of y'all asses needed to chill."

I took the knife from Moms, and Quita pulled out a chair for Monkey to sit in on the other side of the kitchen. I got the dishtowel and wiped the sweat from my forehead. The kitchen was all hot from where Quita had been cooking, and amidst all the commotion, I chose to sit somewhere in between them. I listened as Moms cussed Monkey out about draining her bank accounts, selling dope out of her house, and being the reason she lost her house. It was her who paid for his lawyer, and it was her who paid off the folks he owed for all the drugs he had.

Monkey cussed Moms out about being a ho. He was complaining about her fucking every Tom, Dick, and Eric Lee she knew. I didn't necessarily want to hear that. They went back and forth for about ten minutes. Then, in a fit of rage, I told both of them to get the hell out. My football Sunday had been ruined. My food was cold, and I almost had World War III in my kitchen.

Quita had taken the night off, and with all the drama from the day, peace and quiet was our only desire. It had been a while since she'd been off on a Sunday night, so I wanted to make the best of it. One thing I loved about my lady was she cleaned the house in the nude. I'd rest on the couch and watch ass and titties all over the place. To me, there was no better way to have it.

The sun had started to set, and Quita was cleaning the entertainment system when there came a knock at the door. "Are you expecting somebody?" she asked, dusting off the speakers.

"No, I'm not." I was good for letting your ass sit outside if you hadn't called first. I remembered, though, I'd unplugged the phones. I went to the door and looked out the peephole. It was that damn girl, Noni. I stood there with my eye pressed against the hole like I was Jeannie trying to blink her ass away.

"Who is it, Mo?" Quita asked.

"Uh, Jehovah's Witness."

"On a Sunday night?" She was still cleaning and never seemed too fazed by the disturbance.

"I guess."

Noni kept knocking.

"Those people oughta stop," she said, still rattling jewelry all over the place. "You a better one than me. You already dun stood there too long."

There was nothing else I could do. I had to protect that door. Noni knocked for another five minutes and eventually left. "Finally," I said.

Quita was dusting the end table when she stumbled upon the disconnected telephone cord. "What the hell?" she asked as she picked up the cords from the floor.

"Oh, oh, I did that."

"Uh, what for?"

"I was hoping for us to have some quiet time. Folks been botherin' us since six this morning."

I got her with that. "Awww, that's so sweet," she said still swinging ass and tits in my face. She strutted over to me and sat her sweaty booty cheeks on my lap. My woman never ceased to amaze me. I wanted to hold her and make love to her in every way I could.

"Hey, I have an idea."

"What, baby?" she giggled.

"How about I go run some bathwater, light the candles, get us a little somethin' to drink and you meet in the bathroom?"

"Ooooohhh, lemme find out you tryin' to be freaky."

The candlelight flickered against the white backdrop like a serene spa way off from the rest of the world. I'd put a little Epsom salt in the bathwater to relax our bodies and soothe any aches and pains. The bubbles were just right having made mountains of suds floating in the warm water. I'd started taking my clothes off when Quita yelled, "Mo! Get the fuck out here!"

Sliding into my slippers, I wrapped a towel around my waist and stumbled up the hallway. "What is it, ba . . ."

"Fucking Jehovah's witness, huh?" Noni, standing there with her tote bag, had the biggest grin on her face. Apparently, she'd come back, and Quita had answered the door on her way to the tub. It was an awkward moment because Quita, the ghetto princess, was still stark naked with the door standing wide open.

Noni, assessing the obvious fact that Quita wasn't my cousin, asked, "Is this a bad time for you and your cousin? You seem a bit occupied."

Quita snapped her head at me, "Your cousin, huh?" With her hand clinching the dust rag propped upon her hip, she was so sexy mad.

I stood there with my little knots for boobs at attention from the cold air. My towel draped the real me. Despite my tough shell, I didn't have it in me to hurt Quita to her face. "Quita, this is Noni. Noni, this is my girl, Quita."

Visibly uncomfortable, Noni offered her hand to Quita whose glare had pierced holes in me. She'd slammed the door so hard the whole apartment shook. "Nice to meet you," Quita said. "Have a seat."

"Thank you," Noni replied.

For my own safety, I stayed as far away from Quita as possible. A brush, a plant, a shoe, a book, a brick could be hurled my way at any unsuspecting moment. I actually caught Noni giving Quita the eye as she walked toward the kitchen. "Want somethin' to drink?" she asked.

"No, I'm fine," Noni replied sitting upright in the chair. "Uh, I'm really sorry for imposing. I thought . . ."

Quita interrupted her. "Girl, don't apologize because ain't none of this your fault. It's on that niggah right there."

I popped my head against the wall one smack right after the other. My heart was racing, and I wondered what was going to happen next. The main thing to do was to get Quita to come with me to the back so we could talk. "Quita, can I see you in the back for a minute?" She'd plopped down on the coffee table with her legs open wide right in front of Noni. You could literally see the beads of water forming on that girl's face. She and Quita had connected in some sort of way.

"Quita!" I gestured. "In the back, please. I need to talk to you."

She reluctantly got up from the table with Noni looking away into the kitchen. Quita stomped past me with her arms folded and went into the bedroom. I followed her, thinking of what on earth I could say to fix things. But before I could open my mouth, Quita grabbed me by the face squeezing my jaws together so I couldn't speak.

"One thing you need to know about me is that I don't have to throw shit or hit you to show my anger. I got this, and I already know what I'm going to do to make you suffer for it. If my instincts are correct, she'll be naked when we go back in there, and I want to see what you did to her to make her come to my fucking house at this time of night on a Sunday. Do I make myself clear?"

Who was this woman in front of me? What had she done with Quita? "A'ight," I said as she snatched her fingers away from my face hard enough for her nails to catch my skin. We walked back down the hallway, and I be damned if Noni wasn't what . . . naked!

"Go ahead with yo' punk ass. Show me what you did."

I wasn't as flattered with Noni as I had been the first time. A chocolate girl with a slight Spanish accent, she no longer had anything I wanted. I vaguely remembered her telling me her mother was from Kenya, and her father was from Cuba. Nipples erect, she smiled at me like it was her birthday. I looked over at Quita, who was standing there like a plantation mistress waiting to crack her whip if anything went wrong. I filled my head with images of making love to my lady and not this intruder. Aroused a bit, I took Noni's breasts in my hands. She released a sigh. I massaged them with no passion and no intimacy, but it seemed to not matter to her. Frowning at me and the position I'd put us in, Quita simply watched.

"Turn around," I ordered, and Noni made a circle in the floor. Slowly, I caressed her back making my way down her spine until I reached the top of her ass. Then she bent over, and in the second that I looked at her cheeks spread open before me, Quita disappeared but returned with Master D.

"You forgot something," she said throwing it at me, full speed, harness and all.

Knowing I shouldn't say anything at this point, I picked the harness up from the floor and slid it on. I'd bought a new one where all I had to do was slip every-thing on like a pair of underwear. With my left hand, I fingered Noni's clit, and with the other, I guided Master D into her hole. And I didn't take my eye off Quita, who seemed to be more interested in Noni's reaction. It was Quita I thought about making love to . . . not this woman.

It didn't take much for Noni to cum. She was good for one nut right after the other all night long. Dis-connecting us, Noni turned to face me and pulled me toward her as she made her way backwards to the sofa. In one swift movement, she grabbed her legs and like an acrobat she extended them above her head until her knees touched her shoulders. Agility was an understatement. This girl was a human rub-ber band.

I grinded away inside of her while my eyes remained fixed on the other side of the room. Noni, moaning and groaning, was having the time of her life, and Quita, shaking her head at what used to be a private moment between just us, walked over to me and pressed my ass even deeper into Noni's cut. "Move," she said.

I graciously stopped what I was doing, hoping this was now over. Quickly, I got my towel and covered myself. I saw Quita move closer to Noni, eventually falling to her knees tongue first into her burrow. Noni released one of her legs and folded it like a paper clip and placed it behind her neck. I'd never seen shit like that before in my life. What amazed me most, though was the sensuality between them. Quita knew exactly where to place her tongue, and Noni, well, she knew exactly what she was doing . . . period. "Fuck me, mami," Noni requested.

Quita worked every inch of Noni's pussy with her tongue and hands. As she slinked toward Noni's torso, I watched Quita's breasts dip into her den. Like a dick I'd never seen, she pulled in and out with her nipples imaginatively ejaculating inside of her. While for the average muthafuckah, this was some kinky, above the norm, freakshow-for-you-ass bullshit, but for me, it was what I had been afraid of with Quita continuing to dance for hos at the club. She really did like the taste of pussy in her throat and the smell of it in her nostrils.

Watching them carry on like that irritated me. It had never, EVER been like that with us. I'd blocked all pleasurable sensitivity from my vagina and had learned to focus my energy on giving pleasure and not receiving it. As Quita rose above Noni and positioned herself for them to lock pussies, I was sick. Seeing this as my punishment, I fought back the tears, pounding my fist into the palm of my hand. Quita rocked in place until the motion was replaced with quick, soft bounces making them both let go like I'd never heard either do before, and what made it worse was they smiled about it.

Drenched in water smelling of sex from head to toe,

Quita walked over to me and whispered in my ear, "That didn't feel too good, did it?"

Turning my head away from what I'd just witnessed, I cleared the lump in my throat. "No, it didn't." A tear managed to fall out of the corner of my eye. I don't know who felt the most pain, Mo or Monique.

MAMA MAY HAVE
Mo

A day went by before I was able to say a word to Quita. Quite frankly, she disgusted me. Some nerve I had, right? I'd grown accustomed to being the dominant one, but I also had a weak side.

To try and sort through this anguish, I increased my sessions with Dan. He came by the house one evening after Quita had left for work. When he came through the door, I could tell he was up to something. "How you doing, Mo?" he asked, breezing past me but looking back to see behind him.

"I'm a'ight." I began to close the door.

"Uh, don't do that, Mo," he gestured. "I brought someone with me." Seconds later, Moms appears and comes through the door with the expectation of me being glad to see her.

"Heyyy," she said smiling ear to ear.

"What's good?" I left her to close the door and find her own damn seat. I plunked down on the couch and was like, "Somebody wanna tell me what the hell is goin' on?"

Dan was a little red in the face. He and I clashed before about him inviting folks without my permission to our sessions. I even made Quita leave one time.

"Mo, it's time for some intervention. Some things have escalated beyond your control, and we need to try to bring things back down to earth."

Not even making eye contact with Moms, I questioned, "And having her here is going to help that?"

As gullible as the day is long, Dan said, "Yes, I think so. Just hear me out, will ya?"

I agreed to at least listen to what he had to say. During a couple of sessions, he'd asked me how I felt about Moms coming to try and help me work through my issues about her and about Mr. Luther. I knew I wasn't going to ask her to come, so apparently Dan had gotten her to.

"Now, Mo, your mom is not going to say much today. I primarily wanted her here so she could listen. First, I want you to tell me why you called your mom after you were arrested."

That was a good one. "Um, I thought I needed her. Um, I thought she would be there to rescue me."

"Why didn't you call Quita?"

"Oh, that's easy. I was mad at her. I didn't particularly want to hear her voice right then, so I called Moms."

"Did you feel let down when she didn't come get you out?"

"Yeah, I did, but I was used to it. Things worked themselves out."

"Mo, I need you to know your mom called me that morning. After several months of trying to reach out to her, she called."

Amazed but not fazed, I tossed a look at her but

quickly turned away. "And? She didn't still get me out."

"But Mo, she tried, and that's why we're here like this today. It's time for you to work on forgiveness."

That mo-fo was talking like Job's wife. I couldn't rationalize forgiving her for protecting Mr. Luther and leaving me to fend for myself. I thought about it for a minute, though. She might not have got me out, but she was in court that morning after I'd asked her to be there. "So, mayne, what you want me to do?"

Dan started going through my papers. I was expecting him to pull some shit out of them and then strike up a conversation. Instead, he asked me, "Do you want to begin with an apology?"

Shit, I was looking at Moms like "Go ahead, do it. I'm listening." I mean, I thought he ain't want her to say nothing, but he was running the show. "I guess if that's you want her to do."

Bamboozled by my actions, Dan's ass said, "I was talking about you, Mo."

"And I'm apologizing forrrr . . . ?" Maybe he'd gotten confused on why we were in this situation. *She* was the one who betrayed *me*—her own daughter. *She* was the one who made it a point to make me feel like shit by saying the things she'd said to me. *She* was the one who let that bastard do that stuff to me.

Then Dan's ass goes into something that had slipped my mind. "Mo, you pulled a gun on her. Remember? You threatened her life."

Angry at how it seemed they were trying to flip this shit, I professed, "It was my life that was threatened . . . not hers. Mr. Luther took my innocence away. He could've killed me if he wanted to."

Moms spoke up quickly instantly refuting what I'd

said. "That man would-na killed you. He ain't even like that."

"Now, Ms. Cummings, you promised," Dan reminded her.

Moms acknowledged his request with a simple nod of her head.

"Mayne, she still takin' up for him and shit. I ain't about to . . ."

"Trust me, we're going to work on that. Just work with me, OK?"

"A'ight."

"So, are you going to apologize? We have about thirty minutes or so left, and there are some other things I want to cover."

I thought long and hard about that shit. I didn't one hundred percent agree with what he was wanting me to do, but in all honesty, I did want things to get better. I missed my moms. I called her that morning because I guess my natural instincts kicked in. I needed her. "I'm sorry about pulling my heatah on you." It actually felt good. I saw Moms's eyes light up a little. She didn't say nothing, though.

Dan was pleased. "Mo, I don't think you realize the breakthrough here."

"Actually I don't. Seems pretty upside down right now if you ask me."

"It'll get better. What I've had your mom to do is write that letter you and I had talked about a few times. She doesn't have it with her today, but you'll see it in due time."

"A'ight."

I didn't know we were heading next with this intervention. Dan was taking notes and scratching his head a lot. "This is what I want to do," he said. "Mo, if you don't mind, I want you to talk to us about what happened that day out in the field."

No. Anything but that, I thought. I hadn't blocked it out, but I'd got to where I didn't like talking about it anymore. Was doing this supposed to be part of healing? That ain't the kind of healing I was into now. Healing for me was busting a cap in Mr. Luther's ass. Immediately, I thought about the day I saw him at the store. I hadn't told anyone but Quita about that. I was too ashamed at how I'd handled it. "If that's what you want to do."

"Yeah, let's do that, and then next we'll let your mom talk. This way she can have time to digest what you're about to say."

"Bet," I said. Closing my eyes, I took a deep breath and put myself back there. It's hard trying to return to a place you'd blocked out of your mind. I exhaled, and, when I opened my eyes, there I was in my pink sundress, hair bows, and Mary Janes. "I got to the railroad tracks with my Popsicle. I felt like I was being hunted. I continued through the field. I was his prey, pouncing on me from behind. He devoured my soul and chewed my innocence up like a piece of meat and spat it out."

"So Mr. Luther attacked you from behind? Is that what you're saying?"

My eyes, glazed over with tears, fixated on my moms as she sat there weeping. At times, she was virtually sobbing. I didn't know she was even feeling me like that. While I thought I'd be the one to stop the recollection, it was her. "Look, we can stop right here. I need to get on back home."

Dan was shocked because, for the first time since we started, there was a breakthrough. "Ms. Cummings, you want to leave now? We . . ."

"No, no, no!" she was insistent. "I want to go now, Mr. Dan, and if you not gon take me, I'll get the bus."

"All right, all right. You're obviously upset. We can go ahead and stop." Mr. Dan got his things together and helped moms from the couch. "You did good today, Mo. I'm proud of you."

"Thank you."

Moms went through the door without saying a word to me. She went back to that same ol' shit. I didn't care. Dan stopped in the doorway, turned to me and asked, "Did you talk with your lawyer yet?"

Dan knew everything. He had to in order to blame my issues on my now criminal behavior. "Yeah, I talked to her."

"Look, uh, she's doesn't seem to play too many games. You may want to stay on her good side. I told her there was no way you had anything to do with that rape."

"Thanks."

"I did, though, tell her I'd encourage you to talk to Jamal as soon as possible."

"I'm going to do it tonight. I promise."

"OK, good to hear that. You know, the purpose of bringing up what happened is so we can get you to the bottom of this Mo/Monique thing. You're going to have figure that out. I can talk to you until I'm blue in the face, but the ultimate decision is yours." Moms had gone down to Dan's car and was sitting inside waiting on him. She started honking his horn. "Look, let me go and get your mom home."

BRING THAT BABY HOME
Elise

I was standin' in my house lookin' at myself in the mirror. Listenin' to Monique talk 'bout Mr. Luther brought back my memories of my own pain. At one point I got to thinkin'. I mean, I really got to thinkin'. The way Monique say she was hurt was similar to what happened to me. The difference, though, was she saw who did it to her. I nevah got the chance to see the bastard.

Mr. Luther was a good man as far as I knew. He was always real nice to all the kids. I still felt he talked too damn much to grown folks 'bout their kids' bidness. Since all that stuff went on wit Monique, I really didn't know too much 'bout him. Penny had told me he was pretty sick and her and Mama was lookin' in on him from time to time. Word was he had sugar but was still drankin' lemon-lime Kool-Aid like water. You couldn't tell him nothin'. Penny asked me if I knew he didn't have but half a dick. Say it got gangrene and it fell clear off. The nurse that sit wit him told her that cuz he was hooked up to a catheter and a bag. I figured

Monique had somethin' to do with that. If that was the case, he didn't nevah say nothin' 'bout it to nobody.

Now, I'm not no child like Monique. I'll walk up to your ass and cut your throat and be gone befo' a drop of blood hit the ground. It wasn't hard to figure out he raped me that day in his store, and he know I couldn't prove it. That's why he kept sendin' me all them damn pickles. Suppose he guessed he could fuck my daughter instead.

I called Penny one night and felt like, for the first time in all my life, I needed to talk 'bout me and where I'd messed up. I cried and cried and even told her 'bout what happened to Monique. I told her 'bout how she was lookin', 'bout jail and Cathy, 'bout Eric Lee and Mr. Luther. Next thing I know, Penny was cryin', too.

"So where's Monique now?" she asked.

"Stayin' out in Whitehaven wit the girl."

"Elise, I can't believe you been keeping this to yourself all this time. That baby needs her family."

I felt so bad. I thought she was gonna be on my side. "I just realized sittin' there wit Mr. Dan that he had raped both of us."

"Why didn't she tell somebody?"

I cleared my throat and admitted, "She did try to tell me, but I kept on lettin' him come 'round like a ol' snake. I ain't believe he could do somethin' like that to a chile."

"Well, obviously, you were wrong. You need to tell somebody. I vaguely remember hearing some of the little girls around here talking about him doing something like that. I thought they were just playing around. He needs to be locked up. You see all those old fools who killed folks during the Civil Rights Movement still going to jail."

"Monique not gon say nothin', Penny. She's tryin' to move on."

Penny didn't like where I was goin' wit it. She was ready to fight somebody. "We need to have a family meeting right away about this. We haven't seen Monique in years. You got everybody thinking she ran away for no reason. You need to bring that baby home."

When Mama found out, I was in more hot water. She made me feel like the gum on the bottom of somebody shoe. Nobody seemed to care what happened to me. All they was worried 'bout was Monique. And for once, I was too.

TROUBLE DON'T LAST ALWAYS
Mo

Ifound Jamal at Big Daddy's where he usually was this time of night. He would shoot pool with some of the older dudes and take all their money, so he could get something to eat at the snack bar. I hadn't seen him since we got arrested nearly two weeks ago, and that wasn't no big deal. Some loud mouth fool had probably already told him what was going on. I found him sitting at the snack bar with a chicken plate, a bottle of hot sauce, and a Pepsi. I spun the bar stool around and jumped on it while it was still in motion. "Wassup, fool?" I asked.

He gave me some love and said with a mouth full of food, "Aw, you got it, pardner." Jamal was kind of enough to lick his fingers afterwards. "Dude, where you been at?" Pieces of chicken crumbs were all over the counter, and some smaller pieces were hanging on around his mouth.

"Chillin'. Workin'. Chillin' some mo'."

Jamal never let up from that plate. Taking a bite out of his second chicken leg, "Yeah, me too."

No one was nearby to overhear what I had to say to him, but I leaned in closer to shield our privacy. "Jamal, we need to talk."

"Wassup, yo?"

"They tryin' to put a murdah charge on me."

Finally, he stopped eating long enough to listen. "Where the hell that come from?"

"They sayin' the heatah I had was used to smoke some dude. They keep askin' me where I got it from."

Jamal pushed his plate away and grabbed a toothpick from the holder. "And what you say?"

"Well, I told my lawyer where I got it. You know, she can't say nothin'."

"What she say?" Jamal nervously began to gnaw on the thin piece of wood.

"She just told me to talk to you. Jamal, I can't go down for no murdah." I took my chances with him and just went on and asked him about it. "Pardner, me and you go back a minute. I need you to tell me the truth."

Jamal, digging between his teeth with a now soggy toothpick, guzzled the last half of his Pepsi. "Let's talk outside a minute."

When we got outside, Jamal lit a cig. I wasn't sure what I was about to hear, so I prepared myself. "Wassup?"

I know he was tempted to look underneath my shirt to see if I was wired, but he didn't do it. This wasn't no *Law and Order* shit. I just wanted to know what was going on and clear my fucking name. "I killed my stepfather with it. A coupla days before I met you, I went home to see Moms and check on what was up at the house. Right as I was comin' off the stairs, I hear Moms screamin'. I heard him cussin' at her and all this glass was breakin'. I broke through the door, and he was standin' over her about to kill her. I saw his finger on the trigger, and I knew he was going to shoot her if I came any closer. I couldn't lose my moms, Mo."

To sum it up, Jamal had lied to me. But having been to the same place mentally, I didn't have a problem with it. "I gotcha."

"He starts callin' me all kinds of names and spittin' at Moms. Next thing I know I musta just lost it because I picked up a pillow from the couch by the door, and I blasted three holes in it. One of them hit him in the neck." By now Jamal, my dawg, was cryin'. "He bled all over Moms and the floor. I sat in there with her for almost twelve hours trying to figure out what to do with him. My moms worked at a doctor's office and had all kinds of medical supplies, including a couple of scalpels and saws. It took about six hours to cut him up. We put his ass in a couple of suitcases, and I rolled them right into the Greyhound station and left him on the curb to be picked up with the rest of the luggage. I took his gun and put it in my pocket. That's the gun I gave you."

Damn, and I thought I was demented. "Jamal, mayne, you gave me Stanley's gun?"

"Well, yeah, but you gotta believe me when I tell you I ain't know he smoked somebody with it. I swear I ain't know."

"Dude, I believe you, but . . . Cathy talkin' 'bout somebody saw you."

"Dawg, ain't nobody seen shit. Don't even fall for it. I put that niggah on a bus to Dallas. Do you know how many peeps be in the bus station in the evenings? Hundreds sometimes."

"But they sayin' . . ."

"Look, they gonna say what they want to. You gotta remember what you walkin' 'round here perpetrating as. We, the Black man," he proclaimed proudly with his open palm slapping his burly chest, "ain't nothin' but a statistic. We eitha dead or in jail. They figure we all look alike. You see they had yo' ass down there, and you ain't even no real dude!" he said, laughing. "Do you know how many bruhs sittin' out at the penal farm right now and ain't do nothin'?"

Finding words to show Jamal I understood was useless. "So what am I supposed to do? They tryin' to put it off on somebody."

"Mo, you don't get it, do you? Now, I got the iron from Stanley who may or may not have smoked somebody," he seemed frustrated with me. Jamal started pacing the sidewalk.

"Look, they ain't got nothin' on you. All they tryin' to do is get you to roll on whoever got you that heatah. That shit about a young Black male killing somebody? Shit, that could be any one of us on any given day at any given time dependin' on the po-po's mood. Lemme tell you this, though. You need to stop and think, and I mean really think about what you doing to yourself. It's more to being a man than a dick, and right now, that's all you got to show for it. You ain't gonna never understand what it's like to be one of me because deep down underneath the fro and the dildo, you still a chick. Yeah, I lied to you 'bout Stanley. So what? That's me and my shit and ain't got nothin' to do with you."

Jamal was scaring me. I thought me and him was cool. I felt as if he was trying to make me feel guilty about everything. "So you think I need to give this up?"

"Mayne, you gon always be my dawg no matter what, but I just think you openin' yourelf up to a world of trouble for nothin'. You see what happened the day we was locked up. Even though you was trying to be cool about shit, you was losin' it. If them dudes hadda found out you was a girl, awwww, mayne."

My body was welling up with that frustration again. I was strapped against a society that wasn't ready for me. I understood where Jamal was coming from, but what about Mr. Luther? If I went back to Monique, he would know where I was and hunt me down like a dog and try to kill me—maybe even finish the job he started that day out in the field. Then the inevitable happened.

"Mo, mayne, you cryin'?"

A tear had fallen, and there was no way I could hide it. "I'm a'ight." Clearing the corner of my eye with my finger, I focused and saw the concern on Jamal's face. We'd been homies for a good while, and I knew he always had my back. He walked over to me and sat down on the ledge in front of Big Daddy's. He reached for my hand and held it like family would have. Nobody saw us, and if they did, no one was paying attention. For the first time since I'd known him, I felt Jamal reaching out for the woman in me. I knew he cared a lot, and I was grateful for that.

"Monique, I'll go with you tomorrow to talk to the D.A. I'll fix this. Don't worry about it. I got you," he said assuringly as he squeezed my hand. Just as quickly as he grabbed my hand, he dropped it when this female breezed out the door. "Dayum, girl! You musta jumped off the top of yo' house to get in them jeans. Got dayum," he taunted grabbing his crotch. "And then yo' ass smell good as shit!"

I recognized the fragrance. It was that Anney, Ainney shit Noni wore. Those jeans she was wearing fit on her like faded blue paint. Peeping around a Suburban sticking way out of its parking space, I saw the green

Honda Civic. "Jamal, I gotta go. I'll meet you at 201 in the morning. We gotta be there at ten."

My nig said, "Aw, mayne, wait. Wait! That's you?"

Couldn't do nothing but chuckle. "Holla," and I jogged off to catch up with Noni. I desperately needed her to come downtown, too. After what happened the last time I saw her, I knew it was going to take some persuading. Walking with her fingers stiff with wet nail polish and her keys dangling from her thumb, I caught her just as she reached for the door handle. "Lemme get that for you," I offered.

Noni, surprisingly, was pleasant. "Oh, well, thank you." She flashed her gap with a piece of chewing gum hanging out of her mouth. "How you been doing, stranger?"

Taking her keys from her thumb, I said, "I'm good. What's good with you, sexy?" Folding my arms, I leaned against her car and tried to throw some of my mack on her, but I realized I really didn't have much to say. This was the woman who had let my girl fuck her all over my house, but shit, she had let me do the same thing. She had caught me in a lie, but didn't seem to sweat me about it.

Grinning coyly, she replied, "Nothing much. Working and church as usual."

Church? The nerve. "I see." I didn't want to waste a bunch of time getting to what I wanted. "Uh, uh, uh," I stuttered. "I, uh, got a little problem."

Expressing seemingly genuine concern, Noni said, "What's wrong? Is everything all right?"

"Uh, did you hear about that girl that was raped at school?" I was looking around the parking lot to make certain Quita didn't jump out in a surprise appearance. If she did, I knew I'd be accused of still chasing pussy.

"Yeah, I read about that in the paper. They're still looking for the girl, right?"

"Well, yeah, but, um, they want to question me about it. Before I met you that day, I'd been over to my moms's house, and she don't live too far from the school."

"I read they have a few leads, but the girl isn't talking, nor is anyone else."

"Right. They still want to talk to me, though, to see if I had an alibi."

"Mo, you do. I mean, you were with me, but I can't tell anyone that."

I was fucked. "Damn, yungin', what you mean? I was . . ."

"Get in the car," she ordered, snatching the keys from me. She unlocked her door, got in, and reached over to unlatch the passenger side. A few minutes passed before Noni spoke. Sitting there massaging the silver cross on her key chain, she looked over at me wanting sympathy for whatever it was she was about to say. "Do you realize the position you'd put me in if I had to tell someone I was with a gay woman who looks like a common everyday street thug?"

Whoa, she was hitting a niggah pretty low with all those descriptions. "Noni, are you that mad with me that you'd let me go to jail for something I didn't do?"

"Dear-heart, it's not about you. It's me. If things were different, I'd help you out in a heartbeat, but I just can't do it."

I knew that shit with Quita was going to come back and bite me in the ass. Most of me had been counting on Noni to come through for me, but perhaps that bitch side of her was preventing her from doing it. "Noni, all I need you to do is tell the folks I was with you."

Shaking her head, she quietly said, "No, I can't do that. If my church found out I'd had any involvement with you, they'd put me out."

"How the church gon put somebody out? That's supposed to be God's house, and He loves everybody."

"You know, in the real world, you're right. But my church doesn't operate like that. They'd be on a witch hunt, and I don't want my reputation ruined over this. My private life would be on all but the church covenant. I'm sorry."

I had no choice but to understand. "A'ight." I calmly turned to her acknowledging her sentiment. "Well, you take care," I said as I prepared to get out.

"Mo?"

"Yeah?"

"Do you believe in God?"

Here we go, I thought. I wasn't trying to get into one of these conversations right now. But you know, she did have a valid question. Did I? "I suppose. Why?"

"I know it will seem a little out of place for someone like me to suggest this, but I think you should try to trust and believe in Him. He can work miracles if you let Him."

The church lady was on to something. "Noni, I ain't been to church since I was a little girl. I don't think I got a right to be bothering God with my worries. Besides, I think I've turned my back on Him with all this drama I have going on in my life, especially my thing with Quita."

"Mo, look at me. You, of all people, know I'm not a saint, but it doesn't stop me from knowing God. Tonight when you go home, have a talk with Him, and I promise you everything will be all right."

I nodded in agreement and opened the door. "Thank you, Noni. I'll try that."

Cranking the car, she said, "Oh, by the way, tell Quita I said hello. You two take care of yourselves and remember trouble don't last always," she said, waving as she was putting the car in reverse.

I reluctantly waved back, slamming the door as I watched her back out of my life.

Before I went to the house, I stopped by the job to pick up a few things. Quita loved rag bologna and hoop cheese—the kind with the red rind on it, so I wanted to surprise her. Not too often did I do romantic things for her. I really didn't know how. Sometimes she'd cook my favorite meal—collard greens, cornbread, macaroni and cheese, and pot roast. I had never taken the time to learn how to do it in return.

I left the store and took the bus over to Oak Court Mall to go to Vicky C's for some lingerie. Most of the time Quita was naked around the house, but when we went out, she was particular about her draws and bras matching. I picked her out this purple bra and found two pairs of matching thongs. The ensemble wasn't complete without a bottle of smell good. The sales girl suggested Very Sexy with the body lotion. After taking one whiff, I was sold. I got that for her along with some other important things—like a garter and thigh highs. Having spent more than three hundred dollars on Quita, I left the store feeling like I hadn't spent enough. I stopped in Bailey, Banks, & Biddle and browsed for about ten minutes before any of the sales-people opened their mouths to offer their help.

"May I help you?" a middle-aged man asked. I caught his ass exchanging looks with the security guard.

Quita loved rubies, and I'd spotted a white gold ring

with a diamond and ruby setting. I knew it would look beautiful on her. "How much is this?" I asked pointing at the ring.

He pulled the ring from the case and looked at the tag. "Fifteen hundred," and the bastard put it back in the case.

"Uh, do you mind if I take a look at it, please?"

Again, he glanced over at the security guard. Unwillingly, he took the ring out and held it without ever totally releasing it. I gave him the eye, and in that same movement, he made eye contact with the security guard. "It's the least expensive thing we have," he said.

"OK, well, let me see the one next to it."

He placed the ring back into the case and brought out the next one. "Three thousand two hundred and fifty is what this one costs."

"I see. Well, what . . ."

"Sir, you may find something that more suits your taste in Whitehall Company. As a matter of fact, I believe they are having a pretty good sale."

"First," I said, handing him the ring back, "it's ma'am and not sir. Second, I don't want to shop in Whitehall. I want to shop here, and third, I want that ring before you put it back in the case."

His ass stood there with a light shade of pink rising in his face. "Oh, I apologize. Since you don't have an account with us, will it be cash, check, or charge?"

If it wasn't for Quita, I would've walked out, but I wanted to do this for her. "Actually, I would like to apply for an account," I said, digging in my back pocket for my wallet.

Ol'boy was having issues with me by now. "I'm going to tell you up front the accounts are not easy to get. The finance company has a pretty stringent set of rules. You have to be working and have a major credit card which could, if applied to you, get you instant credit."

Passing him my picture I.D. and social security card, I enthusiastically replied, "Well, that's nice to know. By the way, here's my American Express card which, if I heard you correctly, qualifies me for instant credit."

Now, I might be a wannabe thug who rides the bus everywhere, but I work every day and pay my bills.

All the way home, I thought about what Noni had said. While I was disappointed with her decision, I respected it and was prepared to face whatever was before me. With the gun charge, I hoped that was a wrap. Jamal wasn't the type to go back on his word about anything, especially where I was concerned. Since Noni made it clear she wasn't even getting in it, all types of shit was running through my head. Was the D.A. going to try to make an example out of me? Was I going to jail?

Ironically, Quita and I walked up at the same time. Our conversation between one another had been a little strained after the interlude with Noni. I spoke only when I needed to and rarely had anything to say back to her whenever she was speaking. But today, when I saw her, I wanted to put all that foolishness behind us and try my best to get my friend back. "Hey," I said. Quita looked ravishing as I stepped aside to let her pass.

"Hey, yourself," she said, sticking her key in the lock. She smiled slightly while sneaking a peek at all my bags. "With all those bags, I might wanna think you hit the lottery."

"Who's to say I didn't?" I joked, pushing the door in.

Quita loved surprises, and in our time together, I had never given her enough of them. I guess maybe the bad part about me trying to be spontaneously romantic was that I couldn't hold water when it came to secrets. I was always like a little kid days before Christmas looking for any clue as to what my presents were. I remember Moms always being careful. After realizing I knew her favorite hiding places, she finally started taking everything over to Penny's.

Quita got in the house and went straight to the kitchen. I'd noticed, even while we weren't speaking, that she wasn't feeling her best on some days. She was sleeping in a lot and had missed quite a bit of work. "You want some cake?" she asked.

"No, thanks," I said, placing the bags on the couch. Quita never ate sweets in the middle of the week. She saved them for Sundays after dinner. When she came into the living room, she plopped down with a hunk of German chocolate cake and a glass of milk. "Uh, Quita?"

"Yeah, baby," she said shoving chunks of cake in her mouth.

"What's goin' on with you and all this food? I mean, you polished off a bucket of KFC by yourself. You, uh, ate all the pound cake Moms brought over here, and now you sittin' here eatin' that piece of cake like there's no tomorrow."

Rolling her eyes toward the ceiling, she said, "Nothing's wrong. I'm just trying to put on a little weight."

"For what? Hell, I'm having trouble as it is lifting you . . ."

"Don't go there," she said, throwing her hand to the air.

"What your peeps at the club gonna say when you gain this little bit of weight?"

Quita put the now empty plate down on the table and chugged the whole glass of milk. "Well, I don't really care what they think because I don't work there anymore."

Was I dreaming? "What?"

"I quit last week."

"What you do that for?" I asked, taking a seat on the chair.

Wiping away the milk mustache, she said, "I gave some thought to what you asked me to do. You didn't exactly ask me to quit—you told me. I had a major issue with that whole giving orders thing. One night last week, Mike and nem asked me to step in for another dancer who worked on the men's side of the club. She made pretty good money over there, and it was going to be a one-time thing. I got up on the stage doing my thing, and you know, I was expecting them to really be feeling me. Instead, they were booing me and started throwing shit at me."

"You got to be fuckin' kiddin' me, Quita." She was saying this shit so nonchalantly that I thought she was playing around. "That's why you quit?"

"No, I quit because when I left the stage, Mike and management told me to get back up there. I told them no, and they said if I didn't, I couldn't dance anywhere in the club. So I got my shit and left."

"Babe, why didn't you say something?"

"Uh, for what, Mo? Your ass is banned from the club for life. You know that, right? You know they'll have you arrested again if they catch y'all up there, right?"

"Yeah, I figured that." I didn't care. The place wasn't for me anyway. "But you still ain't say why you eating all this food."

Immediately this huge grin came across her face. "I'm gaining weight for my new job."

"And what job requires you to do that?"

Swallowing, Quita answers, "I'm gonna be in a movie. I'm an actress!"

"Huh?"

"I saw in the paper where they were auditioning people for this movie they're shooting in Atlanta. I went to the audition and got the part. The director asked me if I was comfortable putting on a little weight."

"So, you're like an extra or something? What are they paying you?" I was so happy for my baby.

"Mo, do you not have any faith in me?"

"Yes, I do. I just never knew you had an interest in acting. That's all."

"I didn't, but I was unemployed and prayed to God for a blessing. By no means am I broke, but I don't like not having a job."

"Do you do that a lot?"

"What?"

"Pray."

"Yes, all the time."

"Does it work?"

"Well, I believe so. I've prayed for a job when I was really too young to have one, and I got it. I prayed for someone in my life to love me unconditionally, and I got you. Why?"

This would be the best time to talk about the Noni situation. "I saw Noni today."

Quita didn't say a word at first. She only sat there with her head propped upon her arm looking straight through me. Then she spoke up. "And how was she?"

"She was a'ight. She was up at Big Daddy's getting her nails done when I saw her. Cathy had told me I needed to get in touch with her because she was my alibi for the afternoon that girl was raped."

Resting back on the sofa, she commented, "I can't believe they trying to put that on you. Don't they know you wouldn't hurt a fly no matter how big, bad, and tough you try to be?"

"Well, damn, Quita, why don't you just talk about me like a dog?"

"Baby, you know what I mean," she said, blowing a kiss to me. "Did she say she was gonna help?"

"She told me she couldn't."

"Why?" Quita grew a bit anxious. "What? I mean . . . but Cathy said."

"I can get with you being pissed because I was, too. But she told me I should talk it over with God, and if I believe in Him, everything will be all right. Is it really that easy?"

Sitting there in absolute disbelief, Quita agreed with Noni. "I knew it was some reason I liked that girl. True, her pussy was good, and yeah, she's freakier than most folks I know. But she's right, Mo."

"Is it something you can do with me? I don't have to do it alone, do I?"

Quita laughed, "You probably should. Then once you become accustomed to it maybe we can pray together. Right now, He needs to hear from only you."

Contemplating what I would even say, I confessed, "Baby, for a very long time, I was mad with God for allowing Mr. Luther to hurt me and for giving me the kind of mother I have."

"That's understandable, but you can't be mad forever. Mr. Luther will get his one day, and I truly believe you and your mother are on the way to making things better." I loved me some Quita, and the world was gonna to be all right with that. "What's in the bags?" she sniggered.

"Oh, damn, I almost forgot. I did a little shopping for you today."

"For me?" See what I mean? I didn't do that kind of shit. "You went shopping for me?"

"Yeah, I did," I smiled. "Let's see what we have in here."

Quita and I went through all but one of the bags together. She modeled her lingerie for me and gave me my own private lap dance. That's something Jamal always teased me about—having my own private dancer. I didn't get into all of that with Quita, though. I always insisted she leave work at work. We never talked about what she did, how she did it, or to who she did it to. Maybe that's why it was such a shock to see her dancing for the ladies. When she got to the last bag, I yanked it from her reach.

"What the hell, Mo? Give it here," she whined childishly.

"Nope, I don't want you to tear through this one." I'd gotten the old fuck at the jewelry store to put the ring inside of a much larger box so she wouldn't figure it out. "Um, Quita, I want to say something to you before you open this one."

"OK," she said. "But make it fast before you change your mind about giving it to me."

"Oh, I'm not going to change my mind." I took Quita's hand in mine and said, "I've never loved anyone like you, girl. You came to me and loved me for who you thought I was. Despite how Moms came at you, you still respected her and wanted to know her because she was a part of me. It's not easy for someone to do that. No matter what you decide to do with your life, I'm there. What's in this box is what you mean to me—right here, right now. I love you."

Ol' girl was bawling. Her nose was running, and I watched her hands trembling as she took the box into her grasp. "Mo, I don't know what to say," she murmured, unwrapping the box. At first she was moving along slowly, but the anticipation got to her and ripped the box open, finding my surprise. "Oh, shit! Oh, shit!" she screamed, running throughout the apartment. "Oh, my God, Mo, you don't understand. You just don't understand," she cried.

"No, I don't understand, baby. What's wrong?"

Quita calmly regained her composure and sat down next to me finally catching her breath. "Have you ever wondered why I don't talk about my family?"

"Yes, I have, but obviously it was something you didn't want to talk about, so I left it alone."

Staring down at the ring now on her finger, she said, "Mo, my mother used to walk through the house calling me a black monkey and said I'd never amount to anything. She managed to convince the rest of the family, except Cathy, of it, too, so I don't fuck with any of them."

Blown away, I then understood why she was so insistent about me and Moms getting our act together. "I'm glad you told me. Quita, you're beautiful, and I refuse to let anyone tell you any different."

My baby and I sat up for a while, catching up on our lives and what we'd been up to. She asked me if I wanted her to go to 201 with me, and I turned her down. Although Quita had my heart, I needed someone with me to guard my spirit. Once she went to bed, I went outside and stared into the sky. Next thing I knew, I just starting talking and talking and talking and talking. Whether or not it was prayer, I couldn't tell you, but I felt a sigh of relief when I laid my head on my pillow that night.

As I stepped off the ninth floor elevator, I saw Cathy, dressed in a brown pinstriped pantsuit, sitting in the waiting room. She was going through her briefcase when she looked up and saw me approaching. "Good morning," she said, glancing down at her watch. "And on time, too."

"What's good?" I asked, panning the room to improve my comfort level. Four other people were in there, and I wasn't sure if I wanted everyone else in my business. "Um, do we have to talk out here?"

Cathy rapidly began to gather her things, saying, "No, we can go into one of the conference rooms, but we may want to wait until your friend comes back."

"What friend?"

"Jamal. He was actually here when I got here. We've had some time to talk about this situation, and he told me he gave you the gun for protection from Mr. Luther. By the way, did you know you can still press charges against him?"

"What do you mean?"

"Just what I said. If you can prove what he did to you, then you have a shot."

"Really?"

"Yes, but I have to warn you. Finding other girls to step up and say he did these terrible things to them may be a problem. One thing that angers me in our community is that we keep our mouths shut at the wrong times. Do you think we'll have a problem with that?"

"Well, yeah. Everybody just kinda went on about their business."

Cathy shook her head in agreement. "Mo, like I said, it's not going to be easy. Without substantial proof, we may not have a chance in hell. You didn't report it, did you?"

"No." I knew I could prove he did something to me because I could describe his dick to a tee right down to the day I almost sliced it off. I'd gotten uneasy with talking about everything out in the open. Nobody seemed to be listening, but I didn't want to take the chance of my issues being put in a book somewhere. Right then, in walked Jamal. My man had on a crisp white dress shirt and some nice slacks. "Wassup, mayne? Look at you!"

Blushing, Jamal gave us a little runway strut. "Aw, just a little something I pulled out the dirty clothes," he kidded.

Cathy, laughing at us having a bit of fun before shit got serious, gestured for us to go to the conference room. Me and Jamal nervously sat down.

"Now, I wanted to talk to the both you before we all sat down with Sonny. He's not a nice man. I want you to know that. He's going to come at you with a bunch of questions trying to trip you up, and he's not here to make friends with you."

Me and Jamal was crazy cool. Won't nobody gonna bring us down.

Cathy continued as she pulled out her pen and started taking notes. "Jamal, you told me you gave the gun to Mo for protection, correct?"

"Yes, that's right. I got it from this cat named Sergio."

"Where is he now?"

"Sergio left the shelter a little bit before Mo came there. She never met him."

"OK," she said jotting down almost every word he said. "So, Jamal, you don't know a Melvin Quincy, correct?"

"No, I don't."

Cathy flipped back through her notes before she asked me anything. "Mo, this is what we're going to do. I'm going to talk with the D.A. about getting this dismissed. Since you don't have a record, I may be able to get the weapon possession charge dropped. I got a statement from Quita saying you were protecting her and that the bodyguard had it in for you from the start. I talked with the club's owner, and he's fine with it as long as you promise to stay away from the club."

"I'm a'ight with that."

"Figured you might be." Turning to Jamal and sticking the tip of her pen between her lips, she said, "Jamal, I really think we're going to be OK here. You don't have a record either, and there's no evidence against you in Melvin Quincy's murder. I'll drop Sergio's name which will give them some type of lead. But, like Mo, you've got to stay away from the club."

"No prob."

Cathy closed up her folders and began to put most of her belongings away. I was somewhat relieved, but I still had one more issue to deal with. "Jamal, you can leave if you like. We're done here. If there are any more questions, then we'll give you a call."

Wow, I thought. *This was that easy*. With sweating palms, I waited for Cathy to tell me what I should expect next. "So wassup?"

"Well, now I need to have a word with the D.A. about this madness with you. I may need to talk with him alone for a minute."

"You want me to leave?"

Getting up from her chair, Cathy gave the look of a caring mother. "Nah, I'm going to need you to stay around for a little while – just in case."

"A'ight." I returned to the waiting room and sat down, grabbing a magazine from the table. With it in my lap, I realized I had no interest in it. I leaned my head back against the wall and continued that conversation with God I'd begun last night.

IN DEFENSE OF A LIE
Cassie

It was early in the morning, and I was lying in my usual spot on the sofa. "Cassie, you're going to need to tell me something, baby, if you want me to help you," my father pleaded.

I was so disappointed in him. After hearing him and Mr. Dawson going back and forth about sticking my situation on anybody that fit the bill, I refused to do anything to help either of them. "What is it you want me to say, Daddy?"

"We're trying to catch the girl that did this to you and put her in jail where she belongs. Without you saying she did it, we can't do anything."

"Are you sure about that?"

Daddy's expression changed from that of concern to one of shock. "What do you mean, precious?"

I hated when he resorted to pet names. I knew he was trying to frame somebody for this, and I couldn't let him do that. Daddy always tried to protect me even at other people's expense. "Look, have you ever asked me if I want to go forward with this? Don't you think

I've been humiliated enough? For God sakes, it's all over the news! I haven't been to school in days!" Tears came as quickly as I wiped them away. "Mommy and you have me cooped up in this house, and the only visitor I get is my counselor."

Furious with my tone, Daddy walked over to me and pointed his finger in face. "Do you not realize the position you've put me in with this crap? My name's spread all over the paper and in the news. My reputation is at stake here."

By now, Mommy had come into the room. "Ray, what the hell is wrong with you?"

With his hands buried in his pockets, he shouted, "This is your fault. I told you she didn't need to be at that ghetto-ass school. You let her have her way too much." Wearing a hole in our fresh, new berber carpet, Daddy paused a moment and then looked over at me. "You're not trying to protect her, are you? I mean, you and she weren't—well, you know?"

Mommy stormed over to where he stood, and with her four-foot-eleven frame, she found all the might she could and slapped him in his face. "How dare you, Ray! This is our daughter you're talking to—not one of your sleazy-ass friends. I will not have you degrading her like this."

Rubbing his face where Mommy's palm print rested, Daddy said softly, "I'm strapped, Angie. My hands are tied. Sonny has found someone who fits the girl's description, and they're probably booking her as we speak. Something had to be done."

I really believe smoke was rising from Mommy's head. "Well, I tell you what. If you don't fix it, we're leaving. I won't let this happen to an innocent person, and I'm not encouraging Cassie to be any part of your shit."

Daddy wasn't sure what to do. He'd been on Mr. Dawson's back about holding somebody—anybody—accountable for what happened. I only wanted to move on. "Daddy?"

"Yes, dear," he said, still massaging his cheek.

"Can't I just change schools or even go to a boarding school in another state? Like Georgia, maybe? I'll finish seeing Dan if you want me to."

Mommy smiled with tears in her eyes, and replied, "I'm answering for him, baby. Yes, you can."

A while later after breakfast and once we'd talked about boarding school options, I overheard Daddy in his office trying to reach Mr. Dawson.

A GOOD OL' BOY
Mo

At the last minute Sonny Dawson requested I come
and join Cathy and him in his office. I wasn't nervous or anything like that. I was mainly anxious about
getting this whole thing over with. I believed within
my heart that things were going to be all right. I'd
prayed and left it with God.

"Come on in, Cathy and Mo. You two go ahead and
take a seat," Mr. Dawson said.

He seemed nice. He had that type of southern drawl
that bordered along the lines of redneck and businessman. He'd shake your hand with a smile on his face in
one breath, but in another, he'd smack the horse's ass
at a lynching. Was I going to be a piece of strange fruit
here?

"Cathy, I'm glad you took me up on my offer to come
down here and maybe get some resolution to this situation. It really doesn't make since to waste the judge's
time if we can take care of this off the record. Now, I
got all the information regarding the weapons charge,

and I'm fine with dropping that along with the disorderly conduct charge. What I want to know from you,
Miss Cummings, is what the hell is on your mind? I
mean, you get arrested for loitering and disorderly conduct with a group of young thugs, get yourself locked
up as a man, brought before the judge as a young man,
and you didn't tell anyone any different. Now, I have a
problem with that."

"How so?" I asked. "I wasn't hurting nobody."

Mr. Dawson thumbed through my file, and, after not
even stopping to read a single page, he closed the folder.
"Right. Here's where we are. I have a young lady who
says she can put you in the neighborhood of Forest
Hill High School about the time that a young lady was
assaulted by another young lady fitting your description. Can you tell me where you were that afternoon
from the time you left this building until about seven
o'clock?"

"Sir, I didn't do nothing like that. I couldn't have."

"So are you refusing to tell me where you were?"

"No, not all." I noticed he wasn't relying on Cathy to
say much at this point. I looked at her for approval to
go ahead, and in her you-gonna-be-all right expression,
she gave it. "After I left 201, I took the bus over to
Castalia."

"OK, we've established you were in the area."

Again, I looked to Cathy, and she nodded her head
for me to go on. "Well, yeah, I was over there. I went to
my Mom's house. She lives off Turner."

"And how long were you there?"

"Less than an hour."

"Then what did you do?"

"Well, I left there and cut through the school playground. I caught the bus in Castalia to go home."

"Did anyone see you?"

"I guess the bus driver did, but I mean, I'm telling you the truth."

"What time did you get home?"

"I'm not sure because when I got there I didn't even go in. I went over to Big Daddy's to shoot some pool."

"Uh-huh." Mr. Dawson pulled out his tablet and began writing. "How long were you there?"

"Maybe ten minutes."

Mr. Dawson chuckled, "Must have been a quick game. You lose?"

Was he trying to trip me up? "Actually, I never got to play. I met a young lady, and we went to dinner at China Star."

"Will this young lady vouch for you?"

Before I could answer, Cathy interrupted. "Sonny, we have statements from employees at Big Daddy's and China Star that saw Miss Cummings there."

"I see. What about the young lady?"

Again before I could answer, Cathy spoke up. "Well, she won't come forward because of personal reasons, but I do have a statement from someone who saw them together that evening."

Mr. Dawson was sitting there looking at me with uncertainty. Was he trying to figure me out? "Why do you do this?"

"Do what?"

"I mean, you're sitting here looking like a young man—we almost charged you as a man. But I have a young lady who was raped by someone who's a dead ringer for you. You're gay, right?"

I wasn't sure if I should answer that, but Cathy nudged me under the table. "No, I'm not, sir." That drew alarm from both sides of the room.

"What?" Mr. Dawson asked.

"I said I'm not gay."

"And how is that? Don't you cohabitate with another woman? Weren't you with another woman on the night in question?"

"Yes, I was with another woman that night, and yes, I live with a woman, but I've never identified myself as a lesbian. I . . ." Just as I was about to spill my guts on why I am the way I am, there was a knock at the door.

"Yes?" Mr. Dawson requested.

The door opened, and a woman in a beige suit came in. She smiled slightly at me and Cathy. "Uh, Mr. Dawson, can I see you outside a minute?"

"I'm in the middle of something. It's going to have to wait."

"It can't. I need to see you outside."

Mr. Dawson pushed my file aside and rose from his seat. "Excuse me, ladies," he said, buttoning his jacket.

Closing the door behind him, Mr. Dawson left us, and thankfully he did because I needed to ask Cathy what the hell was going on. "Don't worry about it," she said. "I have a trump card."

"Well, I hope you do. I didn't have nothing to do with what he's talking about."

Mr. Dawson stayed gone for ten minutes before he returned with a blank look on his face. "Miss Cummings, you're free to go." And he picked the folder up and tossed it on his credenza. He completely dismissed the fact that Cathy and me was still sitting there. Then he stopped what he was doing and looked up at us. "Is there a problem?" he asked.

Cathy, gathering her things, said challengingly, "Well, yes, there is, Sonny." She was about to get righteous with Mr. Dawson. "What the hell is going on here? You've got my client going through all these hoops and hurdles for you with this ridiculous interrogation.

You're abruptly asked to leave the room, and then you come back and tell her she can go home. With all due respect, what kind of shit is that?" Like one of those ghetto girls from South Memphis, she struck a pose with her hand on her hip.

Mr. Dawson, who at first was talking like that professional businessman, now had the noose in his hand. "I suggest you stand down, counselor. Don't forget where you are."

A bulldog! That's what Cathy reminded me of. "Listen, I sit in that courtroom day in and day out and watch you send innocent Black men, and some women, out to the penal farm. And you almost sent this one out there because you and your folks are half-ass doing your jobs."

He was teasing Cathy with the noose. "Mrs. Crenshaw, I suggest you and Miss or Mr. Cummings—whatever it is today—get out of my office before I find good reason to put you and it in jail for the next twenty-four hours."

Imagine this. Sitting on the front porch in the summertime with three of your best friends and y'all got a good-ass game of bid whist goin. Y'all drinking Coronas and Smirnoff Ice like they going out of style. You and your pardner are winning, and then somebody smacks a trump card on they sweaty ass forehead. Well, today, Cathy was that somebody with the trump card on her forehead.

"I don't think so, Sonny." She leaned over his desk and got right up in his face. "I want you to think about something. Your deputies had my female client in lock-up with men all night. They couldn't tell a woman with a dildo strapped to her thigh from any other low-life thug on the street. Who knows what happened to her while she was being detained. Then you had her down here trying to stick some ridiculous charges on

her, and you and I both know damn well she had nothing to do with that case. Now, I can slap a lawsuit on
this city AND the county so damn fast it'll make your
head spin with a laundry list of allegations, *or* you can
do something to help me out with a situation concern-
ing M-I-S-S Cummings that happened to her three
years ago."

That noose was put on the table for a moment. Mr.
Dawson didn't have a chance in hell against Cathy at
this point. "What do you need, counselor?" he asked
unenthusiastically.

For two hours I sat with Mr. Dawson and Cathy, re-
calling what happened to me when I was a little girl.
By the end of the conversation, Mr. Dawson had
agreed to have Mr. Luther brought in for questioning.
If what I'd said was correct about the deformity in his
crotch, then he would be arrested and charged.

PAPA MAY HAVE
Elise

The one thing I nevah wished was that I'd nevah met Eric Lee. He was the man that showed me I was a woman on the inside. I learned enough 'bout him in those coupla months to realize I wanted him in my life forever. I ain't know nothin' 'bout havin' churrin when I was wit him, and I ain't lettin' nobody put that off on him. Shit, it take two to tango, and I was dancin' my ass off.

Carrie Ann, Eric Lee's wife, called me 'bout eight o'clock the night before Monique and me was supposed to go and see Mr. Dan. I was plannin' on bringin' my letter wit me so we could get all of that out in the open. I knew I ain't protect Monique like I should, and I was open to doin' whatever I could to make it right.

"Elise?" she say.

"Yeah," I answered.

"This is Carrie Ann, Eric's wife. How you?"

She was closer to his age than I was and nevah seemed to have an issue with me havin' a baby by him.

"Blessed and highly favored."

"Amen," she say. "Uh, I'm down here at the hospital with Eric, and he want you to come down here and sit with him for a minute."

I ain't understand what he want me down there for. Me and him won't like that no more. Like I say, the last time I seent him he come by to borrow some money for some operation.

"What he want, Carrie?"

She got a little quiet on me but finally spoke up. "Can't get into that with you. That's something him and you going to have discuss. He's pretty sick, Elise."

"All right, I'll come down there tomorrow some time."

She got quiet again. Then she say real soft-like, "You can come on now if you can while he's awake. He's in St. Francis in room 624."

Cuz I loved that man the way I do I put my skirt and shoes on and caught the bus down there. Even though I ain't mind goin' out so late, I worried a little bit 'bout how I was gonna get home. It was close to 9:30 when I got there, and visitin' hours was ovah. As I approached the nurse's station, one of the ladies behind the counter looked up at me but kept on doin' what she was doin'. My heart was beatin' a little fast cuz I was expectin' somebody to stop me, but I come on 'round the corner and ain't nobody say a word. I kept on my way lookin' for 624.

The hallway was pretty quiet 'til I got to 622. Then I hears beepin' and machines makin' a lot of noise. When I got to 624, the door was a little cracked, and I saw his name on the little piece of paper outside the door. I peeped in there and seent Eric Lee layin' there with a oxygen mask on his face. His eyes was closed, and Carrie Ann was sittin' in the chair next to him wit her eyes closed, too. Eric ain't look nothin' like he did when I last seent him. His hair was gray and had thinned out like a old man across the top. He was frail wit his body sunk into the mattress. They was runnin' blood and IVs through him. I walked ovah to Carrie Ann and touched her on the shoulder.

"Hello," I said softly.

She and Eric Lee both woke up.

"Oh, hi," she say. Carrie had dun put on a little weight and had put some color in her hair. I ain't know too much 'bout her othah than she and Eric Lee had a baby together.

"I woulda got here sooner, but the bus was late."

Carrie got up from her chair and told me I could sit there next to Eric Lee, and she was gonna get anothah one.

"How you doin', Mr. Man?" I asked.

Wit his hand trembling, he tried to take off the mask, but couldn't catch on to it. Carrie Ann rushed ovah and took it off for him. "You can't leave this off too long, now. This machine'll start to beeping, and you'll have them nurses running down here for nothing."

Eric Lee just smiled and nodded his head at her. Then he looked ovah at me with those pretty eyes of his and asked, "How you been doin'?" Right after that he broke off into a coughin' spell that made Carrie Ann put the mask back on his face for a few minutes while I answered him.

"Doin' all right. Doin' all right. I oughta be askin' you the same thang."

After taking a few breaths in, Eric lifted the mask off his face again. "I ain't been doin' too good, Elise. I got testicular cancer, you know."

He might as well have been speakin' Mexican to me

cuz I ain't understand shit he was sayin'. "What's that?"

"I got cancer of the nuts," he say.

Hell, I ain't know nothin' 'bout that kinda mess, and I ain't understand what it had to do with me. "So what does that mean?"

He started anotha coughin' spell, and Carrie Ann got his mask back on him. Eric Lee rolled his eyes at me and gave her the eye to go ahead and tell me what he couldn't. "We need to let him rest, Elise. Come walk with me outside a minute."

"OK."

Me and her walked down to the waitin' room where nobody was. The TV was on, but she walked right in and turnt it off.

"How's Monique?" she asked me first.

We both took a seat on the couch.

"She's all right. Workin' and tryin' stay outta trouble."

"That's good." Carrie Ann sat back on the couch and folded her arms. "Look, Elise, there's no easy way to say this other than to just say it. Eric Lee is most likely going to die soon."

A bullet had hit me at point blank range, and I was dyin' slowly. I couldn't say nothin'.

"I know you been with him before, so I know you know he ain't got but one ball down there."

I still couldn't say nothin'.

"When he was baby, his momma should've taken him to the doctor and had them to do surgery on him."

I managed to get some words out. "What for?"

"He has what they call undescended testes, which is where one of his testicles stayed in his abdomen but should've been brought down to where the other one was. Since it was never done, it opened him up to possibly getting cancer down there."

I remember the testicle part from the book Auntie Diane had gave me, but it ain't say nothin' 'bout none of this. "So what was the operation he had for?"

"We needed the money to help pay for it because our insurance didn't want to pay for all of it. The surgery, we thought, would remove all of the cancer they found, but it didn't. They got in there and found out they wouldn't be able to help him."

"So he's gonna die soon?"

"Not like tomorrow or next week, but in time."

Naturally, I was hurt but couldn't understand why they couldn't wait to tell me this tomorrow. "So that's why you had me to come out here this late?"

Carrie Ann looked at me like she had somethin' else to tell me but struggled with the words. "No, that's not the only thing, Elise."

"OK, so what's up?"

"With Eric's condition, his doctor wanted a specialist to talk with him about some other things, especially when he found out he had kids."

My heart stopped beatin'. "What you mean?" That bullet was penetratin' my heart.

"Eric Lee can't have kids. He's never been able to have them."

I was dead.

Looking at me quiverin' so bad, she grabbed my hands and held them in hers. "Elise, I know what you feeling. I know what you thinking."

No, she ain't. She didn't know. No one but me knew what goin' on inside of me. "So Monique . . . oh, God, oh God!" I sobbed. My gut was churnin'. I wanted to die-just die. "I want a blood test."

"You can get that if you want, but I'm going to tell

you're wasting your time. We went through that—three times, and the results were the same. Finally, the doctor tested Eric Lee's sperm, and it was nothing but blanks."

Comfortin' me with pats on my shoulder, Carrie Ann say, "Believe me, I understand. I had to deal with my own demons, too."

I ain't care nothin' 'bout her deceivin' Eric Lee all this time. We was in two diff'rent boats. There was no way she could imagine what I'd dun just learned. It went deeper than makin' a man thank he was the daddy of a baby he very well coulda fathered. It went deeper than hearin' Carrie Ann say she'd done the same thang for whatevah reason. It went deeper than knowin' my first true love was dyin'. What it really was I couldn't bear to mention to nobody. I simply asked God to allow me to put my sins in a box and asked for His forgiveness what I had done and what I was 'bout to do.

After the late shift nurse came in and made sure Eric Lee was restin' good, Carrie Ann took me on back to the house. Ain't neitha one of us say a word.

TRUTH HURTS
Mo

I took off work for this session with Dan and Moms. I didn't know what was going to happen or how I would be feeling afterwards, so I asked if we could have the meeting at his office. When I arrived, there was a man, a lady, and a young girl with them. They were filling out paperwork at the receptionist's desk. "Mr. and Mrs. Owens, your insurance will cover all of your daughter's sessions. Here's your card back, and a refund for your other co-pays. I just need your signatures on these documents, and you'll be all ready to go."

Owens, Owens. That name sounded so familiar to me. I sat in my chair and felt slightly uncomfortable because the girl was staring at me—hard. She was a cute girl and all. I couldn't imagine somebody like her needing counseling. When her pops walked by, he rolled his eyes at me and ordered his daughter to join him and his wife as they prepared to leave. That chick kept looking at me like we had been connected at another time and place.

A few seconds later, Moms walked in looking like she'd lost her best friend. Her eyes was bloodshot, and there were huge bags under them. While I wanted the world to know how much I hated her for what she'd done to me, I still loved her. She was my mother. We'd all made mistakes, and I knew she was sorry for hers.

"Hey," I said, but she didn't say nothing back to me.

Her hands were trembling, and she took a seat next to me with her head hung low and not uttering a word.

"You a'ight?"

She still didn't say nothing. She continued to sit there with several folded up pieces of paper in her hand. The receptionist asked me if everything was OK, and I told her that as far as I knew everything was cool. As she sat there puzzled by Moms's demeanor, the phone rang. It was Dan telling her we could come on down to his office.

I got up and waited for Moms to get up, but she just sat there. "I need a minute befo' I come down there. Gone on ahead."

I wasn't going to argue with her. I got my cap and went on down the hall to Dan's office. When I got to his doorway, I peeped my head in and whispered, "Uh, Moms is down there. She said she needs a minute before she comes in here. She lookin' all crazy and shit."

"Really?"

"Yeah. You want me to go get her?"

Before Dan could answer, the receptionist showed up with Moms. "No need. Here she is."

Moms, still looking like something was really wrong, cleared her throat and told us she had to go to the bathroom. "Sorry for being late," she sighed. In her hands were still those folded up pieces of paper. "Y'all start yet?"

Now I know she saw me standing in the door, and

there was no reasonable way we could be having a session like that. "No, we haven't." She walked in past me and grabbed a chair from beside Dan's desk, threw it into the corner and sat down.

Dan was watching her the whole time and immediately realized something was wrong. "Ms. Cummings, is everything all right?"

Wiping what seemed to be stray tear from her face, she said, "We need to go ahead and get started. I got thangs to do."

"OK," Dan said. "We can do that. Mo, go ahead and pull up a chair across from your mom, and I'll close the door."

For the first time in my life, Moms was worrying me. Most times she was trying to get me to warm up to her, and it was me throwing shade to her. I plopped down in my chair and even tried to make eye contact with her, but she kept her head down and was intermittently wiping tears away. Dan was watching her odd behavior and decided to go ahead and get started. I couldn't even get her to look my way.

"Elise, you've got something for me?" Dan inquired.

Moms handed him the pieces of folded paper. Never raising her head, she quietly said, "I need to talk 'bout somethin' befo' we get too deep into this today."

"Well, Elise, you'll have all the time you need to talk in a few minutes. I want Mo to take some time to read what you've written."

"I need to do this now befo' she do that. I need to explain some thangs to her—thangs I just learnt 'bout." The tears started back.

Dan looked over at me to see if I was cool with it, and, if whatever she had to say was going to tell me what was wrong with her, then I was fine with it. "Go ahead, Elise."

"Befo' I start, can you tell me what it is again you called Mr. Luther the day I met you at the shelter?"

"A child molester?"

"Yeah, but it was something else you said."

"A pedophile?"

"Yeah, that's it."

"What about it?"

My curiosity was piqued because this was the first time Moms ever acknowledged even listening to anything Dan told her right after the rape. Moms finally, after several minutes of seeming to go through things in her head, began to open up. "How long do I have?" she asked.

"Take as long as you need, Elise."

Moms folded her arms and began swaying from side to side. "Mr. Luther *is* a pedophile. He *is* a child molester. We growed up 'round that man cuz he had a little corner store where we all shopped. We ain't know nothin' 'bout grown men takin' sex from little girls. That was a time when we just ain't have those kind of worries. We'd go up in there and grocery shop if we had to, but I was always in there for my sour pickles and peppermint sticks. He was a quiet man—nevah could hurt a fly. He sang in the male chorus. He . . ." she sniveled. "He used to tell on us when we was doin' wrong away from home. I ain't nevah pay him no mind. I just went on 'bout my bidness. Your grandmomma ain't nevah told me nothin' 'bout mens, boys, sex, babies, nothin'. What I did learn I got from a book my Auntie Diane gave me. I met Eric Lee when my body was tellin' me to do thangs grown folks do. Me and Eric Lee started havin' sex ovah in the fall. Can't tell you how many times it was, but I can tell you we ain't use no protection. He mighta knowed somethin' 'bout it, but I ain't. Mr. Luther told my granddaddy 'bout it cuz I guess he and Eric Lee was always talkin'. Then one day Eric Lee left. A coupla days later, I was in Mr. Luther's store. There won't nobody in there from what I could tell. All of sudden somebody pusht me to the ground and stole whatever innocence I had left from me. When I heard you tell Mr. Dan 'bout what happened to you out in the field that day, I seent myself out there. I ain't get to see who pusht me to the ground, but I knowed it was him."

I was speechless. I was so angry with her at that moment I could've ended her life right then and there. But I let her continue.

"I know you thought I was protectin' him, but I won't doin' that. I was protectin' me. Mr. Luther was like an ol' woman spittin' venom 'bout stuff he ain't know nothin' 'bout. I had him comin' to the house cuz he say he ain't mind doin' it. E'rybody else was tryin' to get money outta me, and he say he do it for nothin'. You gotta believe me when I say I ain't thank he was doin' somethin' like that to you. I thought you was makin' stuff up. You'd tell a lie e'ry once and a while. I'm so sorry, Monique."

There wasn't much more I could take. Dan was watching me like a hawk, wanting to see, I guess, how I was going to react. I wanted her in the bathroom mirror with Bloody Mary, so she could scratch her eyes out. I wanted the Boogie Man to come from under the bed and take her away. In my childhood, those monsters were my friends. The only monster in my life was the candy man, Mr. Luther. Balling my fists and thrusting them against my thighs, I felt my soul on the verge of implosion. Moms was in her private hell with demons chasing her from the past and finally catching up to her. But I didn't have no sympathy for her.

"Can I have some water?" she asked Dan.

My counselor of nearly three and a half years was dumbfounded. He knew there was something causing Moms to be the way she was, but I'm sure he never imagined this. Walking over to the water cooler, Dan kept his eye on both of us—hoping I wouldn't try to hurt her. He poured the water in the cup and gave it to Moms.

"Elise, um, I know I asked you to write some things down for me. Did you just tell us what was in the letter?"

With eyes full of more water than Niagara Falls, she said, "No, not really. Only bits and pieces."

I'm sitting there thinking what on earth could be in the letter if she just dropped this bombshell. Dan responded with, "Alrighty then. Well, you can continue if you want."

"Last night I got call from Eric Lee's wife, Carrie Ann. She was callin' to tell me he was in the hospital, and he wanted me to come out there. I was thankin' he was needin' so mo' money from me, but when I got to the room, I foundt out he was pretty sick. He managed to tell me he got some kinda cancer in his scrotum. I had trouble understandin' why I needed to know that. Me and him won't together no mo', and he ain't nevah gave a damn 'bout Monique. Anyway, Carrie Ann took me outta the room and tells me he was gonna die fo' too long. Then she told me the doctors was sayin' Eric Lee can't have no churrin, and cuz of this condition, he ain't nevah been able to have none."

I was trying to have no clue as to what she was saying, but my soul wouldn't allow that. "Wait a minute! Oh, God, wait a minute! Are you telling me that old dirty bastard—that, that, that monster—is related to me? Are you telling me he's my father?" I rose from my chair, flung it to the floor, and rushed Moms. I clutched her by the shoulders and tried to shake her until she stopped breathing, but Dan grabbed me from behind. I tussled with him, kicking papers and furniture—whatever I could get to.

"Hold on, Mo! Hold on, Mo!" he kept saying, but I ain't hear him.

Just as I was close enough to jab her in the face, some more people came running in and threw me to the floor. One of those people slammed me to the floor and held me there until I stopped trying to get at Moms.

My adrenaline was running so high I couldn't think. A dagger was in me, and I wanted it to kill me. "I can't believe you! I can't believe you! All this time, all this time." I wept into the floor, piercing hell if I could. Dan did his best to comfort me by offering to let me up if I promised to not try to get at Moms.

"Mo, we can let you up, but you have to promise you're not going to go for your mom. You have to promise me that."

A ton of bricks was on me. I couldn't have gotten up if I wanted to. While I wanted her to have an immediate death, I promised softly, "I won't. I'm good."

Dan and the others lifted me from the floor and helped me back to my feet. In all the commotion, someone had picked my chair up and placed it several feet away from that woman. The receptionist had come in and was comforting her. I didn't care about her pain, even though she was complaining about not being able to breathe. She kept saying her chest was hurting. As far as I was concerned, she was doing a Fred Sanford. The bitch could've died in that corner, and all I would've done was got my shit, turned the light off, and closed the door behind me. Disheveled and out of breath, I took my seat with my face in my hands. I covered my eyes and tried my best to wish all of this away.

Dan, flustered and stunned by what had unfolded before his eyes, told the others they could leave and that he had everything under control. "Wow, uh, are we all OK here?"

The receptionist had left moms with a box of tissue and a bottle of water. They did a few breathing exercises to help with the chest pain. Neither one of us responded to Dan's question.

"Do you feel up to going on, Elise?"

A little hoarse, she said, "Yes, I do."

"Whenever you're ready."

"Monique, I didn't know. I mean, it'd crossed my mind a time or two, but I ain't thank it'd end up like this. You gotta know I'm hurtin' on the inside right now. I want to just die cuz of this."

"Then why don't you just do that?"

"Mo, hold on, let her talk."

Moms went on. "All these years I thought Eric Lee was your daddy. Last night was just as hard for me to hear as it was for you to hear. I told Penny 'bout e'ry-thang, and we tryin' to be here for you."

"All of you can go to hell." Fuck what Dan had to say.

"I wisht there was somethin' I could do to make this not be real, but I can't. The doctors won't even let us do a blood test. It's all a mess right now."

Dan glanced up at the clock and realized we'd gone over our time. "Look, Mo and Elise, we're going to need to stop for today. If you want, we can do another session at the end of the week."

Still steaming, I said, "You know what, Dan?"

"Yes, Mo?"

"I'm done. Now I know why I'm fucked up in the head. It's 'cause of her. All that time I was reaching out to her for help, she kept kicking me to the curb." I walked over to her and screamed in her face, "I tried to tell you what he was doing to me, and all the time, Moms, you knew what he had done to you. Why did you let me go through that? Why did you let me hurt like that?" Finally, my soul burst open. I dropped to my knees and cast my upper body into her lap. "I needed you, Moms. I needed you so bad," I cried. "I became who I am to run away—to hide from the monster. I'm still your little girl. Oh, God, why!" I howled for what seemed like forever. "I didn't make me this way. You did it. You did it, Moms."

I hadn't touched my moms like that since I was a little girl, and I hadn't felt her touch me like she did in twice as long. "I'm sorry, Monique. I'm going to make this up to you. I promise."

Dan got up from his chair and helped me from the floor. Eight very frustrating years for me had come full circle. I didn't know where I was going from there. I didn't know where *we* were going from there.

MONKEY SEE, MONKEY DO
Elise

I walked all the way home from Beale Street. I took Linden and made my way back to Lamar and nevah thought 'bout takin' a bus or hitchin' a ride. Wit e'ry step I thought 'bout my life wit Monique and what, if anythang, I'd evah sacrificed for her. I came up wit nothin'.

When I first met Monkey, he was into some crazy shit. He always talked 'bout how you can kill somebody with anti-freeze and nobody evah be able to tell that what did it. I felt so bad 'bout havin' Mo in this predicament that I wanted to do what I could to make it up to her. I stopped by the shoppin' center on Lamar on the way home and went to the auto parts store.

I got to the house 'round ten o'clock, and after I put my wrap away, I called down to Penny's. She usually went to Mr. Luther's at that time, but I managed to catch her just as she was walkin' out the door. "Hey, there," I say. "What you doin'?"

Penny was gettin' up there in age and hated goin' outside after dark cuz it made her arthritis act up.

"Hey, Elise. Just walkin' out the door to go over to Luther's to make sure he settled in for the night. I sure don't feel like going out tonight. My joints are killing me."

"You take your medicine?"

"Yeah, I took it, but it don't do much for me when it's this cool at night."

"Well, why you gotta go ovah there anyway?"

"To take him this damn Kool-Aid he drinks all the time and to make sure he got his medicine."

"You know, I walked into the house a few minutes ago and still got my clothes on. I can go ovah and do it for you."

Penny ain't hesitate 'bout takin' me up on my offer. I went by her house and got the Kool-Aid. It was in, of all thangs, a huge pickle jar she'd placed in a plastic shoppin' bag. Penny said Mr. Luther go through one of them in a day. As I walked up the steps of the house, I pulled a jar of my own from my pocket and carefully opened it. I twisted the top of Penny's jar and mixed the contents of mine with hers. In the deep of night, I was puttin' an end to my baby's nightmare.

WILL THE REAL M.C. PLEASE STAND UP?
Mo

Cathy was notorious for calling at the crack of dawn and placing unreasonable demands on me. This time, though, she went a step further and came by the house at five in the morning. Quita called me into the living room, and I came out in my boxers, wifebeater, and socks.

"What's good, Cathy? Long time no hear from." I was assuming she was coming by to talk with me about that whole thing with Mr. Luther. "You here with some news about our case?"

Quita, with a lace see-through robe on, cuddled up under my arm to keep warm.

"Mr. Luther was found dead in his house night before last."

Me and Quita sat there in awe. I was happy but refused to show it.

"How?" Quita asked.

"Penny found him when she stopped in to check on him."

I still didn't say shit.

"Was it a heart attack or something?" Quita inquired.

"I'm not sure. With his age and his medical conditions, the medical examiner was thinking natural causes."

I was trying to figure out why she was bothering us at five in the morning with this shit. "Cathy, with all due respect, you know I don't care nothin' 'bout that man. Good riddance, he's gone. Maybe now I can get some real sleep."

Taking a sip from her stainless steel coffee mug, she affirmed, "I understand you feeling that way, but I came by here checking to see if you've talked to or seen your mother."

I looked off in the opposite direction. "Nope, I haven't seen her since the other day at Dan's." That's all I was giving up.

Cathy calmly requested, "Mo, this is serious. I know about the counseling session with Dan. Elise called me very late that night talking really strange. I need to know if you've seen her."

"Well, since you know everything, Cathy, then why the hell should I care where she is? I don't have anything else to say to her. She fucked up her life, and then she turned around and fucked up mine. As far as I'm concerned, she can—"

Before I knew it, Cathy rushed me and punched me in my mouth. "Don't you dare," she bassed at me. "You think you know everything, but you don't know shit. The other night when I talked to her she had virtually lost it. Yes, she's walking around with a lot of guilt right now because of what happened to you, but don't you think she had enough riding on her with her own shit she'd been through? Your great-grandfather was a cold-hearted muthafuckah, and he put your grandmother through hell. Before you continue blaming your mother for this mess, you better get your facts really right."

Damn, Cathy busted my lip, and it hurt like crazy. "I don't know what y'all expect a niggah to do. Mayne, I . . ."

Rubbing her fist, she said, "Look, I'm sorry about popping your ass, but you needed it. For as long as I've known you, you've been blaming everybody else for your issues. While I can understand why you transitioned into Mo, I don't understand why you let that dictate the life you're living. Elise didn't make you go to the store and buy a rubber dick. Elise didn't make you start running the streets with thugs. Elise didn't make you start sleeping with women. Those were your choices, and you need to learn to live with them. You need to accept the fact that no matter what type of underwear you got on, you're still a woman."

Quita, stroking my hand with hers, interjected, "Mo, she's right, baby. You gotta let some of this anger go. Elise doesn't mean you any harm. I know that for a fact."

They both made me sick, and I didn't want to hear it at first. I realized they were making too much sense to me, though, and that's when the tears started. "Y'all don't understand. The one person in this world that I was terrified the most of turns out to be my daddy."

Then Cathy sassed, "And now he's dead. It's time to get over it. Your mother did not, I repeat, did not ask for what happened to her."

"What did she say to you?"

"She told me Mr. Luther was your father, and she was just sick over it. I mentioned we were going to go after him legally, but she didn't want to hear that. All she kept saying was she would take care of it."

"And what was that supposed to mean?"

"I don't know. That's why I have to find her. Do you know any of her friends or past friends?"

"The only person I knew she knew was Monkey, and they weren't the best of friends."

Cathy shook her head. "OK, this is starting to make a little sense. We need to talk to him."

"A'ight." I got up from the couch and went to get dressed.

Cathy and I walked around to Monkey's house and knocked on the door. We'd knocked for a while before he opened it.

"Wassup, fool?" he said with breath so funky it smelled like horses had run through his mouth and shit. He saw Cathy standing beside me and immediately told us to come in. "Counselor."

"What's going on, Monkey?"

"Not a thing," he said closing the door. "Y'all bring some breakfast?"

"Naw, we . . ."

Cathy skipped all the bullshit. "Where's Elise?"

Monkey had the most stupid look on his face. "In her skin, I guess. What you asking me for?"

"You know something, Monkey? It's too early in the morning for games. Where is she?"

Even though they didn't get along, they appeared to have an understanding. Cathy didn't take no shit, and Monkey knew it. I wasn't really sure what their history was, but like I said, they had an understanding. "She in the back," he said, lighting a stick of incense.

Cathy snatched the little brown stick out of his hand. "I don't want to smell that this early in the morning," she said, taking the stick and burying it upside down in a nearby plant.

Monkey pulled another stick out of the sleeve. "This

my house, and I'm doing what I damn well please. You don't run shit here."

"You're mistaken, Monkey. I own your ass, and don't forget that. Go get her."

Before he left the room, he turned to Cathy and asked, "You think just because you helped me out of a tight spot that you can take advantage of me and treat me like dirt?"

"Monkey, why don't you tell Monique, here, how we know each other?"

I wasn't expecting all of this. I did, however, have a bit of curiosity about their dealings.

This cat was standing in front of me looking about three feet tall. He stopped right where he was and took a deep breath. "Four years ago I was in wrong place at the wrong time. You know I was dealing weed and a little caine. I got into a fight with my distributor, and I smoked his ass. Cathy was my lawyer at the time, and I begged her to get me locked up so that dude's peoples wouldn't kill me. Well, she couldn't work that out, and, instead, she hid me out at her house. While I was there, her and her husband got me a new identity. They got me a new driver's license, new social security card, new job, and everything. Your girl ain't no joke."

"So what's Moms doing here?"

That's when Cathy chimed in, "I told her to come here after we talked. Trust me, she didn't want to, but I explained to her I could best protect her here. I didn't know she knew Junior over there. Small world."

"What was all that in front of Quita?"

Chuckling, Cathy insisted, "She doesn't need to know all of your business. I understand she's your girl and all, but you should have limits. Monkey, go and get her please."

Like a little puppy, Monkey headed to the back of

the apartment like his owner told him to. A while later, Moms emerged from the back. Her hair was all over her head, and she was still wearing the clothes she had on in the therapy session. "Good morning, Cathy."

She didn't say a word to me. "Aren't you going to speak to your daughter?"

Moms was still having trouble making eye contact with me. This time I helped her out. I got up and walked over to her and gave her a hug before she could open her mouth. I held her as tight as I could, squeezing her until I felt her gasp for air. "I love you. It's gonna be all right. We're gonna be all right." I reached for her hand and guided her to a seat next to me.

Acting like Judge Hatchett, Cathy slid up to the edge of her seat and extended her hand for moms to grab it. "Tell us what happened, Elise. No one here is going to say a word about any of it after today."

I didn't think Moms had any more tears left, but she found quite a few of them. "I walked home from Mr. Dan's that night."

"You walked from all the way downtown?" I asked.

"Yes, I did. I had thangs on my mind, and I needed peace and quiet to work them through. I thought 'bout the time I'd missed wit you, and all the mistakes I'd dun made. I kinda felt I was followin' in my Mama's footsteps. It run ovah and ovah again in my head all those times you wanted me to hear you, but I won't listenin'. I played it in my mind where I seent him touchin' you and doin' those awful thangs to you. Not one time in my life had I protected you from anythang. I bought you the dresses, the hair bows, and the Mary Janes and treated you like a doll baby and not no real person. I realized that's how I treated your feelings, too. I remembered one time when me and Monkey was talkin' 'bout bumpin' off the mailman and stealin' checks on the first of the month. He told me we could meet him on the front porch on the hottest day of the summer and give him a big cup of Gatorade—the lemon-lime kind. I ain't thank that would kill him until Monkey say we'd put some anti-freeze in it. He won't even be able to taste it. We was gon let him come in the house and sit a spell. Then we was just gon wait. So on the way home I stopped by the auto parts store and got me a gallon of anti-freeze and went home. I called Penny and she say she ain't feel like going to Mr. Luther's house. I offered to go in her place. On my way, I mixed Kool-Aid with the anti-freeze, and I left it for him on the counter where she told me to leave it. He musta drunk it all in one day. I felt relieved 'bout what I'd dun, and now I know he won't be able to hurt nobody else's little girl. I went home and prayed to God again for Him to put my sins in a box so we could move past this. Then I called Cathy and she told me to come here."

This shit was like something straight out of the movies. "So you killed him?" I asked as simply as I could. "I mean, you put yourself out there like that for me? But what if . . ."

Monkey took the reigns on this one. "She'll be all right. That man wasn't no rich White honky, so ain't nobody gonna care how he died. He was Black, old, and ain't have no family. Trust me, she'll be all right."

Nodding her head in agreement, Cathy added, "It's sad to admit, but he's right. Just hang out here for a few more days. Since your family knew so much about Mr. Luther, they'll likely be given the opportunity to make proper arrangements for him."

"Cathy?" Moms asked.

"Yes?"

"Can you take care of that for us? You can go and talk with Penny about it. I'm sho she aint' gon want nothin' to do with it."

"OK, then. I'll tell the coroner."

Days passed, and there was never any mention of Mr. Luther on the news or in the paper. Moms left Monkey's house on the fifth day. When she got home, Quita and I went over and kept her company until she got comfortable with being alone again. Once while we were there, we saw Aunt Penny coming up the street. Moms figured she was coming to check on her because she hadn't seen her since the day she went over to Mr. Luther's. I was fifteen the last time I saw Penny and I knew she would freak out if she saw me as Mo. I went and hid in the kitchen when she knocked at the door.

"Good evening," she said. Her voice told the age of a sweet, old lady whose life had been good to her, and I missed her. "Where you been hiding, Elise?" she asked, coming in and taking a seat. She saw Quita and spoke, "How you?"

"I'm fine, ma'am. And you?"

"Fairly tolerable ain't no count." Whatever that meant.

Moms played it cool. "I was over at Monique's for a few days. You know, once I told her e'rythang she ain't want to be alone. I stayed until we'd dun worked some thangs out."

I stole a look around the refrigerator and caught a glimpse of Aunt Penny. She looked the same—medium brown complexion, small build, pretty black hair, and long legs. "How is she?"

"She fine, she fine."

"Uh huh, did you ask her when she coming home, Elise?"

"No, I ain't askt her. I gotta feelin', though, it'll be soon. You have to let Monique do thangs in her own time. She stubborn as a mule."

"She gets that from you," she said, glancing over at Quita. "You sure are a pretty girl, young lady. Pardon me for asking, but who are you?"

"I'm LaQuita, a friend of Mo's."

Baffled, Aunt Penny asked, "Mo? Who is Mo?"

"Penny, she talkin' 'bout Monique. Remember I told you . . ."

"Ohhhhhhhhhh, that's right. You're her *friend*," she responded teasingly. She extended her hand to greet Quita. "You better tell that girl to bring her ass on home and forget that nonsense. We love her, and we miss her. Nobody's perfect. I don't care what she calling herself these days. Just tell her to come home," she said tearfully. "Just tell her to come home. It doesn't matter who you love as long as you love somebody, and that should begin with yourself."

By then, I was leaning my back against the refrigerator and was silently crying on the inside and on the outside. My family hadn't seen me in years, and I was missing them terribly. Dressed in my oversized Phat Farm jeans, boxers, Rocawear plaid shirt, and Timbs, I gave some thought to who I was and who I used to be. Was there a reason they couldn't coexist? My pick with the black power fist was sticking out the back of my fro, and my pants were buckled around my thighs, exposing my decently shaped butt. I was coming to grips with the fact I'd lost touch with Monique. I never learned to love her; and I'd never let Quita love her either. I realized, in that moment, that the love I had for

Quita was real, so yeah, I was gay. I loved ass; I loved titties; and I loved tasting Quita's sugar walls. Most importantly, I loved me.

Holding my breath, I took what seemed to be the longest stroll of my life. I walked into the living room and stood before my Aunt Penny. At first she glanced over at me and rolled her eyes, but then she did a double-take. "Girl, if you don't take that pick out the back of your head, I know something! Come on over here, and give your auntie a hug!" Penny jumped up from her chair and embraced me. I felt her joy in every squeeze; I felt her shaking with happiness.

"Hey, Auntie," I whispered softly.

"Oh, my baby, my baby," she cried, pushing me away from her so she could get a good look at me. "Let me look at you!" She was spinning me around like the ballerina in a jewelry box she'd given me when I was a little girl. "Well, you don't look that bad. Your mother got me thinking you were looking like a real gang banger," she laughed. "It's nothing a shopping trip to Macy's won't cure."

Dizzy, I reached for her again, and this time it was me embracing her and filling her with the love I'd held back for so long.

GOD BLESS THE CHILD
Monique

Moms, Dan, and me sat in the classroom outside his office. He and I had talked several times without Moms, and we spent the bulk of those times talking about my identity. While I was hard on the outside, I was soft as cotton on the inside. Once I knew Mr. Luther was dead, and I mean like in the ground and with dirt on him, I was ready to live again. That madness with him being my father bothered me for a while, and I understood it was something beyond my control. We don't have any say in who our parents are, and no matter what cards we're dealt from God, we can't fold.

"Elise and, uh, Monique, we've come a long way to get to this point." I was sitting there in a pair of nice Sean John black jeans and a wool ribbed turtleneck sweater Aunt Penny had picked out for me. I had on my usual Timbs, but this time they were from the women's side of Foot Locker and were laced up. Quita had taken me on a shopping spree to Bailey, Banks & Biddle and got me a twenty-inch herringbone necklace. On the same day, she bought me a pair of two karat diamond stud earrings and my first thong. I insisted on a pair of female boxers until I got used to a string up my ass. I'd even stopped wearing the Master D. Instead of the strong men's cologne, I switched to oils so there'd be no confusion. I was whole, and Dan was feeling me. "You're looking good, Monique."

"I feel good, Dan. I really do."

Moms was glowing. She was at peace with where we were. She didn't look worn and weary. "Yes, my baby, looks real good. I'm so proud of her."

"Great, great," Dan said. "Well, both of you know today is our last session. Monique, you have here that you and Quita will be leaving for Atlanta tomorrow, and Elise, you have down here you've gotten a new job and will be moving out to the Hickory Hill area."

Both of us nodded our heads with huge grins on our faces.

"Does either of you want to say something before we close this out?"

To my surprise, Moms went first. "Mr. Dan, all I want to say is thank you for helping us through our problems. Thank you for helping me back to my baby."

Dan smiled. "No problem, Elise. That's why I'm here." He pulled out a brown envelope and laid it on the table. "There's still the issue of the letter you wrote for Monique."

Moms looked at me, and I, with no more worries, gave her my approval to give it to me. There wasn't anything she could say to me, at that point, to make me change how I was feeling. "I want her to have it. There are some things in there she needs to know 'bout."

"Fine." He handed me the envelope. "Monique, is

there anything you want to say? Looking like you're straight out of a magazine," he joked.

I *was* looking rather dapper. Quita had talked me into getting a perm, and I got a cut like Halle Berry had when she first stepped on the scene.

"No, I don't have anything else to say. I simply want to get back to the life God has blessed me with."

Quita and I were ready for our new beginning in Atlanta. Never once did I ever think I would have a girl like Quita who trying to be a daggone movie star. Memphis was only a few hours away, and we'd be back and forth to see Moms whenever we wanted to.

Rising from his seat, Dan opened his arms wide and said, "Group hug!" As he held us captive there, I felt the White boy getting a little weak on us. "You don't know how long I've been waiting to be able to finally say that."

The U-Haul was parked out in front of the apartment, all gassed up and ready to go. Monkey and Jamal came over earlier in the day to help Quita while I was at therapy. When I got inside, I found a case of Coronas with a note signed by Jamal and Monkey. THIS IS FOR THE GOOD TIMES, PARDNER, it read. Moms had told me she was coming by first thing in the morning to bring us some chicken and a cake for the road. Quita was all excited about her new job. The producer got us an apartment close to Centennial Park where they'd be shooting the movie, and I'd already signed up for classes so I could finish school.

All of our furniture was on the truck, but Quita had left out some blankets and pillows for a pallet on the floor. I hadn't seen her all day because her former coworkers were giving her a going away celebration and made a day of it. As far as I knew, they were going to some spa out in Cordova and then to the casino for dinner and drinks. They—Sunshine, Blade, Envy, and Triniti—were crazy about Miss Q, and they had good reason to be. Quita was absolutely fabulous.

I stretched across the floor nude with the envelope I'd gotten from Dan. I pulled out the folded papers, many of them full of grease stains, and put the page numbers in order. When I read the first line, "My gay-ass daughter . . . ," I recognized the hate moms had when she'd started writing it. It had been a busy day, and I, with five Coronas in me, dropped off to sleep before I knew it.

Relaxed on my back with my legs pointed like mountain peaks toward the sky, I woke up with Quita's face buried between my legs—somewhere it had never been. Her liquid punctures began at the very top of me and made their way to my clit—a place where I never knew pleasure existed. There, she hovered with one lick right after the other. She paralyzed me when she grasped the gates to my zone and stuck her pink key into my love cave. My thighs, dripping wet with sweat, shuddered as she turned that key and unlocked my soul. I clutched the back of her head and pressed it against my pussy. Her breathing mimicked my throbbing as I experienced pleasure beyond my wildest dreams. Every stroke of her tongue tickled me like a feather and sent sensuous chills along my spine. Quita slid her tongue along a chute within me and plunged into the undiscovered depths of my womanhood. Unable to control myself, I drew my thighs together, locking her head in position. My body stammered with seizures until it simply fell limp.

Upon her exit, she rolled me over and began a body

massage that commenced at the top of my back and ended at the top of my waist. She lodged kisses in the small of my back while she caressed at the point where my body splits in two. Against my backside, I felt *it* move smoothly down toward my thigh. "Are you OK?" she asked tenderly.

I had no choice but to answer in the same tone, "Yes, I'm fine." With that permission, Quita grabbed my hips and raised me to my knees. Strapped, my woman delicately kissed my skin and sweetly hit it from behind, taking hold of the back of my neck and knocked my rhythm until I told her someone was home.

Gently, I was returned to my first position, and while she brushed her lips across my sanctuary, I imagined bliss—for it was something I'd never known. I held Quita so tightly against me that she was inside of me. "I love you," I whispered into her ear.

"I love you, too," she said, easing her store-bought piece of masculinity which she manipulated as if it were her own into me. Slipping it in and out of me with my lather gushing from within, I busted and so did she. There was nothing more pleasurable on this earth than being fulfilled and blessed with the purity of womanhood.

The End

My Little Secret

by Anna J.

Coming in September 2008

Ask Yourself

Ask yourself a question . . . have you ever had a session of lovemaking, do you want me? Have you ever been to heaven?
—*Raheem DeVaughn*

February 9th, 2007

She feels like melted chocolate on my fingertips. The same color from the top of her head to the very tips of her feet. Her nipples are two shades darker than the rest of her, and they make her skin the perfect backdrop against her round breasts. Firm and sweet like two ripe peaches dipped in baker's chocolate. They are a little more than a handful and greatly appreciated. Touching her makes me feel like I've finally found peace on earth, and there is no feeling in the world greater than that.

Right now her eyes are closed and her bottom lip is tightly tucked between her teeth. From my view point between her wide spread legs I can see the beginnings of yet another orgasm playing across her angelic face. These are the moments that make it all worthwhile. Her perfectly arched eyebrows go into a deep frown, and her eyelids flutter slightly. When her head falls back I know she's about to explode.

I move up on my knees so that we are pelvis to pelvis. Both of us are dripping wet from the humidity and the situation. Her legs are up on my shoulders, and her hands are cupping my breasts. I can't tell where her skin begins or where mine ends. As I look down at her, and watch her face go through way too many emotions I smile a little bit. She always did love the dick, and since we've been together she's never had to go without it. Especially since the one I have never goes down.

I'm pushing her tool into her soft folds inch by inch as if it were really apart of me, and her body is alive. I say "her tool" because it belongs to her, and I just enjoy using it on her. Her hip length dreads seem to wrap us in a cocoon of coconut oil and sweat, body heat and moisture, soft moans and tear drops, pleasure and pain until we seemingly burst into an inferno of hot like fire ecstasy. Our chocolate skin is searing to the touch and we melt into each other becoming one. I can't tell where hers begins . . . I can't tell where mine ends.

She smiles . . . her eyes are still closed and she's still shaking from the intensity. I take this opportunity to taste her lips, and to lick the salty sweetness from the side of her neck. My hands begin to explore, and my tongue encircles her dark nipples. She arches her back when my full lips close around her nipple and I began to suck softly as if she's feeding me life from within her soul.

Her hands find there way to my head and become tangled in my soft locks, identical to hers but not as long. I push into her deep, and grind softly against her clit in search of her "j-spot" because it belongs to me, Jada. She speaks my name so soft that I barely heard her. I know she wants me to take what she so willingly gave me, and I want to hear her beg for it.

I start to pull back slowly, and I can feel her body tightening up trying to keep me from moving. One of many soft moans is heard over the low hum of the clock radio that sits next to our bed. I hear slight snatches of Raheem DeVaughn singing about being in heaven, and I'm almost certain he wrote that song for me and my lady.

I open her lips up so that I can have full view of her sensitive pearl. Her body quakes with anticipation from the feel of my warm breath touching it, my mouth just mere inches away. I blow cool air on her stiff clit causing her to tense up briefly, her hands taking hold of my head trying to pull me closer. At this point my mouth is so close to her all I would have to do is twitch my lips to make contact, but I don't . . . I want her to beg for it.

My index finger is making small circles against my own clit, my honey sticky between my legs. The ultimate pleasure is giving pleasure, and I've experienced that on both accounts. My baby can't wait anymore, and her soft pants are turning into low moans. I stick my tongue out, and her clit gladly kisses me back.

Her body responds by releasing a syrupy sweet slickness that I lap up until it's all gone, fucking her with my tongue the way she likes it. I hold her legs up and out to intensify her orgasm because I know she can't handle it that way.

"Does your husband do you like this?" I ask between licks. Before she could answer I wrap my full lips around her clit and suck her into my mouth, swirling my tongue around her hardened bud causing her body to shake.

Snatching a second toy from the side of the bed, I take one hand to part her lips, and I ease her favorite toy (The Rabbit) inside of her. Wishing that the strap-on I was wearing was a real dick so that I could feel her pulsate, I turn the toy on low at first wanting her to receive the ultimate pleasure. In the dark room the glow in the dark toy is lit brightly, the light disappearing inside of her when I push it all the way in.

The head of the curved toy turns in a slow circle while the pearl beads jump around on the inside hitting up against her smooth walls during insertion. When I push the toy in she pushes her pelvis up to receive it, my mouth latched on to her clit like a vice. She moans louder, and I kick the toy up a notch to medium, much to her delight. Removing my mouth from her clit I rotate between flicking my wet tongue across it to heat it, and blowing my breath on it to cool it bringing her to yet another screaming orgasm, followed by strings of *"I love You"* and *"Please Don't Stop."*

Torturing her body slowly, I continue to stimulate her clit while pushing her toy in and out of her on a constant rhythm. When she lifts her legs to her chest I take the opportunity to let the ears on the rabbit toy that we are using do it's job on her clit while my tongue find it's way to her chocolate ass. I bite one cheek at a time replacing it with wet kisses, afterwards sliding my tongue in between to taste her there. Her body squirming underneath me let's me know I've hit the jackpot, and I fuck her with my tongue there also.

She's moaning telling me in a loud whisper that she can't take it anymore. That's my clue to turn the toy up high. The buzzing from the toy matches that of the radio, and with her moans and my pants mixed in we sound like a well-rehearsed orchestra singing a symphony of passion. I allow her to buck against my face while I keep up with the rhythm of the toy, her juice oozing out the sides and forming a puddle under her ass. I'm loving it.

She moans and shakes until the feeling in the pit of her stomach resides and she is able to breath at a normal rate. My lips taste salty/sweet from kissing her body while she tries to get her head together, rubbing the sides of my body up and down in a lazy motion.

Valentine's Day is fast approaching and I have a wonderful evening planned for the two of us. She already promised me that her husband wouldn't be an issue because he'll be out of town that weekend, and besides all that they haven't celebrated cupid's day since the year after they were married so I didn't even think twice about it. After seven years it should be over for them anyway.

"It's your turn now," she says to me in a husky lust filled voice, and I can't wait for her to take control.

The ultimate pleasure is giving pleasure . . . and man does it feel good both ways. She starts by rubbing her oil-slicked hands over the front of my body, taking extra time around my sensitive nipples before bringing her hands down across my flat stomach. I've since then removed the strap-on dildo, and am completely naked under her hands.

I can still feel her sweat on my skin, and I can still taste her on my lips. Closing my eyes I enjoy the sensual massage that I'm being treated to. After two years of us making love it's still good and gets better every time.

She likes to take her time covering every inch of my body, and I enjoy letting her. She skips past my love box, and starts at my feet massaging my legs from the toes up. When she gets to my pleasure point her fingertips graze the smooth hairless skin there quickly teasing me before she heads back down, and does the same thing with my other limb. My legs are spread apart and lying flat on the bed with her in between relaxing my body with ease. A cool breeze from the cracked window blows across the room every so often caressing my erect nipples making them harder than before until her hands warm them back up again.

She knows when I can't take anymore any she rubs and caresses me until I am begging her to kiss my lips. I can see her smile through half closed eyelids, and she does what I requested. Dipping her head down between my legs she kisses my lips just as I asked, using her tongue to part them so that she could taste my clit. My body goes into mini-convulsions on contact and I am fighting a battle to not cum that I never win.

"Valentine's Day belongs to us right?" I ask her again between moans. I need her to be here. V-Day is for lovers, and her and her husband haven't been that in ages. I deserve it . . . I deserve her. I just don't want this to be a repeat of Christmas or New Years eve.

"Yes, it's yours," she says between kisses on my thigh, and sticking her tongue inside of me. Two of her fingers have found there way inside of my tight walls, and my pelvic area automatically bounces up and down on her hand as my orgasm approaches.

"Tell me you love me," I say to her as my breathing becomes raspy. I fire is spreading across my legs and working its way up to the pit of my stomach. I need her to tell me before I explode.

"I love you," she says and at the moment she places her tongue in my slit I release my honey all over her tongue.

It feels like I am on the Tea Cup ride at the amusement park as my orgasm jerks my body uncontrollably and it feels like the room is spinning. She is sucking and slurping my clit while the weight of her body holds the bottom half of me captive. I'm practically screaming and begging her to stop and just when I think I'm about to check out of here she lets my clit go.

I take a few more minutes to get my head together, allowing her to pull me into her and rub my back. It's moment s like this that makes it all worthwhile. We lay like that for a while longer listening to each other breath, and much to my dismay she slides my head from where it was resting on her arm and gets up out of the bed.

I don't say a word. I just lie on the bed and watch her get dressed. I swear everything she does is so graceful, like there's a rhythm riding behind it. Pretty soon she is dressed and standing beside the bed looking down at me. She smiles and I smile back, not worried because she promised me our lover's day, and that's only a week away.

"So, Valentine's Day belongs to me, right?" I ask her again just to be certain.

"Yes, it belongs to you."

We kiss one last time, and I can still taste my honey on her lips. She already knows the routine, locking the bottom lock behind her. Just thinking about her makes me so horny, and I pick up her favorite toy to finish the job. Five more days, and it'll be on again.

ABOUT THE AUTHOR

When you do what your passion is—your passion being what God gave you the zest and talent to do—the rest falls into place.

Divine destiny is what motivates mother, daughter, author Laurinda D. Brown to do what she does—write novels that portray real people in real life situations. "Growing up in Memphis, TN, and graduating from Howard University exposed me to the diverse sides of human nature and gave me the opportunity to observe people and their situations. I wrote to work through my own emotions, to find explanations for other people's circumstances, and to try to humanize their idiosyncrasies. Writing expresses my take on the world."

Laurinda's books include *Fire & Brimstone*, the 2005 Lamda Literary Award finalist for Best Debut Lesbian Fiction, *Walk Like A Man*, and *Undercover*.

She recently won the 2007 Lambda Literary Award for Best Lesbian Erotica for *Walk Like A Man*.

The author currently resides with her two daughters in Georgia, where she continues to write about life—not lifestyles. She firmly believes that one day we will love one another not for what we are, but for who we are.

Check out Laurinda online at: www.ldbrownbooks.com and myspace.com/laurindadbrown

LOOK FOR MORE HOT TITLES FROM

Q-BORO
B O O K S

DARK KARMA - JUNE 2007
$14.95
ISBN 1-933967-12-9

What if the criminal was forced to live the horror that they caused? The drug dealer finds himself in the body of the drug addict and he suffers through the withdrawals, living on the street, the beatings, the rapes and the hunger. The thief steals the rent money and becomes the victim that finds herself living on the street and running for her life and the murderer becomes the victim's father and he deals with the death of a son and a grieving mother.

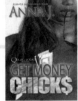

GET MONEY CHICKS - SEPTEMBER 2007
$14.95
ISBN 1-933967-17-X

For Mina, Shanna, and Karen, using what they had to get what they wanted was always an option. Best friends since day one, they always had a thing for the hottest gear, luxurious lifestyles, and the ballers who made it all possible. All of this changes for Mina when a tragedy makes her open her eyes to the way she's living. Peer pressure and loyalty to her girls collide with her own morality, sending Mina into a no-win situation.

AFTER-HOURS GIRLS - AUGUST 2007
$14.95
ISBN 1-933967-16-1

Take part in this tale of two best friends, Lisa and Tosha, as they stalk the nightclubs and after-hours joints of Detroit searching for excitement, money, and temporary companionship. These two divas stand tall until the unforgivable Motown streets catch up to them. One must fall. You, the reader, decide which.

THE LAST CHANCE - OCTOBER 2007
$14.95
ISBN 1-933967-22-6

Running their L.A. casino has been rewarding for Luke Chance and his three brothers. But recently it seems like everyone is trying to get a piece of the pie. An impending hostile takeover of their casino could leave them penniless and possibly dead. That is, until their sister Keilah Chance comes home for a short visit. Keilah is not only beautiful, but she also can be ruthless. Will the Chance family be able to protect their family dynasty?

Traci must find a way to complete her journey out of her first and only failed

LOOK FOR MORE HOT TITLES FROM
Q-BORO
BOOKS

NYMPHO - MAY 2007
$14.95
ISBN 1933967102

How will signing up to live a promiscuous double-life destroy everything that's at stake in the lives of two close couples? Take a journey into Leslie's secret world and prepare for a twisted, erotic experience.

FREAK IN THE SHEETS - SEPTEMBER 2007
$14.95
ISBN 1933967196

Librarian Raquelle decides to put her knowledge of sexuality to use and open up a "freak" school, teaching men and women how to please their lovers beyond belief while enjoying themselves in the process. But trouble brews when a surprise pupil shows up and everything Raquelle has worked for comes under fire.

LIAR, LIAR - JUNE 2007
$14.95
ISBN 1933967110

Stormy calls off her wedding to Camden when she learns he's cheating with a male church member. However, after being convinced that Camden has been delivered from his demons, she proceeds with the wedding.

Will Stormy and Camden survive scandal, lies and deceit?

HEAVEN SENT - AUGUST 2007
$14.95
ISBN 1933967188

Eve is a recovering drug addict who has no intentions of staying clean until she meets Reverend Washington, a newly widowed man with three children. Secrets are uncovered that threaten Eve's new life with her new family and has everyone asking if Eve was *Heaven Sent*.

LOOK FOR MORE HOT TITLES FROM

Q-BORO
B O O K S

OBSESSION 101
$6.99
ISBN 0977733548

After a horrendous trauma. Rashawn Ams is left pregnant and flees town to give birth to her son and repair her life after confiding in her psychiatrist. After her return to her life, her town, and her classroom, she finds herself the target of an intrusive secret admirer who has plans for her.

MICHELLE McGRIFF

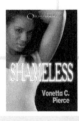

SHAMELESS– OCTOBER 2006
$6.99
ISBN 0977733513

Kyle is sexy, single, and smart; Jasmyn is a hot and sassy drama queen. These two complete opposites find love - or something real close to it - while away at college. Jasmyn is busy wreaking havoc on every man she meets. Kyle, on the other hand, is trying to walk the line between his faith and all the guilty pleasures being thrown his way. When the partying college days end and Jasmyn tests HIV positive, reality sets in.

Vonetta C. Pierce

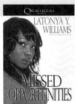

MISSED OPPORTUNITIES - MARCH 2007
$14.95
ISBN 1933967013

Missed Opportunities illustrates how true-to-life characters must face the consequences of their poor choices. Was each decision worth the opportune cost? LaTonya Y. Williams delivers yet another account of love, lies, and deceit all wrapped up into one powerful novel.

ONE DEAD PREACHER - MARCH 2007
$14.95
ISBN 1933967021

Smooth operator and security CEO David Price sets out to protect the sexy, smart, and saucy Sugar Owens from her husband, who happens to be a powerful religious leader. Sugar isn't as sweet as she appears, however, and in a twisted turn of events, the preacher man turns up dead and Price becomes the prime suspect.

TONY LINDSAY

LOOK FOR MORE HOT TITLES FROM
Q-BORO
BOOKS

DOGISM
$6.99
ISBN 0977733505

Lance Thomas is a sexy, young black male who has it all: a high paying blue collar career, a home in Queens, New York, two cars, a son, and a beautiful wife. However, after getting married at a very young age he realizes that he is afflicted with DOGISM, a distorted sexuality that causes men to stray and be unfaithful in their relationships with women.

POISON IVY - NOVEMBER 2006
$14.95
ISBN 0977733521

Ivy Davidson's life has been filled with sorrow. Her father was brutally murdered and she was forced to watch, she faced years of abuse at the hands of those she trusted, and she was forced to live apart from the only source of love that she'd ever known. Now Ivy stands alone at the crossroads of life, staring into the eyes of the man who holds her final choice of life or death in his hands.

HOLY HUSTLER - FEBRUARY 2007
$14.95
ISBN 0977733556

Reverend Ethan Ezekiel Goodlove the Third and his three sons are known for spreading more than just the gospel. The sanctified drama of the Goodloves promises to make us all scream "Hallelujah!"

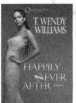

HAPPILY NEVER AFTER - JANUARY 2007
$14.95
ISBN 1933967005

To Family and friends, Dorothy and David Leonard's marriage appears to be one made in heaven. While David is one of Houston's most prominent physicians, Dorothy is a loving and carefree housewife. It seems as if life couldn't be more fabulous for this couple who appear to have it all: wealth, social status, and a loving union. However, looks can be deceiving. What really happens behind closed doors and when the flawless veneer begins to crack?

LOOK FOR

COMING JAN. 2008
ISBN: 1-933967-37-4

Attention Writers:

Writers looking to get their books published can view our submission guidelines by visiting our website at: www.QBOROBOOKS.com

What we're looking for: Contemporary fiction in the tradition of Darrien Lee, Carl Weber, Anna J., Zane, Mary B. Morrison, Noire, Lolita Files, etc; groundbreaking mainstream contemporary fiction.

We prefer email submissions to: submissions@qboro-books.com in MS Word, PDF, or rtf format only. However, if you wish to send the submission via snail mail, you can send it to:

Q-BORO BOOKS Acquisitions Department
165-41A Baisley Blvd., Suite 4. Mall #1
Jamaica, New York 11434

*** By submitting your work to Q-Boro Books, you agree to hold Q-Boro books harmless and not liable for publishing similar works as yours that we may already be considering or may consider in the future. ***

1. Submissions will not be returned.
2. **Do not contact us for status updates.** If we are interested in receiving your full manuscript, we will contact you via email or telephone.
3. Do not submit if the entire manuscript is not complete.

Due to the heavy volume of submissions, if these requirements are not followed, we will not be able to process your submission.